Praise the Lord
and
Pass the Poison

PRAISE THE LORD *AND* PASS THE POISON

A CHRISTINE RANDAL MYSTERY

AMANDA CALDWELL

CRACKERDOG PRESS · SEATTLE

Praise the Lord and Pass the Poison
Copyright ©2022 Amanda Caldwell

All rights reserved. No portion of this publication may be reproduced by any means without prior written permission from the publisher with the exception of brief excerpts for articles and reviews: Crackerdog Press, www.CrackerdogPress.com

Cover illustration by Lauren Wayne

First Printing, October 2022.

Printed in the United States of America, 2022.
ISBN-13: 979-8-9871214-0-5 (Paperback edition)
ISBN-13: 979-8-9871214-1-2 (eBook edition)

For Steven,
my Rob

Chapter 1

"Aren't you going to get out?" my husband asked, arm resting on the steering wheel. The heat was cranked and chugging to ward off the chill of the Indiana winter evening that threatened to seep into our thirteen-year-old Toyota Corolla.

We sat in the dark parking lot of the office complex. This late in the evening, the only other cars were also here for the music team practice in the room our church rented on the top floor.

"I'm considering it." I pulled the visor down to check that my eyeliner hadn't smudged. My dark blue eyes are my one truly fine feature, so I liked to play them up.

"Practices going really well, huh?" Rob said.

I rolled my eyes at him but wasn't sure he could see me in the dim illumination of a single security streetlamp. I couldn't see much of him but the tousled spikes of his glossy-straight hair. He knew my feelings on the matter.

"I don't know if it was such a good idea to make me the praise team leader," I said finally. The streetlight glinted off the lenses of my glasses, so I would have to trust the eyeliner was intact.

"Interim praise team leader," Rob corrected.

"Thanks for reminding me." I touched up my lip gloss and studied what I could see of my reflection: pale skin, dark lips, and darker hair waving out around my head before dissolving into the black. Good enough.

"I just think you should get them to make you the team leader in fact," he said. "Maybe pay you a little somethin'-somethin'."

"Yeah, right. And I really deserve it, considering what wonderful leadership skills I've shown so far."

"Yeah," Rob said, "for one thing, you're late."

I swatted him on the shoulder.

"You know," he continued, "you don't have to go in."

"Yes, I do," I protested. "The church service will be more awful than usual if I don't corral them into at least mediocrity."

"I meant you don't have to be interim praise team leader," he said. "You could let it go to someone else, take a load off."

I sighed. "I kind of wanted to do a good job," I whispered. "It's just—the teens don't listen to anyone over 20, the long-timers don't listen to anyone under 40, and I'm too...un-mom material for the other women my age. And they don't get that they're all too untalented not to need my help."

"I hope you don't start out meetings with that speech."

I swatted him harder.

Rob laughed. "Seriously, though: what if we tried to get to know them better? Invite people over for dinner, make friends. Maybe they just don't know you. Who's the one who had us over a month or two ago for tacos? Sammy or something?"

"Tammy," I corrected.

"So we could invite her back. We could make, like... frozen pizza."

I snorted. "But our place always looks like an overstuffed thrift store. We never put anything away."

"Then we'll rent another place for dinners and pretend we live there," Rob said, taking my hand for a squeeze. "Now you better get in there before they give up on you and go home."

I consented to open my door and reluctantly release my seat belt to unfold myself from the Corolla. The brittle winter air of Northwest Indiana sucked my breath away as I left the heated interior.

"Knock 'em dead, hon," Rob called after me.

I shut the door with a satisfying chunk.

I flapped my arms again in a futile attempt to get the singers and band to stop talking and start the music. "Team." No change. "Team!" I said, louder, and half of the eyes swiveled toward me. Good enough. "Are we ready to start? 'King of All Kings,' from the top."

The pianist gave a nod and started the intro. The drummer picked up the beat half a measure in, and I allowed it for now. Best to get through the dang thing at least once before tackling perfection.

"Glo—," Walter sang in a confident bass.

"Kiiing," Barb sang simultaneously in a bloated soprano.

The other six singers stared blankly at the two false starters.

"We're starting on the verse," Walter said.

"No, we're starting on the chorus," Barb said.

"You're both wrong," I said, too tired to be diplomatic. "We just talked about this, remember? We're starting with the tag. To be different." A goal I was now regretting.

"All glory to you, Lord Jesus," I clarified, muffling a sigh as I wondered if that sounded more like a newfangled curse than a proclamation. "Again."

"Right, Christine," Walter said to me. "Sorry." Despite

being older than I by a couple decades, Walter was one of the only members who tried to respect my position as interim praise team leader. Maybe as a school principal, he knew how tenuous respect could be, and how hard it was to earn.

I shot him a weary smile and signaled the drummer this time, who gave a proper click-off, and everyone more or less muddled through for once. I ignored the off notes from half the singers and the lack of originality of the guitar part. I winced that half the singers flubbed the words since I knew not everyone was as good at memorizing as I was and wanted to be gracious. I even managed to tune out the amateurish trumpet player whose mother insisted he'd make a fine addition to the praise band but who so far just tootled along with the melody, in an apparent attempt to drown out everyone else.

By the time we had finished "King of All Kings," I had had it. But it was no good. They had to run through "My Heart Is Yours," because it was a new song this week and I knew the team would suck on Sunday if they didn't try it at least one more time.

"'My Heart,' again, please." I tried for a strident tone to cut through the chatter that immediately resumed upon the conclusion of any song, but at twenty-six my vocal abilities didn't extend to commanding instant obedience. This praise-team leader gig was my first real shot at leadership. Sure, I'd gotten it only because I was the oldest person who was foolhardy enough to volunteer. The fact that I was the relative newcomer at this church also undermined whatever meager authority I had.

I tried yelling again, giving it my all. "'My Heart Is Yours'!"

The group stared.

"Thank you," Dylan Ruiz, the bassist, said. He was cute and young and made me feel uncool every time I looked at him. Everyone snickered.

Well, at least I had their attention.

Or so I had thought. "Barb," Walter called. Dissension from Walter, of all people. The night had really gotten out of hand. "Can I have one of those cough droppy things?"

Tammy started to cough. "I could use one, too," she gasped out. Both my allies deserting me in my time of need. Apparently half the team was in serious need of medical attention from all the strenuous practicing.

I sighed and waited out the new interruption. Why had I ever agreed to lead the praise team?

I could picture the fateful decision, sitting around the table at the worship planning committee meeting, the members of whom had invited me there especially. Older and wiser possibilities had declined or were too busy running businesses or families, they let me know in oblique terms. The other candidates were even younger than I was and had less musical experience. Would I be willing to head up the praise team, just until the church could launch a proper search for a permanent placement? Six months later, here I still was.

My selection had happened a year and a half after Rob and I had moved to Northwest Indiana from Illinois, where we'd stayed for a couple years after graduating college. Rob worked with a graphic design firm and had gotten the transfer to Indiana just after our marriage. We accepted it because we had no place better to go.

In our new area, it had taken us several months of church shopping to settle on New Vision Community Fellowship, a place about forty minutes from our home in Mansardville, and one we had visited only because someone from Rob's work knew someone there. We had tried out other churches closer by, but most had been very traditional and we had failed to connect with anyone. We picked New Vision as the friendliest of the options.

Maybe too friendly, I thought on a sigh, as Barb, the resident cough-drop distributor, got up from her seat and walked through the practice room to the table piled with the group's belongings.

"My bag's here somewhere," she said. She began sifting through winter coats and moving aside backpacks. "Hmmm." Now she sounded worried. "I had it under my coat."

The group, much to my dismay, moved en masse from their seats and instruments. Half shifted toward Barb and the table, to duplicate her search by ineffectually moving coats on top of areas cleared by another seeker. The rest wandered around the large-windowed office space that doubled as an acoustically dreadful practice studio, poking into corners and shifting chairs, expecting a handbag to pop out at any moment.

I sank into a seat to watch. I resolved to keep a jar of cough drops on the piano from now on. And maybe tea with honey, piping hot to greet all my musical charges. And throat massages. Oh, yes, I'd like to throat massage them all right about now.

Barb Vanderwal was in her fifties but maintained a stylish middle-aged look, with short-cropped hair, and sporting trim lime-green slacks tonight. She was, like ninety percent of the population of the church, of Dutch descent, as her blond hair, now turning artfully to gray, attested. She was one of the old-school members of New Vision, if the pioneers of a five-year-old church could ever be termed old-school. Now that the church was getting bigger, praise-singer wannabes had to audition for the privilege of joining, but Barb had been grandfathered into the praise team. To be polite, I supposed she sounded very good in the shower. I knew for a fact that the soundboard always turned her mic down on Sundays. Barb knew everyone who was anyone in the church, and many more besides, and she was always available to offer a dinner out to newcomers, a dinner delivered to new moms, or a cough drop to any people with a tickle in their throat. You could often hear a rippling wave of rustles coming from the vicinity of her row during the sermon.

Rumor was she had them imported from Austria or Switzerland, but that they were better than Ricola and were made with some secret blend of beneficial herbs. They tasted vile, but otherwise they wouldn't be healing, everyone reasoned. After I had first joined the praise team as a duly auditioned singer and had once been handed one without prompting after clearing my throat a few too many times, I had eschewed any further offers, despite the touted benefits.

I viewed the ruckus now. Jim Vegter and Walter Kappas, our two male singers, worked as a masculine team, sorting the jackets into one pile and lining the bags up along one side of the catch-all table. Walter, another New Vision old-schooler in his late forties, had reached for his own dark gray trench and was helpfully flapping it to see if a pocketbook fell out, while Jim felt up a backpack from one of the younger members. Kirsten Lindquist, our keyboardist, came along behind and began hanging the jackets over chair backs, although I couldn't see what good that was doing. Maybe she was trying to help determine if anything else was missing.

Two of our women singers, Gretchen Plantinga and Heidi Abbing, were fraternal twins in their nineties. They were the seventh and eighth children of a German immigrant mother and a Dutch immigrant father, they had told me at a potluck when I had been awkwardly stuck in the corner with them until extricating myself for more Jell-O salad, and they were the only people I knew who apparently spoke fluent Dutch, when the mood struck them. It was striking them now as they searched together for the bag, the broad and tall tenor Gretchen poking a yardstick into a leaning pile of large notepads in a corner, and stooped and white-haired soprano Heidi rattling off something intense and mystifying, the way another language

13

sounds to the unfamiliar ear. I wondered why a search for a handbag required such a private and voluble conversation.

Tammy Dykstra, the hoarse-throated instigator of all this hubbub, tipped back chairs to peer underneath the legs and brushed at fliers and brochures left on tables, as if a purse might be hiding beneath a stack of trifolded paper. Tammy was sweet, a soft-voiced but welcoming woman in her mid-to-late thirties with long, thin limbs and dark hair she always wore up in a simple style. She headed the singles' ministry at New Vision, though that had the more alluring name of One-on-One. I thought that sounded kind of sexy, but from the church website's pictures of group outings, I wondered if I'd want to belong to it if I weren't recently married. It did not look as exciting as the name made it sound.

Penelope Tenpas, another singer, was the only one besides me sitting out the hunt, but she had a reason. She was a new mother who managed to combine holding a baby with singing through use of some sort of wrap. Occasionally Gopher, for that was what she inexplicably had named her son, would contentedly gurgle and coo inside his fabric confines, but whenever he started fussing, which was most of the time, Penelope would automatically bounce in place, her voice jolting along with her plump body. If he started wailing, she would bounce all around the large room, or take him outside if he reached too many decibels to sing over. Penelope called him high-spirited in an apologetic but affectionate tone. I just called him loud. It was too soon to say whether Gopher had inherited her red ringlets, but it was undeniable he had inherited her clear soprano voice. Right now he was surprisingly calm. In the relative silence of the search, I could hear him slurping away inside. Penelope took the handbag hunt as opportunity to switch sides.

Barb appeared flummoxed, and ran from one side of

the room to the other, her lime green legs a whirl, keeping everyone apprised of her scattered thoughts with a running commentary: "I know I brought it in with my jacket, because the strap caught on the seam, and I thought I heard a little tear, and I thought that was weird, because my jacket's suede. But then I didn't see anything wrong, so I brought it in, and I put it on this table so I could take off my jacket and look more closely at it, but, see, there's nothing wrong. I can't imagine where my purse is now, though."

Nineteen-year-old coolio Dylan Ruiz watched the scene with his melting brown eyes that peered out from beneath a fall of exquisitely effortless hair. It was the type of hairstyle that said he was too cool to care while still playing up his features perfectly. He was half-heartedly flicking through papers on a table, but he offered the first helpful idea. "Why don't you check outside anyway?"

"Right." Barb nodded, relieved to have someone offer a suggestion. She found her astonishingly purple suede jacket draped around a chair by Kirsten's ministrations and dug out car keys. "At least I keep these in my jacket!" she exclaimed, clutching them in triumph. As she lifted them in the air, a small object fell loose and onto the typical gray-blue speckled office carpet. She leaned down to pick up the paper-wrapped item.

"Found one!" she exclaimed. Tammy jumped, the chair she was tipping falling back forward with a thunk. "Here's one from my pocket." Barb held out her treasure. "Who wants it?" she asked, swiveling between Walter next to her at the coat table, and Tammy across the room. Tammy coughed again, and I wondered if it was pointedly.

"Tammy can have it," Walter said in a gentlemanly way, absentmindedly patting the pockets of his conservative tweed suit coat, as if another stray cough drop might have teleported in there. "I'll just go get a sip of water."

Barb nodded and moved over to Tammy, who had

15

gazed back in silence while awaiting the verdict. Barb held out her fist, and Tammy extended one thin palm to accept the drop.

"Thank you," she whispered, unwrapping the prize and popping it in her mouth.

Tammy was so quiet that attending dinner at her house had been almost excruciating. Rob and I had had to keep up all ends of the conversation. Still, I appreciated her effort in extending friendship.

Barb nodded happily at Tammy's grateful acceptance of the drop and turned on her heel to head out to the parking lot.

"Well, I'll be!" we heard Barb say from the corridor. She poked her head back in, and the rest of her soon followed, including one orange leather handbag. "It was here out in the hallway. How did it get there?" She shook her head, but her indulgent expression suggested a fond acceptance of her own forgetfulness.

"Now that you have your pocketbook back, I'll take one of those drops, too, if you have one," Jim said, clearing his throat, presumably the better to demonstrate his need. His voice did sound somewhat hoarse. That was the problem with singing below the range of human hearing as he was ever wont to do. It was nice to have two basses, but I had to keep reminding Jim to sing up an octave and keep pace with the tempo. It always sounded like he was still singing the hymns of the more traditional church he had transferred from rather than the kickier modern praise choruses.

"Sure," Barb said, digging through her bag. "I have some right...hmm..." She stuck her hand in farther and wiggled it around, face scrunched. She removed her hand and opened the bag wide to stick her face close to the opening. She flipped her reading glasses from headbanding her short graying hair back to her face, the better to search the confines. "I swear there was a pack right in this little pocket." She looked up at the group, blue eyes wide through the lenses. "That's the oddest thing," she said. "That's the second pack that's gone missing this week!"

"Oh, well," Jim said, smoothing a hand over his shaved bald head. "It's not a problem. I'll just go get a little cup of water, too." He cleared his throat again and followed Walter out the door into the corridor, where a communal water bubbler stood between the restroom doors. They reentered in a couple moments with cone-shaped paper cups in hand, sipping away.

I stood. It was time to regain some semblance of control over my herd.

"'My Heart Is Yours,' then," I once more attempted. The group reassembled, including the youth. Teenagers Avery DeHaan and Zachary Brown walked in from the hall—I hadn't even seen them leave, but now here they were on their way back, heads together and giggling. They made a striking contrast—Avery's light brown hair newly blue-streaked and Zachary's cherubic blond curls, the envy of any female. Thirteen-year-old Avery adjusted her dork-chic glasses and gazed up at Zachary with an almost-four-teen-year-old's devotion but what looked like a twenty-five-year-old's awareness of her effect on the opposite sex. Dylan's attention was riveted on them, and his mouth twisted in more than its usual devil-may-care sneer. Potter, the trumpeter whose mother had earned him a place on the team, emerged from under a desk in the far corner, dusting off the knees of his jeans, and retrieved his trumpet. At fourteen, he was the youngest in the group after Avery, and he kept quiet except when honking his horn. He was Ethiopian by birth and had been adopted into a doting family here in Indiana, though I often wondered how well he dealt with being the only dark-skinned kid in a family of very, very white people.

The room finally was settling back to normal. Fellow instrumentalists Blaine Grotenhouse and Hal Dormer restacked some boxes they had moved out from the wall. Everyone really had been thorough and completely irrational in the search, I mused.

Sixteen-year-old Zachary settled in to the congas, while forty-something Hal, gray ponytail swinging, took the big drum set. I knew I was going to catch it from Zachary's mother, who considered congas subpar and would want to know why I hadn't allowed her son to play the real drums. She never did believe me when I told her Zachary enjoyed all forms of percussion and that, as a team, we appreciated variety. Zachary never seemed to instigate or be aware of his mother's behind-the-scenes manipulations to catapult him to stardom. He would frequently skip practice, and then his mother would berate me for not letting him play on Sunday.

One last song, and we could all go home. It was 8:55 already, and I had hoped to wrap up by 9. I had discovered that Midwesterners were nothing if not punctual, so we had been muddling through since 7:10, allowing the time it took for me personally to arrive and prepare. In one-plus years in the region, I still hadn't gotten the hang of being on time for anything. Fortunately, everyone had a key card to the practice space and was able to get in upon an early arrival.

Tammy coughed. Barb looked at her and smiled. "There's the herbs kicking in," she said.

Tammy smiled, but it looked a little weak. She raised one slender hand to her throat and coughed again.

Walter, sitting next to her now, gave her a friendly swat on the back.

Tammy's mouth opened, but no voice came out, only an alarming wheezing. Her tongue protruded as she seemed to be gasping for air.

Time as well as all of the other team members froze. Finally, Kirsten broke the spell, leaping from the piano bench. Kirsten had been a nurse before she became a young and busy mother to five children under five, the most recent additions being triplets. "Call 911," she said to Barb, in the no-nonsense voice befitting a mom or a nurse.

I felt ashamed that I hadn't yet done anything so useful. I considered adding my own phone call, but Barb was already digging her cell out of her recovered handbag.

I moved to where Kirsten was supporting Tammy with one arm behind her back. Tammy had half-risen from her chair in an instinctual effort to move toward air. Walter put his own arm around her from the other side, and Kirsten swept a confident finger into Tammy's mouth, dislodging the remnants of the half-dissolved brown lozenge.

But Tammy's paroxysm continued, so presumably she hadn't just been choking on the cough drop. What else was there to do?

"Avery," I said, turning to face her and relieved I had thought of something practical. "Go downstairs to open the door for the paramedics." The office building where we rented a top floor room had an entrance that required the same key card to get in after hours and automatically locked behind anyone exiting. Avery nodded and got up to leave, her forehead furrowed with worry, and, with a disturbed backward glance at Tammy, Zachary trotted along behind.

Barb had given the pertinents over the phone but was still talking to the 911 operator and shouting out ineffectual instructions to Kirsten, who had Tammy lying on the floor and was kneeling beside her, speaking in a low voice, "Relax, just relax your throat. Just breathe. That's it. They're on their way." Kirsten ran a hand over Tammy's dark hair, mussed out of its usual neat twist.

Walter had removed his suit coat to wad beneath Tammy's head as a makeshift pillow. He now stood over the two and started praying, "Father God, please take care of your daughter Tammy."

Tammy began to throw up onto the Berber carpet, and Hal turned his face away, while Potter raised his trumpet case to right below his eye line. Gretchen and Heidi murmured imprecations in Dutch but kept their eyes on the situation. Walter continued his prayer, eyes half-closed and hand outstretched over Tammy's horizontal form.

Penelope was weeping silently, tears rolling down her pale face and onto her baby's bald head. She had the boy out of the sling now and on her shoulder, and she snuggled him close, rocking back and forth with her body angled out of the line of vision of the spasming body on the floor.

Finally, the paramedics burst through into the room, and all the less helpful among us scattered to the fringes to watch them work. It was all a blur of tubes and gurneys and medical orders, and in minutes Tammy was loaded, white and unhopefully silent, onto a carrier and ferried out the door and to the elevator.

I sank down and stared at the spot on the rug she had soiled.

This had not been a good rehearsal at all.

Chapter 2

"How'd practice go?" Rob asked, staring at our small-screen and very unflat TV. The thrift shop had given it to us for free to take it off their hands. I had bummed a ride home with Walter, and our talk the whole way had been nothing but Tammy's sudden sickness, of course. Neither of us had had much helpful to say except how awful it was.

I stood in the doorway until Rob looked up.

"Oh," he said at the look on my face.

"It was awful." I sank next to him on the futon, trying to ignore the DVD he was watching, a superhero flick from the library.

"Is Sunday going to be that bad?" he asked, finally hitting pause.

"It wasn't practice itself. Well, I mean, it was terrible as usual. But mostly it was this awful thing that happened at the end. You know how we were just talking about Tammy Dykstra?" An image flew into my mind of our visit to her house, of Rob and me sitting at her scarred oak table and chowing down on concoctions from the taco bar she'd set up.

21

"Uh-huh," Rob said, still not sensing the dramatic gravity here. Maybe he also was having a taco flashback. "What about her?"

"Well, it's not good. She got really sick, or was choking or something, and collapsed."

"What? Seriously?" Ah, finally.

"The paramedics had to come and bring her out on a stretcher and everything." I paused, my hands in my lap. "I don't know what I'm supposed to do. Should I call the prayer chain, I guess?"

"I guess. What happened?"

"I don't know. She was sucking on one of those lozenges Barb always hands around..."

"Ugh," Rob said.

"Yeah, enough to make anyone sick, right? I don't know how people can stand those things." I shook my head and tried to get back on point. "But, anyway, we started singing that new song, 'My Heart Is Yours,' which I agree is gag-worthy—sorry—" I shook my head to clear it. "She just started choking or having a fit or something."

"Did you do the Heimlich?"

I frowned. "I didn't really do anything. I was just sort of paralyzed, shocked, you know? I've read about first aid plenty but never had a call to practice it. But then Kirsten came over. You remember Kirsten with the triplets?"

Rob nodded. "I remember about the triplets. Was that fertility treatments or what?"

Sidetrack. "She's not saying," I said.

"So—yes," Rob said.

I nodded. "A-ny-way," I continued, "she's also a nurse, so it was handy to have someone competent. She took charge, told Barb to call 911, and then started calming Tammy down so she might be able to breathe better. She was wheezing like a broken whistle."

"But did she get out whatever was choking her?"

I tried to remember the order things had happened.

"Well, Kirsten did sweep her mouth out, and the lozenge came loose, or what was left of it. But then she was still breathing heavily, and she eventually even threw up on the rug. So I don't think she was just choking, you know? Maybe she was allergic."

I looked at my husband.

"Do you think I could call the hospital? Would they let me know anything if I'm not a relative?"

"Do you know which hospital?" Rob asked.

"No, good point." I frowned again. This grown-up stuff was hard. How did competent adults deal with situations like this? I had always felt a lack of respect in my leadership, and every once in a while it occurred to me that this disrespect was perhaps earned.

The phone in my pocket chirruped, and I gasped.

Rob nodded toward the general vicinity of my pants. "Maybe that's someone from church right now."

I flipped it out and saw a new message and realized I hadn't turned the ringer back on after practice. I was pretty much the only praise-team participant who heeded the repeated requests for phone courtesy during rehearsal. I swiped to my voicemail and set it to speaker for Rob's sake.

"Christine, this is Barb. I don't know if you're home yet—"

I jabbed a finger to call her back.

"Hey, Barb," I said, out of breath from my vigorous finger motions. "I just got in."

"Just awful about Tammy, isn't it?" she said.

"Yeah, I know. Have you heard anything?"

"Mm-hmm. Walter called the hospital and they have her in the ICU." See, other people did somehow know which hospital to call and how to get information out of strangers. Where did I learn that kind of skill? "It sounds like she's not doing so well."

"I can believe it," I said, remembering her face drained

23

of color and animation under the oxygen tubing and clear tape.

"I'm just activating the prayer chain so we can lift her before the Lord," Barb continued. Oh, man, she managed the prayer chain as well. At least maybe I could figure out how to participate in that.

"Am I supposed to call someone next, then?" I asked.

"Oh, no, we all have our lists of people to call, so it's taken care of." Naturally. "But keep her in prayer."

"Of course," I murmured.

"Talk to you later, then," Barb said.

"If you hear anything," I blurted before she could hang up, "will you let me know?"

"Sure," Barb said unperturbedly.

We hung up.

I sank onto the futon and stared at the screen as it went black. I guess now it was just a matter of waiting and seeing. Meanwhile, my mind couldn't stop circling around one recurring thought.

I turned to Rob. "Wanna go get some Taco Bell?"

The next day a knock on the door woke me. Rob had already left for work, but it was still early morning, too early for someone to be visiting me. I squinted at the alarm clock: 11:45, and yup, the dot was on A.M. Who the heck would come over at this hour?

I guessed it might be UPS, though we hadn't ordered anything. The mail lady came at a decent hour of the afternoon.

The knock came again, just as insistent as the first time.

It sounded too confident to be our seven-year-old neighbor, not to mention too high up on the door. When we moved in two years ago, he determined we were an incredible source of free boxes to build forts with, and he hadn't stopped coming around at odd intervals since. We didn't know his name, so we just referred to him as Box Boy. But Box Boy never knocked more than once, and if we ignored him he went away. From the third emphatic knock, I knew whoever this was was not going away.

"Just a minute!" I called, stumbling over my feet as I walked the opposite direction to the bathroom to grab the robe I barely ever wore. Fortunately and surprisingly, it was on the hook where I last remembered seeing it. As I pulled it on, I caught a glimpse of dark bedhead so evil that my eyes refused to take it in, so I rushed back to the door as quickly as it was groggily possible to.

Our peephole was useless unless the person had gotten bored enough to step back and stand across the hallway under the light. I figured this person was too determined to have gotten bored of disturbing us. I gave it a shot, but it gave me no viable information, except that from the height of the dark blur and a general impression of feminine shapeliness, it was indeed not Box Boy.

I ineffectually fluffed at my hair to make my waves behave and opened the door on the chain.

A badge was pushed up into my face, causing me to take a step back in surprise.

"Detective Madari," came a no-nonsense female voice to match the authoritative knocks. "Murphy Police."

"Just a minute," I said, and pushed the door closed so I could unlatch the chain. I hesitated a moment. I had learned from daytime talk shows that you should always call the police station to verify the identity of unexpected police visitors, but I didn't even know where to begin. How did you call the police station without using 911? Did I have time to look up the non-emergency number online before the so-called detective's patience ran thin? And if she were indeed an impostor, would 911 be my best option after all, only then it would be too late?

Oh, whatever. I slid the chain back, and let my visitor

in, even though I knew she was a stranger and I was pretty certain she was carrying a gun. Probably she was harmless, right?

Detective Madari was in plainclothes, though that seemed too dull to describe the spotless wool coat and skirt suit she was wearing. She seemed sturdy enough in her heels, but I wondered if she could run after a perp in them. I looked at her severe features and decided I never wanted to be someone she was chasing.

"Mrs....Song?" She was staring at an electronic tablet.

I arched my neck to see what she had written down, and she frowned at me.

Whoops. Apparently she didn't want me cheating off her notes. Too late for her, though. I had found what I needed.

"Yes, Song," I said, my voice sounding too loud to my ears.

"Spelled as it sounds?" she prompted.

"Yes," I said, taking my volume down a notch. "It's Korean. Not that I am. My husband is. I mean, American. Korean-American." I heard the babbling but couldn't stop the flow.

"Hm." She seemed to be barely listening anyhow.

"But it's not my name."

That got her attention. "Excuse me?"

"That's my husband's name. Rob Song."

"We have information that a Christine Song lives here."

"Information from whom?" I was a copy editor by trade and relished the sound of the "m" on the end of my correct use of the latter word.

Detective Madari pursed her thin lips. "From a Barbara Vanderwal."

"Ah." Well, that explained it. No one at New Vision seemed to understand why a wife wouldn't want to take her husband's name. Particularly her husband's perfectly spellable, pronounceable name, as opposed to most of the Dutch surnames New Vision was prone to. "Sometimes I go by that name at church, because it's easier."

"An alias?" Madari asked, stylus poised above her tablet.

"Um, if you like."

She wrote down this information about my alternate identity. Detective Madari was probably in her mid-thirties. I noticed that her face stopped just short of pretty, mostly because the bones were too prominent, as if even too much skin would have been in excess.

"What is your legal name, then?"

"Christine Randal. One l. C-h on the Christine." She scribbled some more. "I used to go by Chris, but there are like fourteen thousand Chrises at our church, so I decided it was easier to go with Christine now. I considered Chrissy, but everyone thought it sounded too much like a cheerleader."

Madari looked up with incisive gray eyes and for the first time in my life gave me an actual visual of an iron gaze. "You have a lot of names to go by."

I wasn't sure what to respond to that, but decided that stopping the outpouring of useless information was in my best interest.

"Can we sit down?" Detective Madari said. She looked over my shoulder at my unmade futon bed with clear uncertainty that such a thing would be possible. To save space while being thrifty, Rob and I had rented a one-bedroom apartment and converted the bedroom into our office. I used it for the at-home editing business I was trying to build up, and Rob used it to play computer games when he got home from his job as a graphic designer. We rarely had friends over, since no one else we knew rented. No one seemed to want to drive out to Mansardville from the ritzier areas of Northwest Indiana, and certainly no one wanted to visit a cramped apartment when they all had multi-bedroom, multi-story houses to entertain in.

So a futon seemed practical and was one of those things that made perfect sense to us. We had bought it with the expectation and solemn promise to each other that we'd fold it up into a couch every day and make it back into a bed each night. That had lasted one day after we bought it on special financing from the futon store. Since then, it sprawled in all its queen-size glory across our living room, and we perched on it sideways, leaning up against the curved-wood arms, to watch TV or read. Despite its comfortable spring-loaded expanse, I could see where my rumpled sheets might not look inviting to sit on were I a stranger.

"In here," I said, leading the detective toward the office in back.

She looked over the disarray of boxes and papers in the erstwhile bedroom with no less suspicion, but I wheeled out Rob's office chair for her and turned it to face my own, gesturing for her to take a seat while I plopped down into mine, the hydraulics making a little wheezing squeal as they settled to the proper height. In the brighter office lights, I could see the detective's hair was a striking deep brown with shimmering chestnut ribbons that looked like the natural envy of any highlight enthusiast. She had it pulled victoriously straight back into a tight knot. I wondered how irritated she felt at the extravagant color.

"Aren't you curious what this is in regards to?" Detective Madari asked as she settled into Rob's chair, feet planted firmly despite her skirt suit, and tablet ever at the ready.

"Of course," I said, feeling sheepish that I'd let myself get bogged down in minutiae. That was one of my problems with building up my home business as well. I'd mean to, say, write an online ad to attract clients, and in my keyword optimization testing I'd end up being distracted by

28

a link to compare celebrity baby bumps. Before I knew it, the whole day was gone and Rob was home from his salaried position asking how much I'd gotten done today and looking more than a little envious that I got to be a kept woman.

"We're gathering information on the death of Tammy Dykstra."

I felt my stomach thud. "No," I breathed. "She died?"

"Last night at Graybeal General. Didn't anyone tell you?" She held her stylus poised between two fingers and looked at me curiously.

"No. Well, at least, maybe they left a message..." I picked up my cell from its charging station on the desk and flicked away the lock screen to check for icons of incoming texts or calls. "No."

I could tell Detective Madari was taking in my loner state, but she continued. "Yes, she died of acute ingestion of nicotine."

"Ooo." I felt my mouth round into the little sad sound. "That's bad."

"Yes." The detective tapped once on her tablet with the stylus. "And so we're interviewing all the witnesses to the incident so that we can investigate the murder."

"The what now?"

Detective Madari looked at me blankly.

"Tammy was murdered?" I whispered.

"I've just said as much. She had a fatal blood level of nicotine."

I mirrored her blank stare. "That's not from smoking too much or something?"

Detective Madari cocked her head, presumably the better to gauge if I were as ignorant as I looked. "No, Mrs....Ms. Randal. Nicotine in this amount could not have been accidentally ingested by a reasonable adult. This was intentional." She reached into a pocket at her side and pulled out a small digital recorder. "Please tell me everything that happened last night, beginning with when you left for—choir practice, was it?" She pressed a button. "And I'll just record this conversation. Is that all right with you?"

I nodded, since she'd already begun to.

"Please verify your acceptance vocally."

"Yes," I croaked. I wanted to ask her if I could call my lawyer, only—I didn't have a lawyer. I guessed it was best just to get this over with.

Detective Madari set the recorder on the desk between us. "Now, precisely what happened last night?"

I tightened the belt of my robe where it gapped over my pajamas, feeling suddenly very vulnerable.

Chapter 3

Rob called from work while I was looking up nicotine poisoning online.

"I'm bored," he said. "Talk to me."

"How can you be bored at work? Aren't you doing work?"

"I'm waiting for a meeting to start. I already went to the bathroom and got some animal crackers from the vending machine. I've run out of ways to amuse myself."

"I'm glad to know I'm your last choice." I got up and walked to our little one-butt-wide kitchen. Animal crackers didn't sound half-bad.

"I figured you might have something to amuse me with."

"How do you know I wasn't hard at work editing?"

A sound suspiciously like a snort came over the line.

"Well, you're not exactly Mr. Productivity yourself today," I said. No animal crackers in the junk cupboard. I settled on Doritos.

"What are you crunching?" Rob asked.

I told him. "They're nacho cheesier."

"Good idea," he said. I heard a faint jingling. "I have

just enough change left. Do you mind if I spend a Great Sand Dunes quarter?"

I thought over our collection. "No, we have the sand dunes. It's the Everglades I've been looking for. But should you be eating Doritos? Won't they make your meeting uncomfortable?"

Rob was somewhat lactose intolerant. His lactose intolerance didn't bother him at all—it just bothered anyone else who was in the room with him after he'd slipped up. "Maybe that will just make the meeting shorter," he suggested. "Fine, I'll go with barbecue."

I heard the clanging of coins into the machine as Rob went after his prize. In between our crunches, I broke the bad news.

"Tammy died," I said. Rob could handle blunt.

"Oh, no," he said. "That's too bad."

"There's more," I said. "She was murdered."

"Murdered," Rob echoed. "Well, that's not amusing, but it's certainly intriguing. I've never known a murder victim before."

"You couldn't even remember her name, so I don't know that you can say you knew this one, either."

Rob gave a verbal shrug.

"She was poisoned," I added. I could hear Rob literally chewing things over. "Don't you want to know how I found out?"

"I assume Barb called you," he said after a swallow.

"Don't assume," I chided. "Barb's left me in the lurch. It was a detective."

Rob gave a little choke on the other end. "From the actual police?" he said. "Are you a suspect?" He sounded much too enthusiastic about the idea.

"I don't know," I said. "I don't think so. Or maybe we all are."

"Did you ask for a lawyer?"

I gripped the cell phone tighter. "Should I have?"

"We don't know any lawyers."

"No, I know."

"Murder." Rob breathed out heavily.

"I know." I hadn't been able to concentrate on anything else all day. How could someone have been murdered, and right in front of me, too?

"Well, I have to go," Rob said, suddenly brisk. "Our meeting is starting."

"Bummer for you," I said, snapping back to the immediate. "See you later."

Rob tossed off a "later" and disconnected. I tongued the last of the orange crud off my fingers and tried to ignore the lure of crime solving via Google and get some work done.

"So it couldn't have been an accident?" Rob wasted no time continuing our phone conversation as he set his laptop bag down on the office floor, leaning it against his desk, and shrugged his thin arms out of his winter jacket, letting it drop in a pile. This was why our place was always a sty—neither of us had much sense of how to keep things picked up.

"I don't think so," I said, still in my jammies but sans robe. I had swiveled away from facing my laptop screen to look at Rob. "It was a mega high dose, and it shouldn't have been in food in the first place." I chewed on my lip, ripping off a satisfying strip of dead skin before deciding I should call it quits. "But do you think it's possible Tammy wasn't the target? I mean, what did she ever do to anybody?"

Rob had finally made it to his own desk chair and sat down. He tended to do everything deliberately, so everything took a while, even a 3-foot walk, despite his lithe build. I swiveled back toward my screen to peer at his oval face over the top. The fronts of our desks kissed so that we could make goo-goo eyes at each other while working on our computers.

Rob leaned back in his office chair, the plastic and metal rubbing and creaking. "It wasn't a very surefire way to kill a specific person, was it?" he mused. "I mean, Barb gives those drops out to everyone, so how could someone who spiked it know that Tammy would get that one in particular?"

"Well, I didn't get to tell you everything that happened last night. There was something kind of weird, but then it was overshadowed by Tammy's collapse. Barb went looking for a cough drop to give Tammy, and her purse was missing. Later, she found it randomly out in the hallway, but now there weren't any cough drops left."

"How did she give one to Tammy, then?" Rob asked, leaning forward on his desk, long fingers crossed like a teacher quizzing a student who'd just admitted a mistake.

I had trodden this same ground so many times with Detective Madari during the interrogation earlier today that I felt repetitive telling it to Rob, even though I realized he didn't know any of it.

"She was getting her keys out of her pocket to go check her car for the purse, and a single cough drop fell out of her coat pocket."

Rob pushed back in his chair again. "Well, that's weird."

"Yeah," I said. "I guess the killer could have put the poisoned drop in the coat, then stole the others so that the poisoned one would definitely be used. But then..."

"But then, how would the killer know Tammy would get the drop?" Rob pursed his lips to one side. "Unless Barb's the killer."

I guffawed. "Seriously? Barb?"

Rob looked at me solemnly. "Well, it has to be someone, Eggs."

That gave me the shivers. Not my nickname—that was

a long-standing joke between us. But that someone hated Tammy enough to kill her, and that I probably knew the killer.

"Does it have to be someone we know? Someone from the praise team?" I asked.

"Well, it really only has to be someone Barb's in contact with, I guess," Rob said. "Especially if it was a random target, and Tammy just ended up unlucky."

"Maybe Barb was the target!" I exclaimed.

"That makes even more sense," Rob said slowly. "Sure, she gives plenty of those drops away, but let's assume logically that she eats at least two herself for every one she gifts. I can always hear her clicking those things between her teeth or smell them on her breath...uhh." Rob gave an exhalation of disgust.

"Although," I said, "the killer did have to be at praise team practice, to steal the purse and the extra drops."

"Weeell," Rob said, drawing out his thought, his deep brown eyes semi-focused as he gazed up at the ceiling, "that's assuming first of all that Barb herself didn't just leave her purse out in the hall or forget to restock on drops. But if they were stolen, it's possible it was by someone else entirely."

"Yeah," I agreed, dubious, "but that would be a pretty big coincidence. This whole thing with the lozenges, and then someone dies from one minutes later. Although it could all just be random, just some messed-up person who tainted a bag of drops, and this happens to be where it ended up." My logical musings went unheeded, though, because Rob was deep in thought.

"Oh!" He shot forward in his chair.

I jumped.

"Did Tammy ask Barb for the lozenge?" Rob's eyes were wide.

"Yeah," I told him.

"Oh," Rob said again, but much more subdued this

time. "Never mind then. I thought if Barb had just volunteered it, then for sure it must have been her."

"You really have it in for Barb, don't you?" I asked him.

"Well," Rob said, "it's not like I want her to be a murderer, but she does criticize all my website designs."

Rob volunteered for New Vision by redesigning the church's outdated website and now maintaining it, since no one else was competent enough to take over as webmaster. Far from appreciating the untold unpaid hours he had put into the project, Barb kept nitpicking about font choices and color schemes and suggesting alternate menu wordings. Rob nodded and pretended to take notes in person, then blasted her to me in private.

I shrugged, conceding the point. "I generally like Barb, but she can be a bit much at times. But still—a murderer. I don't want to even think it."

Rob shrugged, too, apparently still convinced she was the prime suspect. And maybe, to the police at least, she was.

I thought further. "Doctoring the drop must have been beforehand, though, right?"

"Did you say it was nicotine poisoning?" Rob asked.

"That's what Detective Madari told me."

"What's that mean, like crushed up bits of cigarette?"

"Well," I said, happy to have studied at Google U, "you actually concentrate tobacco into a syrup and use the purified and intense nicotine as a liquid."

"So it couldn't have been accidental?" I shook my head in agreement. "And it would have been hard to doctor the drop mid-practice."

"Though not impossible," I said, "if the killer had a syringe at the ready."

"Barb would have had the best chance, regardless," Rob said.

"Barb doesn't use tobacco, though."

"It's not a controlled substance," Rob said.

36

"I wish we could just talk with everyone." This speculation thing was kind of fun, but I needed some actual facts.

"Line up the suspects?" Rob said.

That gave me an idea.

"I should call her."

"Barb?" Rob said. "The murderess?"

"Stop it," I said. "Out of concern and an opportunity to express our mutual horror over Tammy's death and share what happened with the detective...and, incidentally, to wheedle some information out of her. It will be fun, like we're investigating. Rando and Eggs strike again."

Rob and I had met on the newspaper at Blanchard College in Illinois—he laying out and I editing. We had gone on our first date as "just friends" to the March Mingle, Blanchard's non-dancing answer to a formal dance. That year, the school had hired a murder mystery troupe to entertain us all, and we had been sat at a table with nitwits who had somehow managed to best Blanchard's arduous application process. Since we had been in a whimsical mood and drawn only smiley faces on our nametags, our table was convinced we were part of the troupe and kept pumping us for clues. One character the mystery mentioned was a cross-dressing gentleman who went as Mrs. X when in the drag-queen mood. No one at our table could seem to fathom the cross-dressing angle, and soon they were all accusing me of secretly being Mrs. Eggs.

Rob and I had taken that as our cue to escape into the hallway of the rental hall, laugh until our sides hurt, and then lean in closer to dispel any lies we'd told ourselves about being just friends. Later on, we discovered that our solution to the mystery was indeed the correct one, but we'd missed out on entering it for a prize thanks to our impromptu getaway. We never regretted that for a moment. Thinking about it again made my mouth quirk up in a smile, and I looked at Rob for an answering one.

"Be careful," was all he said.

He was serious. This wasn't a dinner mystery game.

I shook it off and picked up navigated to the PDF of the church picture directory on my computer to confirm Barb's number. I thought I'd try her home line first, so as not to seem extra pushy.

I scrolled to the Vs. There was Barb, smiling back at me, her hands resting on her husband Adam's shoulder as she leaned in to him. Adam's smile seemed camera-fixed, but Barb's was her usual enthusiastic genuineness, reaching all the way to the sparkling blue eyes under her cropped gray-blond hair. There were definitely things that bothered me about Barb. For one thing, there was her unthinking elitism. For instance, when friends of ours were moving into their grandparents' house in the country, she told them, "You'll have to keep horses, of course. Everyone in the country does." Our friends, who were moving to save costs after their house had been foreclosed on, stared at her blankly but nodded. Later, they told me they could maybe swing a stick horse—used. And then there was her unconscious expectation that everyone would agree with her opinions, as when she told Rob everything that was wrong with his website redesign, or when she bossed around the worship planning committee with whatever spontaneous suggestions sprang into her head. It didn't occur to her that she wasn't an expert or that her opinions might hurt other people's feelings. She didn't mean to offend. Despite her faults, I couldn't help but find her likable. I couldn't see her being spiteful, and certainly not enough to murder someone.

My finger poised to dial her number, I looked across at Rob, who had begun doing some tippity-typing on his computer, presumably checking his email as was his wont on arriving home. "I had a thought," I said to get his attention. He was not the most observant person in the world. He looked up, absently pushing back the one lock of shiny black hair that never stayed out of his eyes, and then adjusted his glasses for good measure. Rob had resisted the Lasik-or-contacts trend that had aptly swept New Vision, but more from a phobia of having anything touch his eyeballs than resistance of the status quo, which was my stated reason. I found Avery DeHaan's insistence on wearing clunky frames endearing, considering she had perfect vision. "Why would Barb kill someone with her specialty cough drops? She must know it would be traced back irrevocably to her."

Rob was silent a moment. "Why do murderers do anything risky? But a lot of them do, and then they're caught. I don't know." He thought a minute longer. "But it does make more sense that she'd have been framed rather than use that method. Then again, that's a method she could be sure would work. She certainly had the best access to the cough drops and had a habit of distributing them. She could be sure the poisoned one got into the right hands. Mouth. Whatever."

I nodded. "But then there was that moving of her bag and the theft of the other cough drops."

"Although she could have staged that herself, to make it look like someone had tampered."

"You're determined to make it her," I said, smiling.

"She seems like the obvious suspect," Rob protested. "I know it might seem like she's too obvious, but that's usually whodunit."

I pondered this. "Do you think we watch too many murder mysteries?" I asked Rob. "It's not like we're actually going to solve this thing by talking it over."

"Probably the police are more effective at this sort of thing than we are," Rob conceded. "But you might as well call Barb and satisfy some of our curiosity. What harm could there be in that?"

I shrugged and dialed, worrying once more at talking with a potential killer.

"Barb?" I said when she answered. "This is Christine Randal from New Vision."

"Christine!" Barb said, sounding as enthusiastic as ever. "I meant to call you earlier to let you know." Here her voice finally dropped in timbre, to suit the news. "Tammy unfortunately didn't make it."

"I know," I said. "A detective from the Murphy Police was here earlier, collecting my statement."

"You, too?" Barb said. "We had them over here as well, and so did Kirsten and Walter, though I thought that was because we'd been the ones helping Tammy."

Well, that stung. But what had Barb been doing to help, beyond dialing the phone?

"Maybe they're interviewing everyone," I said.

"I don't believe it's murder," she said, as confidently as if she assumed I would agree with her.

"Why's that?" I said. "The detective said the levels of nicotine were astronomical."

"There's no way my cough drops have any poison in them." Barb sounded calm. "I have one in my mouth right now."

I could feel my eyes bugging. "Barb!" I gasped. "Spit it out!"

"It's fine," she said. "It's from my stash that just came in the mail today. I order them from England, you know."

"I thought it was Austria."

"Nope." I could hear her sucking. "It's a British company. Local herbs."

Local herbs to them, poison to us? "I can't believe you're not worried about them."

"The lab must have made a mistake," Barb said. There was no reasoning with her certainty.

"Did you ever find out where the other ones went to, the ones missing from your purse?" I asked instead, which sounded pleasingly to my ears like a good question an amateur sleuth would ask.

"No," Barb said, sounding idly puzzled rather than alarmed. "Isn't that strange?"

"Did you leave your purse out in the hall, or did someone move it there?"

"I couldn't say," Barb said. "I don't remember leaving it out there, but you know."

"Is it possible you had just run out of lozenges, since you just ordered more?"

"Hmm," Barb said, "it's possible. I don't really remember. I thought I had some in there, but I just usually do."

Well, this was no help at all.

"The detectives asked all these same questions," Barb said.

"Detectives?" I said. "There was more than one?"

"Two of them," she said. "One to talk, one to take notes."

What did it mean that they had sent two to Barb specifically? I thought Rob must be right that she was suspecto numero uno, whether she knew it or not. That made me feel a little better, at least. I rated just one cop at a time.

"Do you know when the funeral is?" I decided to switch tacks.

"I'm not even sure who Tammy's family is," she said. "She didn't have any at New Vision that I know of. I'll let you know when I find out."

Sure she would.

"It's too bad it's an alto," Barb said, slurping on her lozenge.

"What?" I hadn't kept up with Barb's change in topic.

"It's too bad we lost an alto. We don't have as many of those."

I couldn't argue with that. I would have to point out to Rob that Barb apparently wouldn't have killed off anyone who sang harmony, since we were a rarer breed.

"Now it's just you, right?" Barb continued.

I hoped she wasn't suggesting someone was targeting altos. We were a generally well-liked bunch. "It's okay," I said. "Avery can pitch in with harmony, but she has such a strong voice I like keeping her on melody if possible."

"I can sing louder, if you like," Barb said helpfully.

"Um, thanks, Barb." I think I managed to sound sincere.

"Sure thing. See you on Sunday!" Life went on. Poor Tammy.

"Well?" Rob was staring at me, waiting for my report.

"She says she doesn't know if her bag was moved or not, or if the lozenges were stolen or not. Oh, and two detectives came to interrogate her. But she didn't sound worried at all. Get this—she was sucking on one of those lozenges!"

Rob looked as gobsmacked as I had been. "She did it," he said. "Only she would know which ones were poisoned."

"Riiight," I said. I hadn't thought of that. "Well, there you are, then." I dusted my hands. "We've solved it. Shall I call the police and gloat?"

"Nah," Rob said, "Let's go to Wendy's. I have a hankering for some chili." He leaned over to retrieve his jacket from the floor.

"Weren't we going to check out a Bible study tonight?"

Rob stopped with one arm in a sleeve and one out. "What?"

"We've been talking about trying out one of the church small groups."

"Tonight?"

"Well, the one at Walter Kappas's house is tonight, and I'd rather that there's someone we know there."

"Someone you know," Rob corrected.

"You'll like Walter," I said. "He's nice."

"Or a murderer," Rob said.

"He's one of the Watchkeepers." The Watchkeepers

were New Vision's snazzy version of an elder board. "He's a Christian high school principal."

Rob gave a shrug that suggested this proved his point.

I shot him a look. "We already determined Barb did it," I reminded him. "Hey, maybe Barb will be there tonight."

"That will make my life complete," Rob said, looking even less enthusiastic. "What time do we have to leave?"

I jiggled my mouse so I could check the time. "Now." I got up to start getting ready. If Barb was there, she'd have something to say about my being late, as usual.

Chapter 4

When we arrived at Walter's house, a roomy two-story in a subdivision, his porch lights were off and I almost tripped over some tools and shovels left lying out in the driveway. Walter apologized for the darkness when he opened the door, clad in his usual school-principal suit with his retreating fringe of brown hair backlit by the interior lights, and belatedly illuminated the cluttered path we had just traveled. I wondered if he'd turned off the lights on purpose because we were late.

Since the meeting had already started, it was perhaps fortunate that Barb wasn't part of the group after all. The gathering did include a few familiar faces from praise team: Walter and his wife Belinda, Jim the basso very profondo, and Zachary, the teenage drummer. I was surprised to see him at a Bible study, I suppose because I was age-biased enough to think it would be all adults. He was slumped in a flowered easy chair in Walter's living room and staring rather morosely at Wren DeHaan, who was Avery's younger sister and who was at present scrawling in some sort of workbook at a table in the corner. His blond curls caught the glow of a table lamp and haloed his grumpy face.

"The girls usually tag along," a booming voice announced. I turned from handing my coat off to Walter and saw Gavin DeHaan, the drama team leader, gesturing from his place on the couch from me to Wren and then in a large circle, I guess to suggest two girls.

"Where's Avery?" I asked.

"Out tonight." Gavin's voice seemed to know no volume control. I felt sheepish on his behalf, not to mention on my own, since we were interrupting whatever had been going on before our late arrival.

"We'd just started," Belinda Kappas said, as pleasant as her husband and seeming to read my thoughts. Her shoulder-length salt and pepper hair was held back neatly by a tortoiseshell headband.

"Where?" Zachary interjected, the corners of his mouth diving.

Everyone turned at his nonsequitur of a question, but he was looking at Gavin.

"Oh, Avery," Gavin said after a—what else?—dramatic pause. "She's out with Dylan at his band rehearsal."

"Is she playing in it?" Zachary asked, sounding confused rather than suspicious.

"No, no," Gavin chortled, his broad face and prominent cheekbones creasing and rising in interesting wrinkles set from a lifetime of dramatic expressions.

"She just likes to observe," Gavin's wife volunteered from where she sat squished beside her husband on the rose-velour couch, the better to give Jim the full final cushion on the end. "Because she's going into music performance." In contrast to her husband's thundering voice and granite-hewn features, Marjorie was a mouse of a woman, with lank blond hair that blended into her fair skin and a voice that barely rose above a whisper. She looked to be not much older than we were, and I wondered that she had two near-teen daughters.

Zachary's brow furrowed as if he couldn't quite piece together the information he was receiving.

Another praise-team parent pair were present, our bassist Dylan Ruiz's mother and father. I was not at all surprised to see that Dylan was not interested in attending a Bible study, Avery or no Avery.

I nodded at the smoothly elegant Alexander and Mora Ruiz though I didn't know them very well, because unlike the other youths' parents, they left me pretty well alone. Dylan presumably was raised Christian Reformed since his father was also a Watchkeeper at New Vision, but I was never sure if he kept going to church because he got something religious out of it, or if it was just because he needed an outlet for his bass playing. Despite my instinctive distaste for his personal style that mocked my own bland appropriateness, including tight jeans and metal wristlets, I had to admit that his bass skills were among the best that this group of musicians and eager would-be musicians had to offer.

Alex Ruiz was the owner of several car dealerships. I wasn't sure if Dylan's parents were proud of their son's musical abilities or merely tolerated them. Mora had sworn Blanchard College, Rob's and my alma mater and a tough school to get into, had been Dylan's first choice, yet he was currently attending community college. Indiana folk tended to stay close to home, but I wondered if Dylan's choice had anything to do with wanting to keep his band together.

The only person I couldn't place was a diminutive yet sturdy woman sitting in a straight chair. Middle-aged with boy-short dark brown hair, she perched alertly on the edge of her seat with a fancy-looking pen poised above a red leather-bound diary. She smiled at me, and I smiled back, wondering where I'd seen her before.

"We'll get started, then," Walter said, clasping his hands together in an eager-beaver way. "Let's pray."

Rob and I sank down onto the tasteful wall-to-wall carpet next to Belinda, since all the available seats were taken, and bowed our heads. Despite the current lack of seating, the room could fit all of us with ease. Like most Midwestern houses we visited, I noted an astonishing dearth of clutter and wondered if they would come minimalize our space for us. There was one tall oak bookshelf with a dozen books against the side wall, one sumptuously framed painting of a cottage over the sofa, and a decorative flowered swag curtain over the window at my back, and that was all.

After the short prayer, Walter gestured toward us. "I forgot," he said with a chuckle. "Does everyone know Rob and Christine Song?"

Everyone nodded, and I didn't bother to correct the last-name conflation. Rob glanced at me with his social-rabbit face, and I read his thoughts that he was not so privileged as to know everyone in return.

"You remember Gavin and Marjorie from the drama team," I broke in out of pity, nodding their way. "And that's Avery's sister Wren over there."

"Hi," Rob squeaked when Wren turned to eye him from under a fall of blond hair, then turn back to her work without comment. I assumed it was some sort of home-school assignment from Gavin.

"And you know Walter and Belinda." I smiled in turn at Walter, who stood kitty-corner from us against one wall, and Belinda, next to us on the carpet. I noted for some reason that they were the only married couple not sitting together, but I supposed that was what came of host duty. They waited patiently as I hijacked their group.

"Have you met Alexander and Mora?" I said. Rob smiled noncommittally.

"I think we've met in passing," Mora said smoothly. With her sleek raven hair and twin sets, she looked like she came from money. "We're Dylan's parents."

"Ah," Rob said, as if that cleared things up. I knew he probably had no idea what our bassist's name was.

The unfamiliar brown-haired woman's chair was next to the loveseat Alexander and Mora were sharing, but I paused in giving out her name.

Obviously a keen observer, she broke in before the pause could become awkward. "I'm Valerie Dejong." She smiled pleasantly at both of us. "I'm the editor of the church newsletter."

"The InSight," Rob said.

Valerie beamed assent.

"And that's Zachary, one of our drummers, and Jim, one of our singers," I finished, smiling at both. Zachary was still pondering the missing Avery too hard to notice. Jim nodded gravely back, his bald head gleaming in the overhead glow of recessed lighting.

"Terrible thing last night," Valerie said, obviously grasping the praise-team connection among many of the attendees. She took her smile's wattage down a few notches out of respect.

"Mmm," I murmured in assent.

Mora clicked her tongue, whether in distaste of murder or our mention of it, I wasn't sure.

"I heard nicotine poisoning," Valerie continued. "I imagine the police will be looking hard at all the church members who smoke or chew."

Somehow the same speculation Rob and I had indulged in sounded more obnoxious coming out of Valerie's mouth.

Jim gave a little hiccup, and in focusing on him, I was surprised to note that he looked near tears.

"Did you know Tammy well?" I asked him solicitously. "I remember her mentioning an outing with you when we were over at her house."

There was a pause while Jim swallowed. "We were in One-on-One together," he managed.

I knew Jim less than some of the other members, because he'd joined just a few months previously. I knew he owned a handyman company, supplying tools and manpower for homeowners seeking improvement. Maybe his deep bass voice was art imitating life, an attempt to sound like a jackhammer. He had been attending a traditional but slowly dwindling Christian Reformed church in Nederland, Illinois, when he jumped ship over to New Vision, with its casual dress, catchy sermon titles, and electrified music.

New Vision was what was known as a seeker-friendly church, meaning it tried to attract people who wouldn't otherwise attend a worship service, with mixed success. One of the criticisms of such newfangled churches was that most of the people attending were like Jim and only "stolen" from alternate churches. Our pastor hated the word "stolen" used in that context, because it was the choice of people like Jim to move over from less captivating church options, but I could understand the frustration the traditional churches must have when faced with newcomers like us. It was a frustration I shared in that it seemed like the people coming into the church were looking more for an entertaining show than to commit to a position of serving or leading. That said, here I was heading up the team that provided Sunday morning's main entertainment, so maybe I wasn't one to talk, and at least Jim in this case was volunteering and plugging himself into the community, through praise team, this Bible study, and, I was now discovering, the singles group.

"She seemed like a big part of that group," Walter said from his station against the wall, where he'd seated himself on the carpet as well now, seeming to be his usual courteous self by buying Jim time to become composed.

"She was," Jim said, after taking a deep breath. His voice was a little less strained as he continued. "She was really into photography. We led a photography class together for the group."

"I saw the photos on the website," Marjorie whispered, swiveling her torso to face him and then immediately turning back into her husband. "They were really good," she spoke into his side.

"On the church website?" Valerie said. She jotted a note to herself in her book.

Jim nodded, as if once more he couldn't trust himself to speak. It was hard to imagine this tough construction worker–turned–business owner tearing up, but here was the proof.

Walter must have taken pity on him or decided it was time to resume the evening's discussion, or both. "Well, we'll get started with this week's chapter, then," he said briskly to the group at large.

He handed us two slim volumes penned by Mike De Jong, the leader of the forerunner seeker church, Birch Park. Everyone who was anyone at New Vision reverenced Birch Park as the mother ship. New Vision didn't yet have the cachet of a megachurch like Birch, nearby in Illinois, not that they weren't trying. Part of the hold-up was not having the budget of a white-collar megachurch, in no small measure because our congregation was about 200 to Birch's 20,000 or more, but that didn't stop the leadership of New Vision from dreaming big and using all the resources Birch handed out like so much manna.

For the next hour, we read illustrative anecdotes and answered multiple-choice questions. I doodled in the margins of my book with the pencil Walter had had passed over to me.

"What do you think, Christine?" Walter called from across the room. I jolted out of my reverie and looked in surprise at my scribbled note: "Why Tammy?" It was underlined, and I'd added a couple inappropriately cheerful upside-down flowers onto the stems of the Ys.

What did I think?

I wasn't sure which question we were on. "I'd say C," I

improvised. Wasn't that the most common multiple-choice answer?

"Interesting," Belinda said at my shoulder.

I nodded.

Thankfully, Gavin broke in with his opinion and I was free to return to my previous thoughts.

What had Tammy done to deserve being killed? Barely anyone knew her, apart from the One-on-One contingent. She was always quiet, but in a cheerful way, not like Zachary's detached, mom-led participation. She showed up on time (I thought) and had her music ready and got along well with the other praise team members. Well, obviously, I thought, retracing my letters to bold them, she didn't get along with at least one person.

Rob noticed what I was doing and caught my eye to frown at me. I tipped my book toward him, and he gave a discreet shrug.

"What answer do you have, Rob?" Walter asked him. His principal's eyes must have been trained to catch out any student having private conversations and passing notes in class.

"C," Rob said after an awkward pause. I hid a smirk and ignored his subsequent glare my way.

We turned the page just as I was coloring in the teensy hole in the A. I resolved to think about the question later and devote my attention to the conversation, since it had been my idea to attend. It turned out the topic of the study was discipline, and tonight's chapter was about focusing on the task at hand. Go figure.

After finishing out all the questions, Walter allowed us to have a somewhat meandering conversation before he led us in prayer again.

"There are snacks in the kitchen," Belinda announced with a smile as people began to stand and stretch their legs.

As I watched the group file into Walter and Belinda's

spacious kitchen ahead of me, I also saw Zachary pull himself out of his chair and go stand near Wren, staring down at her until she looked up from where she was gathering up her supplies into a colorful tote bag.

"Yes?" she said superciliously. At only eleven years old, that kid had a thing or two to teach even Avery about precocious self-confidence, I thought. Not to mention me.

I missed the rest of their conversation as the crowd cleared enough to let the stragglers through, and Rob had put a gentle hand at my back to usher me through the kitchen door, cutting off my eavesdropping. Behind Rob, we left Valerie still fumbling to close her pen and red diary, even though I'd have thought those would have been easy enough to pack away.

Rob and I grabbed lemon bars and homemade Chex Mix from two platters on the kitchen island and ate alternately out of each fist. The kitchen looked startlingly new, as if it had just been remodeled. I noticed a single hole where a dishwasher would fit and wondered if that was the final piece of the puzzle. The granite counters, stainless steel appliances, and cherry cabinets with ceiling-high molding were a far cry from our cramped galley kitchen, with its 1980s particle-board cabinets and mismatched appliances. At least most of ours still worked.

With my mouth full, I moved out of the way as Valerie finally made her appearance at the snack location.

I found myself face to face with Mora Ruiz, Dylan the bassist's mother.

"Good to see you here, Christine," she said, taking a genteel nibble from a single lemon bar that perched on a paper plate in one thin hand.

There were plates? I looked back toward the island, and sure enough, I couldn't imagine how I'd missed them. Oh, well. "It's good to be here," I said. I bent my head down to my lemon bar hand to take a bite off of the top.

"I trust Dylan is behaving himself in praise team," she

said with a subdued chortle.

I smiled. "Absolutely. He's one of the best musicians we've got."

She accepted this with a gracious nod.

I took a mouthful of Chex Mix and then stood there for a moment hearing every crunch in the lull in our conversation. Mora politely looked off into the distance, half-consumed lemon bar balanced on her plate.

When my mouthful was down to soggy remnants and I couldn't take the awkwardness anymore, I cast about for some suitable conversation gambit. "Hey," I said. Mora turned back toward me with one eyebrow slightly raised. "I hear Dylan's planning to go to Blanchard College next year."

I could have sworn Mora's cool smile turned a fraction icier.

"Yes, is he transferring from the community college next year?" I hadn't heard Valerie come up beside me, but now there she was, pen once more in place above her red diary. She was even shorter than I'd realized from seeing her sitting down. Her close-cropped head barely reached my elbow. "I love to write features on our young scholars."

Mora wasn't pretending to smile anymore. I wondered at the drop in temperature in this part of the room.

"Rob and I went to Blanchard," I said quietly. "Just, you know, if Dylan wants any advice." Mora looked resolutely at me and hadn't turned toward Valerie once, but I wasn't sure that Mora saw me, either. I filled my mouth with more Chex Mix.

"Kind of you," she murmured. "We're not sure if Dylan will be attending Blanchard after all."

"Oh?" Valerie said.

Mora's mouth compressed before she deliberately re-donned her smooth mask. "He's enjoying Boyle Community College more than he'd thought. Plus, he has his band to play with, and they're looking to record an album next year. And Blanchard is very expensive."

I nodded at that last one. "Tell me about it," I sighed, remembering the zeroes on the checks I wrote out each month for our student loans—and the coordinating zeroes in our checkbook.

Valerie scribbled a note in her book. "Well, tell him to call me for an interview if he does decide to transfer." Mora gave the slightest of nods, still not facing the elfin newsletter editor. "I like to keep tabs on all of our congregation's good news."

"Are we talking college?" Walter had sidled up to us. "That's been a big change in our house, too."

Belinda overheard and smiled our way. "Yes, we're empty nesters finally." She moved to stand on the other side of Mora, still leaving space between herself and her husband.

"How fun," I said to Walter. "How many children do you have?"

Walter paused, and Belinda laughed. "Trying to tally them all up?" She turned to me. "Two, one a freshman this year and one a junior."

Walter smiled tightly. Maybe he, too, was thinking of all those zeroes.

"Well, I think Alexander is ready to leave," Mora said, sweeping me a gracious nod as she left our corner of the kitchen to rejoin her husband. He held out a tan fur cape that he suavely wrapped around his wife after she approached. I wondered if it was real fur and decided that it probably was a well-kept antique. I studied Alexander's pristine dark gray wool greatcoat that covered an expertly tailored suit jacket and slacks and wondered at such a family caviling at the price of any college.

I left Valerie writing notes to herself and allowed myself to be drawn back to the snacks. I needed some more Chex Mix, and this time I piled it onto a plate, the better to balance a cup of apple juice in the other hand.

Wren was picking up the juice when I pulled up a paper cup, so she held the bottle over mine.

"Thanks," I said. I was taking a sip when I glimpsed movement out of the corner of my eye.

"Oh," I said. Wren was occupied putting the cap back on the juice after pouring her own drink. "I think your mom's ready to leave." I waved my Chex Mix plate hand toward where Marjorie was waving timidly from the door to the kitchen.

"She's not my mom," Wren said into her juice cup.

"What?"

Wren pulled the cup down from her mouth. "She's my stepmom."

"Oh," I said.

"She's, like, twenty-eight." She examined one fingernail as she spoke and studiously ignored Marjorie's half-hearted attempts to flag her over. "She'd have been sixteen when Avery was born."

"Huh," I said. "That's funny." Was it?

Wren tossed back the rest of her juice and pulled her tote bag up higher onto her shoulder. "See you around," she said. She expertly tossed her cup into the trash as she walked out of the kitchen and right past her stepmother.

Zachary brushed by her on his way toward the snack island. I watched him approach and reach over me for the juice, wondering if he would get around to saying hi. He grabbed a lemon bar and leaned back against the island, chewing.

I decided it was up to me. "Hey, Zachary," I said.

He looked at me with his bland blue gaze as if surprised to see me so close. "Oh, hey."

"I meant to ask," I said. "Did you and Avery and Dylan see anything suspicious when you were out in the hall yesterday?"

"What?" His mouth dropped open enough for me to see partially chewed bright yellow filling.

"At praise team, when everyone was looking for Barb's purse," I said, "you three were out in the hall together. Did you see anything?"

"I was going to the bathroom," he said, returning to chewing.

I wasn't sure what to say to that, so I was gathering up just one more plateful of Chex Mix when I saw Rob approach through the thinning crowd.

"Split another lemon bar?" he asked me.

"I'm game."

He held out a gooey half, and I offered him a sip of my juice.

Then we left the kitchen to reenter the living room and wait for Walter to bring out our coats.

"Whose is this?" He was holding aloft a puffy black jacket with a company logo and smiling. "Just joking," he said, handing it to Jim. I recognized the logo was that of Jim's handyman company.

That reminded me. "Walter," I said.

He paused in handing Valerie a bright red jacket to match her diary. "Hm?"

"You were sorting jackets that night that...you know, Tammy's incident."

Walter nodded solemnly, passing along a moth-holed black hoodie to Zachary, who pulled it on and up over his bright curls.

"Did you feel anything odd in the pockets or anything?"

He stopped where he was, my own parka clutched in one fist. I reached out to take it, but it took some tugging before he let go.

"What do you mean?" he said. The remaining group members were also staring at me.

"I don't know, like bulky," I stammered. "I just thought, since Barb's cough drops were stolen, maybe you stumbled on something that would give a clue where they'd gone to."

Walter chuckled. "Afraid not," he said, smoothly resuming his coat distribution.

"Oh, well," I said. "Worth a shot." I waited for Rob to retrieve his jacket and shrug into it, and then I took his arm as we made our way out into the chilly January night.

"Thanks, Walter," I said along with the others leaving at the same time. I waved with the hand holding Rob's and my Bible study books and carefully navigated around the tools in the driveway this time.

"Come back next week!" he directed good-naturedly at the two of us, his breath a white fog in the night air.

"Sure thing," I called, stamping my feet on the sidewalk while I waited for Rob to hurry up and unlock the car. My key fob had stopped working long before, and we'd not yet justified replacing it.

Rob settled himself and put on his seat belt before becoming aware that he was missing a wife beside him. He belatedly popped the passenger door locks. "I thought I'd pressed it twice," he said in apology as I shivered into my seat beside him.

"I hope yours isn't dying, too," I said between my chattering teeth.

He turned the engine to purring life, and I had hopes that the heat would start to warm me up just about the time we got home.

Rob had other plans, however.

"I'm famished," he said. "How about Wendy's now?"

I glanced at the dashboard clock to confirm that the night was still young. "Absolutely."

Chapter 5

I was idly checking my phone before bed when I recognized an email from a foreign address. Sure enough, it was an urgent editing request from one of my best clients, a cadre of German scientists studying infant car safety. Could I please edit this research journal submission to APA guidelines and have it back by tomorrow? Since I had trouble figuring out time zones across the pond, I figured I'd better stay up and finish rather than try to get up in time the next day.

The next afternoon, when I arose, I found Rob spending his Saturday goofing off on his computer in our home office. I grunted at him as I entered the bathroom across the hall. He waved.

I came his direction after I'd finished up. "How's it feel to be a kept man?" I lumbered over to my desk chair and peered through my eye boogers in his direction.

"Feels pretty good," he said. "I could get used to this. Is this what you do all day when I'm at work?"

"Dunno," I said. "What are you doing?"

"Spider solitaire," he said.

"Nah, I'm more a Candy Crush woman."

"Have you considered my suggestion about getting New Vision to pay you?"

"What, for being a crappy interim praise team leader?"

"They could make your a permanent crappy praise team leader," Rob said casually. "Wouldn't they pay a permanent leader?"

I shrugged but then realized the gesture was lost, since his eyes remained glued to his little floating cards. "I don't think they'd pay someone without any experience or talent," I said.

"I think you undervalue yourself," Rob said, eyes still on the screen.

I shrugged again but didn't add any verbals this time.

Rob must have finished a game, because he pushed back from the desk. "I've been waiting for you to get up to have some breakfast. Tater tots?"

"With melted cheese?"

"But of course, ma petit fromage." Rob had figured out precisely what cheesy products he could buy to avoid digestive indignities.

I made kissy lips his way and pushed the button that would slowly bring my laptop alive.

Bored while waiting, I picked up my phone. I decided it was time for my monthly check-in with my parents. They lived in Virginia, because my dad worked for the State Department. They were a lot more settled now than we had been growing up. I sometimes wondered how I was living in Indiana after a childhood spent in locales around the globe.

"Hey, Mom," I said when she answered.

"Daughter!" she exclaimed. "How are things?"

"Kind of exciting, actually," I said, preparing to launch into a recounting of Tammy's death.

"Good, good," she said. "Now let me remember what I wanted to tell you."

"Okay," I agreed, after a pause. I waited out a run-through of which people from the church I'd attended in high school were pregnant, getting divorced, or in the hospital.

When she let down her guard, I broke in. "Did you maybe see on the news about Tammy Dykstra's death?"

"Hm?"

"It happened at praise team practice. Right in front of me."

"That's terrible!"

Finally, a reaction. "Yeah," I said, "it was poisoning."

"Ugh," my mother said in rejoinder. "I had the worst case of food poisoning a few weeks ago. Really took it out of me."

I tried to insert a flustered correction, but the Mom Train had left the station.

"Well, I have to get going, honey. It's time for dinner here, you know."

There was nothing for it but to say goodbye.

When I hung up, I realized a call and text had come in while I was on the call with my mom, as abbreviated as it was.

The text was from the legitimate Mrs. Song, Rob's mom. "How are you? Please have Rob call me."

Ah, my weekly reminder text to nag my husband. Rob never called his parents, and he never checked his voicemail, for the dubiously good reason that he'd forgotten the passcode he'd set for it and also how to change it. Rob's mom had never gotten the hang of email or texting more than a sentence or two, which would be something Rob might actually respond to. I often thought Rob's mother and mine should trade children—Rob couldn't care less about keeping in touch with his family, and they never let him forget it.

"Call your mom!" I shouted toward the kitchen.

"What?" Rob shouted back.

"Never mind," I yelled louder. I'd already pushed the

button to hear the call I'd missed and didn't want to talk over the voicemail.

"Hi, Christine, it's Kirsten. I'm somehow missing my sheet music to —" There was a crash and a scream, and Kirsten's voice sped up. "I'll call back later. Bye."

The robot voice told me she'd left her message a good forty minutes before, so probably whatever had broken had been cleaned up by now. I dialed her back.

Apparently there was no good time to speak on the phone with her, however. I could barely hear her over the apparent world war at her house. "Who is this?" she said for the third time.

"Christine! From praise team!" I screamed again.

"No!" I jumped before I realized she wasn't talking to me. "That's not where the cat's food goes!" Kirsten's voice changed timbre as she reengaged with me, though she still had to speak loudly to overpower the din on her end. "I'm sorry, Christine, I'll have to call you back when they're all napping. Assuming that heaven blesses me so..." I could barely make out the last sentence, but I took it to be a from-her-mouth-to-God's-ears sort of aside.

"Sure," I said, rethinking Rob's and my timetable for having kids, and wondering whether an only child would be a good idea.

Kirsten's mention of sheet music reminded me that Penelope had had an idea for a song we could do in praise team, but I needed to run it by the worship planning committee first. As long as the directory was still open on my computer, I scrolled to her picture, which had been taken before Gopher's birth. Penelope looked serene in a Pre-Raphaelite way, if lonely.

Perhaps this wasn't a good time to call mothers in general, I tried to think over the wailing. This was quashing my enthusiasm even for only children.

"I'm sorry, Christine," she said, or I thought so. Did she have the phone right next to the baby's mouth? "I think Gopher's teething, and he won't eat or settle. I'm going to have to call you back."

She sounded close to tears herself. I thought about suggesting that screaming was perhaps Gopher's way of protesting a very silly name, but thought better of it. "Sure," I said. "Hope you get him...um, happy again."

"Thanks," she said weakly before disconnecting.

"Taters are ready," Rob announced from the doorway as I was hanging up.

"Perfect timing," I said.

"Did you get to return your call?" he asked, handing off one paper plate to me.

"Yes and no," I said. "There was too much screaming for a conversation to take place."

"And we're still considering having children?"

Apparently Rob and I thought alike.

"Hey," I said over gooey, melty, cheesy tater tots, topped with an artful drizzle of ranch dressing, "what did you think of the Bible study last night?"

"I thought it was interesting to see people's reactions to Tammy's death," Rob said immediately.

"What do you mean?"

"Well, Jim was the only one who was really sad, wasn't he? But he was in One-on-One with her."

"Do you think he went one-on-one with her, if you know what I mean?"

"Yes, Eggs, I know what you mean."

"It seems like no one else really knew her outside of the singles group."

"Who else would have been in One-on-One with her?" He raised one of his bold eyebrows to hold off any more of my jokes on the name.

"I don't know," I said, spearing another tot. I mused on my lack of knowledge about my own praise team compatriots until Rob interrupted me.

"What's the guy with the wild white-blond hair?" Rob

gestured with his fork above his head. "Blake?"

"Blaine."

"Right." He chewed thoughtfully. "I've had a few conversations with him about design stuff."

"I don't know if he's part of the group or not."

"Who else is single in the praise team?"

"Um, I don't know. The young folks, obviously, but they're not likely to be part of One-on-One. I think that's more for adults."

"What about those old twins?"

"Gretchen and Heidi? It's possible, I guess, but I don't recall seeing any nonagenarians in the church pictures of One-on-One outings."

"What about that bassist, the guy whose parents were at the Bible study?"

"Dylan," I confirmed. "He could be. He strikes me as the unconnected sort, but what do I know?"

"Who was the guy at the Bible study?" Rob asked.

"Zachary?" I said. "The kid obsessed with Avery's whereabouts?"

"Yeah," Rob said. "What about him?"

"Well, he's one of the youth I was referring to," I said. "But I guess I'm just being ageist. If he's old enough to attend a Bible study, I guess he's old enough to be in the singles group."

Our dinner and our recounting were interrupted by the ring of my phone. I balanced my tater tot plate on the edge of my desk, rotating it so the few remaining taters were weighing it down so it wouldn't tip off. I'd hate to lose one. Then I was free to swipe to accept the call, leaving only a meager smear of grease on the screen.

"Christine? This is Penelope calling back."

"Penelope," I said. "I hope Gopher's all right?"

"He's fine," she said. Fine? The kid sounded like he had been spitting out a lung, but mothers knew best. "I should have a few moments while he's asleep." She sounded anxious, and she was talking in a half-whisper that made me strain to hear. I had the impression she was trying to hide her movements from a jailer.

"How old is he?"

"Three months," she replied.

"Great age," I said, which was my standard response to all ages I was told. I figured it sounded positive and as if I had some knowledge of child development. I secretly thought three months sounded a little too larval still for comfort. Probably the kid was just unhappy to be on the outside.

"He's sweet," Penelope said, still whispering. Maybe it was more like talking nice about an abusive spouse.

"Did you happen to know Tammy?" I asked, remembering Rob's and my conversation about One-on-One.

"No." Penelope sounded surprised by the abrupt change in topic.

"We were just wondering, Rob and I—" Well, this was awkward. What stream of consciousness had induced me to bring up this topic? "I was just wondering if anyone really knew her."

"No," Penelope said again, but in a less agitated tone. "I know she was part of the singles group. She invited me to join, but I felt kind of...awkward, you know, as it was."

Awkward? Singles group? A light dawned. Why had it never occurred to me that Penelope was an unwed mother? That explained why the baby was with her everywhere she went, and why I never saw anyone spotting her.

"Right," I said, as if I already knew all about it. "I could see that. So you did talk with her a little, then?"

"Just when I first came to church and filled out one of those little cards—you know, where you say what groups you might be interested in, and of course at praise team a little. But mostly I've just had my hands full with Goph—" A wail cut her off in mid-name. I swore I could hear a muffled curse on her end.

"I have to go," she said, not bothering to keep her voice low anymore.

"Good luck," I said. I realized after I said it that perhaps it was not the most diplomatic of goodbyes, but Penelope had already clicked off in any case. And here I had wasted the whole conversation easing into the point of it, which was to secure delivery of the sheet music. I would have to call her again later, I realized, sighing at my telephonic inefficiency.

I perked up when I saw my remaining lukewarm taters. The cheese had congealed a bit at this point, but my mouth wasn't picky.

In the evening, Rob and I decided to take in a second-run flick at the Draper Movie Theater.

At a stop sign on our way, I glanced over idly to the surrounding houses and watched a tall, gray-haired woman help a stooped, white-haired woman maneuver her way up the icy sidewalk.

"Hey," I said to Rob, pointing. "It's Gretchen and Heidi."

"Who?"

"The twins, the old Dutch twins."

"Oh, right." Rob seemed unimpressed with my sighting.

"Oo," I said, just as Rob had gotten a break and was pulling through the intersection. "We should stop."

Rob hesitated on the gas but then thought better of it and zoomed into his turn to keep ahead of the cars that were catching up behind him.

"No, I mean, pull over," I told him.

"What? Why?" Rob obediently put his blinker on, though, and drew to the curb a few blocks down from where I'd seen the nonagenarians alight.

"I'm almost sure Heidi said she knew the song Penelope mentioned. Maybe she has the music for it, and that would save me some legwork."

Rob looked at the dashboard clock.

"We're early for once," I pointed out.

"Only because we were going to stop for something to eat on the way," Rob said.

"We'll get popcorn there."

Mention of the salty, buttery treat seemed to appease him slightly, so I pressed on.

"It will take only a minute," I promised. "I'll just dash in and back out."

Rob pulled forward toward the next right turn, then made a circuit around the blocks until we were back at Gretchen and Heidi's house and could pull into the driveway behind their behemoth town car.

I undid my seat belt and had my hand on the door handle before I realized Rob hadn't moved since putting the car into park.

"You're coming in with me, aren't you?" I asked.

"I figured I'd just wait here," Rob said.

"You don't want to leave the car running the whole time." I paused with my legs half in and half out of the car.

Rob clenched the wheel tighter. "I thought you were just running in and out."

"Come in with me," I said, closing the door over any further argument.

I waited until Rob grumpily extricated himself, and we made our way to the door together, walking cautiously over the poor job of shoveling that had been done. I wondered if Gretchen did the shoveling herself.

Gretchen and Heidi lived in Bruce, which was next door to Mansardville. Bruce was an odd mix of inner-city-esque boarded and barred street fronts, industrial wreckage, and small-town blue-collar Americana. The sisters lived in one of the quainter parts. My understanding was that Gretchen had never married while Heidi was a long-time widow. They gave the impression of having lived together for ages, though maybe that was some twin phenomenon.

A decorative wreath covered much of the screen door. I awkwardly knocked around it.

When that produced no results, Rob took over, yanking open the screen door entirely and pounding on the inner wooden one.

I danced around on the small front step, trying to keep warm while we waited. Rob was about to knock again when I heard a mix of snuffling and shuffling inside. I held up an arm to warn him off, but he had already lowered his hand.

"Who is it?" a low voice called querulously.

From the gruff tones, I assumed it was our female tenor. "Hello, Gretchen," I said. "This is Christine from praise team."

I always had a moment's pause when using the first names of people a generation or more older than my parents, but New Vision had a casual vibe to it, and I would have felt equally awkward calling her Ms. (or did she prefer Miss?) Plantinga.

"Pardon?"

I repeated the last half, trying for a little louder and more forceful without screaming.

"Christine," she said finally, and there was a jangle of a door chain. Rob and I waited out the opening of the deadbolt and the doorknob lock, too.

Gretchen unconsciously began reshutting the door when she saw a man standing beside me.

"This is Rob," I said quickly, but loudly. "My husband."

The inner door opened widely at last, and we were ushered in.

From blizzard to inferno, I thought, shedding layers as quickly as I could without giving the impression of a striptease. Gretchen and Heidi must keep their thermostat permanently at roast if it could be this hot when they'd just arrived home.

Heidi made her way cautiously into the foyer, her cane tapping on the hardwood.

Rob obstinately kept his jacket on, telling me while informing the twins, "We're just here for a second."

"Pardon?" Heidi said.

"You are here for a wisit?" Gretchen said at the same time.

"I wondered if you had the song Penelope mentioned," I yelled over to Heidi. "The one from your old church."

She responded so quietly that I felt rude for having shouted. "Oh, yes," she said. "I know the one you talk about. Let's see." She slowly made a circle back around and tapped her way into the drawing room beyond, where an upright piano held a collection of Hummel figurines atop lace doilies. She lifted the embroidered lid of the piano bench and leaned her cane against the side so that she could use both hands to pick up a stack of music within and start thumbing through.

Gretchen watched for a moment solicitously. Apparently assured that Heidi could manage, she waved us past her sister toward the seating area at the farther side of the drawing room. I was almost sure they would refer to it as such, or perhaps parlor, rather than something as modern as living room. "Please," she said.

I gave Rob an apologetic smile and allowed myself to be ushered into a stiff armchair, with another ubiquitous doily on the back and plastic coating on the armrests. I thought about our off-white glider with the off-gray arms and considered adding the same treatment when I got home.

"You like Butterkuchen, or?" Heidi absentmindedly asked from her stooped position at the piano bench.

I stared back blankly. Surprisingly, Gretchen glared at her sister. I wasn't sure what to make of that.

"All right," I finally answered for both Rob and me, unsure as to what I had agreed.

Gretchen smiled stiffly and left, to return a moment later bearing a plate of cake slices. That looked innocuous enough. Then Rob caught my eye and raised a brow meaningfully. Unfortunately, I couldn't imagine what meaning he thought was attached. He inclined his head toward the cakes.

I tried shaking my head so that Gretchen wouldn't see, but apparently her eyesight was sharper than her hearing.

"What's wrong with them?" she asked.

"There was a poisoning death recently," Rob said.

"Rob!" I exclaimed, feeling my cheeks flame even hotter than the thermostat setting warranted.

"Ach, um Himmels willen," Gretchen muttered. She yanked up a piece of cake, tore it in two and shoved one half in her mouth. She chewed, chewed, chewed, and finally swallowed. There was a dramatic pause, and then she handed Rob the other half.

"They're fine."

He nodded and accepted the half-slice graciously.

I picked up my own and started in on enjoying our pre-popcorn treat.

"I'll just be packing up, then," came a voice from the doorway. Surprised, I looked up to see a stranger in the house—a tall man, with slick fair hair, and a tool belt around his waist. "I'll be back tomorrow to patch up the shed roof as best as I can so you don't get any more snow in there."

"Sank you, Albert." Gretchen nodded to him. She turned to me. "Our great-nephew. He does some work for us."

"Ah," I said, hearing the young man's tools clanking as he walked out of sight.

"Terrible thing about Tammy," Heidi said from over at her post. She licked a finger and dug into a new stack of sheet music.

"Mmm," I murmured around a bite of butterwhatsit.

"Terrible," Gretchen agreed. "Barb has called earlier asking if possibly we knew Tammy's family, in case the church should plan a memorial service, but Heidi and I have not known Tammy well."

I nodded, considering her curious grammar. She must have been a monolingual Dutch speaker until late in life. Her word order reminded me of some of the mistakes my German editing clients routinely made.

"Tammy came out of Kentucky, I understand," Heidi said from the piano bench.

I nodded, but this was news to me.

"Terrible thing, to die without family and close friends around. Tammy invited us to one of her singles parties, but, well, that wasn't really...something for us."

"I understand," I said.

"I can't find it," Heidi announced, setting down her last armful of music. "I am sorry."

"That's all right," I said. "I can get it from Penelope later. I just thought, as long as I was in the neighborhood..."

"Thank you for the cake," Rob said, already rising. I made the mistake of glancing at him and catching the roll of his eyes back at me. His thick black hair had wilted and stuck to his golden-tan forehead, now flushed a peachier color than usual, and I imagined the shirt inside his zippered parka must be sticking to his back, since mine was, and I had already removed jacket and cardigan.

"Hey," I said, "as long as I'm here..." Heidi had shuffled over to the settee by me and perched on the edge. She peered at me like a little bird out of her pale blue eyes.

"Did either of you see anything while you were searching for Barb's cough drops? I was just wondering."

Heidi broke off my gaze, and Gretchen spoke over my last sentence with a short, "We didn't find them."

"No, I know," I returned, "but did you see anything else suspicious? I noticed the two of you were talking about something."

"It vas girl talk," Gretchen said, her accent suddenly becoming even more Dutch. "Sisterly tings."

I wondered if the resurgence of her native accent meant an increase in her stress levels. I had obviously touched some sort of nerve in mentioning what she and Heidi had been discussing.

"You seemed pretty intense," I said, trying to back out of the topic but inadvertently prolonging it. I really needed to work on my conversation skills. I tried adding a little laugh that was supposed to sound off-handed and merely sounded nervous.

"Ve are Dutch."

Gretchen knew how to end a conversation.

"Thank you for the bu...cake," I echoed, standing to join Rob.

Gretchen showed us to the door. Her goodbye was polite enough, but her eyes were grim.

Chapter 6

Rob and I were able to forget the awkward encounter in the dark of the theater, the movie action chasing all thoughts of real-life villains out of my head. It was a good time until halfway through, when the film unceremoniously halted and the lights came on.

Rob and I looked around, surprised, but no one else seemed distressed. The other patrons were calmly filing out into the lobby, some leaving jackets and bags behind.

Rob and I looked at each other and decided corporately to follow.

Out in the shabby but chandelier-lit lobby, there was a table set up with cake and punch. I couldn't help but shoot another look at Rob. He widened his eyes back at me.

I looked around for someone collecting cash for the goodies, but they appeared to be free of charge. Everyone else was just milling around, enjoying a little dessert and chatting to neighbors. We joined the clutch around the cake table and walked away with our second sugary prize of the night, finding an empty wall to lean against. Had we just wandered into Maybury?

"Fancy meeting you here," said a voice at my right ear.

I whipped my head that direction.

"Blaine!" I said.

Blaine also held a plate of cake and cup of juice, and his wild wheat-colored hair made a spiky pattern where it met the dark wall behind him.

Rob stepped forward to smile around me at Blaine.

"Hey, Rob," Blaine said, confirming my suspicions that Rob had met Blaine multiple times in the past but simply neglected to remember his name. "Did you notice the new A-boards at New Vision?" Blaine snickered.

Rob groaned. "What were they thinking? Light turquoise on yellow is visible from a car how exactly?"

I bobbed my head between the two designers, trying to remember if I'd even noticed the A-boards. Not that I knew what an A-board was.

"And I hate that awful font," Blaine was saying. "It's everywhere."

"Did you like the kerning on the new banner?"

Blaine and Rob guffawed in unison.

It looked like this conversation would keep going throughout the whole intermission if I didn't break in, but all I could think to talk about was Tammy.

"Did you know Tammy through One-on-One?" I interjected.

Blaine blinked pale eyes behind his thick-rimmed glasses but turned to me agreeably. "Yeah. We knew each other some."

He stacked his empty cup on top of his empty plate so he could gesture with the free hand.

"I've been thinking about this a lot lately, actually."

"Really?" Rob said.

"Yeah," Blaine said, "trying to replay any conversations I had with Tammy, trying to figure out if anyone had a motive to kill her."

"Really," I echoed.

"We're not the only amateur detectives?" Rob said, flashing a look at me. I shrugged.

"No," Blaine agreed earnestly. "We've got to figure this thing out."

"Or, you know," I inserted halfheartedly, "the police could handle it."

Blaine waved a dismissive hand. "We know things the police don't know," he said. "Like that Tammy was fired recently."

"Fired?" I said.

"By Walter." Blaine held each of our gazes meaningfully in turn.

"Really." I couldn't think of another word to use, apparently.

"She worked at Nederland Christian School," Blaine elaborated. "But she got canned last week."

"Awkward," I said, imagining attending praise team practice with my ex-boss.

Blaine nodded.

"Were any of the kids on the team her students?" Rob said, apparently trying to gather more potential suspects and motives.

"No, she wasn't a teacher," Blaine said, his hair bobbing a beat behind as he shook his head. "She worked in administration. As I understand it, her official position was as some sort of receptionist, but she had duties in soliciting donations as well, you know, for scholarships and such."

"That, my dear Watson," Rob said, nodding at me, "is motive."

"Motive for whom?" I said, feeling my brow furrow. "Motive for Tammy to kill Walter, more like."

"Well," Blaine said eagerly, as if he'd considered this objection before, "we don't know why Tammy was fired. Maybe there was some gross mishandling of funds, or she found out something fishy."

74

"Cherchez le cash," I said, improperly.

"Penelope works there, too," Blaine said, but he was unable to continue his line of thought since just then the overhead chandeliers began fitfully flickering on and off. I thought it was some sort of brownout at first, but I noticed the other patrons filing back toward the theater, dropping their crumb-laden plates into a big garbage can before disappearing through the swinging doors.

Rob and I began to follow when Blaine stopped our progress.

"We need to investigate," he said. I turned back from dumping my trash. Blaine's pale eyes, magnified slightly behind his lenses, still looked dead serious. Like ours, those were no vanity glasses. "I want to catch this guy, too," he said.

"How do you know it's a guy?" I asked him, hearing similar lines from Columbo and Murder, She Wrote echo in my head.

"See," Blaine said, "I knew it. I knew you guys would have the makings of a good detective."

"Or at least a television one," Rob muttered. He'd watched the same shows with me.

"I have other skills," Blaine said quickly.

I arched an eyebrow in silent invitation.

"Computer skills," he clarified. "Among others. They might come in handy." He studied his fingernails. "How much information have you gotten out of the police?"

"I haven't tried," I said, skeptical.

"I have the police report," Blaine said, still studiously avoiding our gazes.

"Anyone can get that," Rob said. "They're public record."

I glanced at Rob, surprised. Were they? How did he know?

Blaine looked straight at Rob this time. "Well, how would you like to see the autopsy report?" he asked quietly.

"What?" Rob and I shrieked in unison. A teenager in a theater-issued polo who was packing away the last of the cake sent us a glare.

"We could go in on this together," Blaine continued, whispering. "I know I could be of use." Why on earth was he auditioning for us? Had we inadvertently garnered a reputation for nosiness, or was it just that I was the praise team director and therefore the de facto investigation leader? "I mean, Tammy was my friend." Blaine was continuing his spiel. "Not a best friend or anything, but we were in One-on-One together." He ran a hand through his Einstein-esque hairdo. "Now, I don't necessarily have the people skills you do."

I made what could only be termed a scoffing noise.

Blaine apparently took this as a sign that I was questioning his contributions, and hurried on. "But I could bring other skills to the table. And between the three of us, maybe we could come up with something the police haven't."

Rob held out his hand. "We're game if you are, partner."

Blaine shook Rob's hand while I shook my head at Rob's premature show of loyalty to the person whose name he couldn't remember a few hours before.

We could hear the movie's soundtrack resuming inside the theater. Rob put one hand on the swinging door.

"Aren't you afraid I might be the killer?" Blaine said, stopping us one last time.

Rob shrugged. "If you are, we'll catch you for sure now that you're working with us."

"What was that?" I asked Rob in the car afterward.

"The thing with Blaine?" he asked. "Or the intermission reception?"

"Gosh, I'd almost forgotten how weird that was," I said, "given how much weirder that conversation with Blaine was. Have we somehow gotten branded the amateur detectives in this case?"

"Pretty cool, isn't it?" Rob said, grinning at me as we waited for the light to change.

"I don't know," I said. "I guess. If we had any detecting skills at all. So far, we've kind of struck out."

"Oh, come on," Rob said. "You're no fun. We're highly logical—"

"What are we, Vulcan?"

Rob ignored me. "—so all we have to do is use the little gray cells."

"I'm sorry," I said, "but are you appointing yourself a kind of Poirot, and am I Miss Lemon?"

"Oh, you're at least Hastings," he said. "But, seriously, don't you want to figure out what's going on? Get it right before the cops do?"

"Yeees," I said slowly. "But it seemed more like a lark when it was just the two of us speculating. It's somehow weirder and...real-er...now that a third person wants to investigate alongside. When Blaine said it could be him, it really hit me for the first time. What if the killer really is someone we know? Someone we like?"

"It's probably not even anyone in the praise team," Rob said, flipping through radio stations. "For all we know, it's some monster from the cough drop company back in England, who gets his kicks from randomly sending poisoned tidbits across the ocean."

"Well, that's no fun," I said, illogically. "It would be much more interesting if it were someone at church."

Rob laughed at my hypocrisy, settling the radio on classical when every other station on our preselected channels was in the midst of a commercial. "At any rate," he said, "I'd really like a look at that autopsy report if Blaine was serious."

"Yep," I said. "I think they're eventually publicly available, but if he has some source for getting a look at them early, that would be super helpful. And if he is involved somehow, like you said, now we'll have him under our gaze."

When we walked into our apartment, I had to go into the office to get my pajamas from the dresser we kept in there. I had worn my fancier jeans for our big evening out, but they were half a size too small. They were bearable only if I hadn't had two slices of cake and a tub of popcorn, plus a large diet soda.

I released the button and zipper and breathed a sigh of relief. I took my cell phone out of my pocket and placed it on the dresser. It had been almost out of juice, so I'd turned it completely off for the movie, and now I rebooted it. I was contorting myself to undo my bra when I saw the message light flash onto the screen after it came to life.

Scratching my back to get rid of that post-bra itchiness, I pressed the play button and turned it to speaker.

Three messages in a row of hollow static. A persistent telemarketer. Good thing I'd had it off for the show. Delete, delete, delete. A message from Blaine already, telling me he wanted to email me a PDF of the autopsy and some notes on the police investigation but wasn't sure what email address to use. He was certainly eager.

I was making a note to call him back, but the first pen I grabbed was out of ink. Rather than throw it away, I placed it back in my pen canister to try it again later and make sure. And this was how I ran into these problems, I reminded myself. But there was no time to think about that now. I grabbed a pencil instead and was pleased to see the point wasn't entirely worn down or broken off. Blaine had already sped past his number, and it wasn't the same that he'd called from, so I tried to hit the back button to replay his message now that I had a writing instrument.

Either I was too late or I hit the wrong button, because a new message began.

"Christine," said a horrible deep mechanical voice. "You are not the one called to solve the killings." The voice sounded like a demon robot. I stood transfixed, half-dressed and clutching a pencil. "It is mine to avenge, I will repay, saith the Lord." There was a click, and then the messaging service's much more neutral female robot came on to tell me what time it had been left. I missed it, though, over the pounding of my heart in my ears.

Rob walked into the room and saw me standing in my undies. "Nice look," he said, unbuttoning his own movie-going duds. "Care if I join you?"

"Rob," I said, pointing to the phone. "It's awful."

Rob listened to the current message, a telemarketer with a thick accent. "Hello, may I speak to Mrs....uh...Song?" Pause. "Hello? Hello?"

"Aggravating telemarketers calling all day," Rob said, hitting delete, "even on the weekends."

"Rob," I said more urgently. "The message before that one!"

Rob furrowed his forehead but obediently started pushing buttons. He pushed too many times and we listened to Blaine's message again.

"Wow, that's dedication," Rob said. "Our little sidekick. Are you going to call him back?"

I looked down vacantly at my pencil, realizing I had once again forgotten to write down the number, so intent was I on what was coming next.

But then the evil voice was playing, and Rob and I both stopped thinking about Blaine and telemarketers and just listened.

"Well." Rob looked as rattled as I felt.

"What does that mean?" I cried in a low voice. "Is that from the killer?"

"It's probably not a rival amateur detective," Rob said.

"Or the police. Not their style."

"Don't joke!" I said. "It's just horrible."

"It's obviously done with some voice modulator," Rob said, having switched to thoughtful. I took reassurance from his Sherlock Holmes demeanor. "Anybody can pick up one of those things at Radio Shack."

"Is there any way of knowing whether it's a boy or a girl?"

"Not without seeing their parts in person, babe," Rob said, looking me up and down. "Speaking of which, it's hard to have a rational conversation with a topless chick."

I walked past him and pulled open my pajama drawer. I belatedly drew on my PJ bottoms and stretched a camisole over my head.

"That's better," Rob said. "I guess." Rob reached over me to open his own pajama drawer and took out what he needed. "Now we can scheme about how we're going to catch this perp."

"You're using law-enforcement speak already," I said, feeling better now that we were both talking about it.

I closed the pajama drawers up for both of us and then opened the top drawer for comfier socks than the thin trouser socks that didn't stretch out the inappropriate ballet flats I'd worn out into the snow and ice. At home, I was a plain cotton kind of gal.

We hadn't stopped my voicemail's litany, but the other two messages had been one more telemarketing attempt plus a call from Rob's dad this time, ordering Rob to call his mom. Rob murmured a reminder to himself that he really should call his family sometime. I worried briefly that if he did, they'd order him to hightail it out of the state, away from murderers, and back to San Francisco, where they lived. However, the chances of Rob actually following through on calling back were slim. Rob had managed to delete that message, but the others had been saved by default and I would have to get to them later. I flicked to the call log and saw what I had feared: The menacing call was listed as Unknown Caller.

"'It is mine to avenge,'" Rob was saying. "That's a Bible verse."

"I think it's from the Old Testament," I said.

"But then quoted again in the New Testament," Rob said. "By Paul or Jesus or someone."

"That pinpoints it," I mocked.

"Hey," Rob said, "you went to Blanchard, too."

I assumed a pious expression and pulled a Bible off the shelf, flipping back through the onionskin pages. "I'll just consult my concordance." The concordance had verses indexed by subject matter.

"Vengeance?" I mused aloud, wondering what keyword might have it. "Revenge?"

Rob snorted at me and fired up his laptop. "I'll just look it up online."

"Oh, is this a sword drill?" I said. "The race is on."

I picked my first keyword guess, but that was a no go. "Revenge" was a hit, though. There were three instances of the phrase: Deuteronomy 32:35, Romans 12:19, and Hebrews 10:30.

I flipped to the first, only to discover Rob was already reading it out loud from his computer. I harrumphed and waited for him to read the others. Hearing them read, though, even in context, didn't fill in any more gaps for me.

"It might not be literally meant," Rob said. "Maybe it's just a warning not to take revenge yourself."

"I'm not revenging nothing," I said ungrammatically but passionately. "Maybe the messenger was referencing this Hebrews one: 'For we know him who said, "It is mine to avenge; I will repay," and again, "The Lord will judge his people." It is a dreadful thing to fall into the hands of the living God.' Are we being judged, or are we being the judges?"

"I don't know," Rob said. "Is there a way to figure out what a psychopath means?"

"I mean, as far as judging other people goes, we were just trying to figure out who's breaking God's rules," I said, my voice rising, "like the one about, oh, not murdering people!"

"I'm on your side," Rob said. "I know we're not vigilantes. But maybe this creep thinks you should keep your nose out of his business."

"Hey, what's that about?" I said. "He called my personal phone, and he said just my name, didn't he? 'Christine.'"

Rob thought about this. "That is kind of spooky."

"What did I do?" I wailed. "It was Blaine's harebrained idea to form a detective squad."

"You do keep asking people questions about Tammy," Rob pointed out.

"I know, but that's just...conversation," I said.

"You've asked Walter and Gretchen and Heidi whether they found the cough drops. And you've been asking people whether they were in One-on-One with Tammy."

"It's just something that's going on around us," I insisted, incensed at being misunderstood. "I was just talking."

"Uh-huh," Rob said, sounding unfairly dubious. "You don't have to convince me. Apparently, the killer didn't see it that way."

"Oh, my gosh," I said, sinking down into my office chair. Even my comfy pajamas weren't soothing me. "Then it must be someone at church. To have been around me this weekend and gotten nervous."

"What I want to know," Rob said, "is why the voice said 'the killings.' Plural."

I looked up at him in alarm. "Has there been another one, do you think?" I whispered.

Rob shook his head. "I don't know, but I think you

should call the police and let them know that the killer called you and left a nasty message promising more deaths."

"But is it the killer, then, or just a concerned citizen who thinks God will bring the killer to justice without any human intervention, thank you very much?"

Rob chortled. "Like a giant finger pointing from the sky and a booming voice saying, ''E done it'?" He laughed some more.

I waited it out. He sobered.

"You do believe the killer will be brought to justice, don't you?" I asked him.

"No one deserves to have life snatched from them," Rob said, "particularly not on God's turf. I imagine he's a might testy about that."

I envisioned God as a feisty old man, waving his fist at murderers to get off his lawn.

"Well," I said, "maybe God would like some help." I actually felt better, thinking that maybe I could do something little to help solve this terrible puzzle and put such a mean-spirited person out of commission.

Rob laughed again. "You and Blaine will make a great team."

"Should I call Detective Madari now?" I said. "I hope she can do some fancy-dancy triangulating to trace who left it. That should clear up these murders in no time."

Rob looked doubtful. "Well, it's too late tonight," he said, looking at the plain white wall clock we had unnecessarily hung up but that fit in well with the office décor. "What say we try to forget creepy messages and go watch some Monty Python? I've gotten myself in the mood."

That sounded as good a plan as any to me. As long as I fit some chocolate chip cookie dough ice cream in there somewhere. Now that I was in my stretchy drawstring PJs, my stomach had quite recovered from its earlier malaise and wanted redress for being squished for several hours.

Who was I to deny it after treating it so badly?

"Make sure the doors and windows are locked, though," I said, unexpectedly nervous about emerging from what seemed the relative seclusion of the office.

Rob looked at me sympathetically and draped an arm around me to give a squeeze. "Can I get you a tisane?"

I shook my head at him, shaking off my fears at the same time. I was safe at home, and Rob was here, and all we had been doing was talking about suspects, not actually stepping on anyone's toes. I smiled up at my partner in crime investigation. "I'm Miss Lemon. That's my job."

Chapter 7

Before I knew it, it was Sunday morning and I was groggily realizing that the bell was tolling for me. Or, to be more precise, the clock radio was. Rob snoozed it one more time but nudged me and sleepily said, "Fifty minutes."

I squinted over at the red numbers. Shoot, he was right. Okay, okay. I fumbled for my glasses on the collapsible tray that did multiple duty as my nightstand and dining table and made my unsteady way toward the bathroom, my feet protesting the cold linoleum as I arrived.

A hot shower and a lot of caffeine-laden diet soda woke me up sufficiently to drive us to Murphy Middle School an hour later. Yes, we were, as always, late, and I knew Barb would notice. I had made up some time by driving slightly more than usual over the speed limit, but I was still five minutes behind schedule. I left Rob in the car, the engine running to keep it warm, and sprinted toward the middle school's side door. Rob preferred to read a book in the parking lot until it was closer to the time the service started. He found that if he tried to relax indoors, he was invariably put to work doing something unbearably dull, like stuffing fliers into the bulletins or operating the machine that showed the movie clips to illustrate the sermon. Refusing wasn't in his nature, so he avoided the issue completely by staying out of the line of sight. There were always more jobs to do than warm bodies to do them, but Rob felt like I volunteered enough for both of us.

I left him peacefully wasting gas and producing carbon emissions and stepped into the warmth of the middle school cafetorium. Set-up teams came in every Sunday morning even earlier than the praise team did and cleared out the long benched tables and filled the empty space with rows and rows of folding chairs. They hauled in sound equipment and heavy speakers and wired the space for sound. They put up A-board signs in the parking lot assuring people that the middle school was indeed doubling as a church and directing traffic to the appropriate lot and pedestrians to the appropriate entrance. Eventually, cheerful volunteers in bright yellow-green safety vests would stand out and wave folks into the lot and reinforce the signs' arrows by pointing in the same direction. The cafetorium retained its ceiling banners touting Murphy Middle School as the champion of some sport or other in some year or other, and its posters on the surrounding walls exhorting the students to fight back against bullying, and a lingering scent of floor polish and cafeteria food, but it was surely and efficiently being transformed into a church.

Even now, the back of the cafeteria was a hive of activity, with the week's greeters folding bulletins and featured ministries setting up miniature information booths to recruit people before and after the service. Valerie Dejong sat with Jared Scheele, the co-editor of the church newsletter, at a table folding the latest issue of InSight. Rob and I had talked with Jared, a lanky technical writer in his late twenties, a few times by the coffee and cookies after the service—for some reason, fate kept seeming to bring us together to have the same awkward get-to-know-you conversation each time. I gave them a little wave, keeping my distance, and Valerie looked back at me with her ever-avid gaze.

"You're late!" I heard yelled across the open space. I turned toward the voice. It was Barb, standing halfway toward the front of the auditorium near one of the sound technicians, a sunny vision of yellow blouse, floral jeans, and high-heeled white boots amidst the misty dimness of the cafetorium. "We'd almost given up on you!"

I checked my watch—seven minutes overdue. I needed to move to a less efficient culture. "Sorry!" I gave a little wave.

Despite my egregious tardiness, my team was nowhere near ready to rehearse. The sound team was still adjusting mic cords and wasn't ready even for sound checks. Kirsten was at the electric keyboard chatting with Hal. Zachary the other drummer was nowhere to be seen, but that wasn't a shock. Probably he was smoking out of the backstage door, beyond his mother's reach. His mom sometimes complained in my hearing about how Zachary picked up the smell of cigarette smoke from hobnobbing with "those other musicians." I never corrected her impression. Barb was still interfering with the sound techs' work. Blaine was riffing on his guitar, and Dylan was fiddling with his amp. Gretchen and Heidi were sitting in the front row of seats on the floor, chatting with a couple other volunteers on a break, all of them on the older side of average for New Vision. Avery, Potter, Penelope, and Jim were all missing. I sighed.

I was about to settle in to wait it out when I realized this was my chance to talk with both Kirsten and Hal. I moved over to the twosome hanging out by the electronic keyboard where Kirsten was pushing buttons to program her preferred settings.

"Hey," I said casually.

"Sorry I didn't call you back," Kirsten said, not sounding particularly apologetic. "I found the music I needed after all. Grace had made an airplane out of it, but I rescued it." I couldn't remember if Grace was her three-year-old or her four-year-old.

"Glad to hear it," I said. I stood there awkwardly for a beat. "So..." I could feel it coming out of my mouth before I could stop it, but it was the only conversational topic I could seize on in a pinch. "Did either of you know Tammy well?" No wonder the unknown message leaver thought I was nosy.

"No," Kirsten said, sounding bored and idly fluffing her blond Mom haircut. "I heard she was from Kentucky. Barb said that's where the memorial service would most likely be held."

"Oh," I said. "Well, that's that then." Now what would I talk about?

"I knew her," Hal said staunchly. Hal Dormer was an eager forty-something who had played in a garage band in high school and loved reliving his glory days. Every once in a while he shook his graying hair out of its ponytail to bounce around his face while he drummed with his eyes half-closed.

I looked at him in surprise at his admission. "From where?"

"We were in One-on-One together," he said. For some reason, I had thought Hal was married, but maybe the woman I saw him with often, gray hair in a matching ponytail, was just a long-term girlfriend. "We planned the camping trip to Caboose Lake."

"Right," I said. Kirsten still looked bored. I knew she couldn't be in One-on-One, and I knew she'd taken time off from the praise team until just a few months ago, with all her childrearing obligations. But it was possible she knew something just from having been a part of the church for so long. I decided I'd better include her in the conversation. "And you?"

Maybe it wasn't the best segue. Kirsten blinked clear blue eyes. "I don't think I ever said more than two words to Tammy," she said shortly.

"Until her death," I said.

Kirsten blinked again, and her blond brows lowered. I really needed to work on my transitions.

"I mean, you did such a good job calming her down."

Kirsten's brows relaxed nominally. "Well, I have medical training. As a nurse, I know what to do in such situations."

"I'm glad one of us did," I said, and meant it.

"I just wish it had been more," Kirsten finished quietly.

"It sounds like there was nothing more you could have done," I said to comfort her. "She'd already ingested the poison, right? And you did get out half the lozenge."

Kirsten's mouth twisted wryly. "Yeah," she said half-heartedly.

"How did you know to call 911 right away?"

"What do you mean?" Kirsten's eyes narrowed slightly.

"You had Barb call 911 even before you got the lozenge out. Why didn't you start with that?"

"Nurse's training," Kirsten said shortly, and stopped at that.

Something else occurred to me. "You were hanging up coats," I said.

Kirsten stared at me again. Rob was right. I had an obsession.

I turned toward Hal to include him, too. I could feel his attention slipping. Did police ever have two people to interrogate at once? It was hard enough just to carry on a group conversation.

"And you were searching the boxes, right?"

Hal nodded.

"I was just wondering. Did either of you see anything out of the ordinary? Did you see Barb's extra cough drops anywhere, for instance, or feel a strange packet in anyone's pocket?"

They both shook their heads.

"The police have already been over all of this," Kirsten said pointedly. She tucked strands of her blond hair behind her ears in a business-like fashion and turned toward her music stand.

I smiled tightly. I wondered if Kirsten was the anonymous caller, so annoyed did she seem by my intrusion into the investigation.

But things were starting to happen on stage finally, so I dropped my line of thought. The sound techs were finally ready to check the levels, so we singers moved toward the front to pick out our mics. There was the usual tussle over who had the brightest and lowest; some of the singers had personal favorites. Avery was magically present at the mic stands, though Penelope was still absent. I saw Jim walking up from backstage with Zachary, which fueled my suspicions that perhaps they'd both been smoking outside. When they walked to the mic stand, I could feel the cold air radiating from their clothes, and I smelled at least one smoky aura. There was even a little fleck of something dark on Jim's white church shirt. Potter's mother ran up to the stage to let us know poor little Potter had a cold ("poor little Potter" being her actual phrasing), so that solved one mystery at least. Walter and Barb were already singing lines into their microphones in response to the tech guys' directives. Walter held his microphone awkwardly in his left hand, his right bandaged due to some sort of home-renovation accident. I had to give the man props for showing up after what must have been a late night at the emergency room.

"Where's Penelope?" I asked Walter, who was closest to me.

"How should I know?" he said. My eyes widened at his unusual snippiness, but I chalked it up to his injuries.

We couldn't wait for Penelope, because our precious practice time had already been cut perilously short with the extra-long sound setup. The players for today's dramatic skit were tapping impatient toes in the wings, wanting to rehearse, and our pastor, also a Chris and one of the reasons I had to go by Christine in this church, was just as anxious to get his cordless lapel mic calibrated. Everyone wanted to finish before any early-bird congregants showed up, particularly as the first to arrive tended to be newcomers to the church. Regular attendees knew the services never started on time, despite Barb's strong preferences. We began our songs, and I hurried to finish directing what little rehearsal time remained to us before we were booted offstage. I only hoped Jim and Walter didn't take this opportunity to forget all the syncopation I'd drilled into them at the last few rehearsals.

The tension level ratcheted up a notch just as we were preparing to rehearse the final song.

"Praise team," said a loud voice. I looked, and it was Gavin DeHaan leading the way onto the front of the stage, a coterie of dramatists in costume behind him, blocking our line of sight to the lyrics monitor. I sighed, signaling the instruments to wait.

"Yes?" I said.

"Are you almost finished?" Gavin boomed, his dark eyebrows rising as he gestured expansively at his posse. Gone was his joviality from the Bible study, and his prominent jaw looked chiseled out of granite. "My drama team needs to practice on stage to get the blocking down, preferably before everyone arrives." He gestured pointedly toward the rear doors, as if the hordes were waiting outside to tear them open.

"We have one song left," I said.

"You're five minutes over already," Gavin said, pointing to his large-faced watch.

I held in my sigh and forced a smile. "Things always run a bit behind," I said. Then I purposely turned my back and signaled the instruments to begin, praying we could get it in one take and relieved that Gavin and his troupe retreated to the wings.

We didn't. Things fell apart so completely halfway through that we had to start over from the top. To make matters worse, all sound dropped out entirely during our second try.

I could feel the breath from Gavin DeHaan's sigh all the way from the wings to center stage.

All I could do, though, was stand around ineffectually as sound volunteers scrambled around on stage, picking up cords and yelling back and forth to the people stationed at the soundboard. There were numerous tweaks attempted and plugs moved, but nothing was fixing the problems. Pastor Chris, a measured yet charismatic man in his thirties with sandy red-blond hair and matching tidy beard, ascended the stage in the middle of the hubbub, holding his wireless lapel mic in one hand and looking put out.

"Can someone hook me up for a sound test?" he said into the ether.

"Uhhh," Gavin DeHaan very audibly sighed again. "The drama team still needs to run a tech rehearsal."

One of the head sound guys paused in his mad rush to look back and forth from Gavin to Pastor Chris. "Sorry, Pastor. Sorry, Gavin," he said. "I hope this will be fixed by the time service starts."

Back his head went down as he pulled out cords and shouted instructions.

Pastor Chris retreated down the steps, mic cord dangling uselessly from one palm, slapping sermon notes against one leg clad in dress slacks.

Gavin flapped his arms at his drama team. "Let's go

92

rehearse in the teacher's lounge, then."

"Christine," a voice called behind me. It was Blaine, un-slinging his guitar. "Are we done here? I'm supposed to be in the drama today, too."

I suppressed a sigh and nodded pleasantly for him to depart.

Since the teacher's lounge was taken, I gestured for the rest of my group to congregate in the back hallway, where we talked through the intro and order to the last song. The other musicians wandered off then, but I had the singers sing it through in its entirety, humming and improvising the instrumental interludes for them. They didn't laugh at me, which was a plus.

I once again clapped out beats with the group for Walter's benefit, since he never seemed to get the hang of what he called the synco-whatsit. I knew Walter had a pacemaker due to a congenitally iffy heart and wondered if I could get it upgraded to include a metronome. Not that that would help Walter learn to clap on the off beats; he was as white as an middle-aged Dutch Christian Midwesterner could be. Today he seemed even more arrhythmic than usual, unable to clap at all due to his injured hand, and unexpectedly distracted. Maybe his pain medication was wearing off.

If we could all just get through the service intact, I could wheedle Rob into taking us somewhere fancy for brunch, like Denny's. Unlimited refills and mozzarella sticks, baby.

I was wandering through the hallways to kill time when I decided to stop off at the teacher's lounge bathroom. I figured the drama team must be done rehearsing by now, so the lounge should have been clear and free. As I rounded the corner—smack—I ran straight into Gavin DeHaan, who had been heading out of the room.

"Oops," I said, rubbing my arm where I'd hit the doorframe on rebound.

Gavin still hadn't spoken. He seemed to be holding his breath, and his temper. But from the way he was hopping, I figured he'd done something to one foot.

"My toe," he finally croaked out.

"Oo," I said sympathetically.

"I hit it on your big clodhopper of a shoe," he wheezed.

Hey, now. I looked down at the offending footwear. Maybe they were a little clunky, but that's what made them so practical. I had learned my lesson when my ballet flats had gotten soaked the previous night. I couldn't help it if the toes were perhaps reinforced. It saved me from hitting my toes on things and, you know, hurting them.

"My toe," Gavin moaned again. "That's just what I needed today."

"Um, sorry," I said. I was trying to edge around him to get to the restroom and out of his warpath.

He hobbled off without looking back at me. Very dramatic, that guy.

When I reached the stage, everyone was already waiting, poised and hushed behind the red curtain. I counted faces and was relieved to see no one missing, with the exception of the ailing little Potter. Even Penelope had arrived at some point, though she was avoiding eye contact with me by tilting her bright red curls to block her view. We had a general rule that if you didn't attend a rehearsal, either Thursday night or Sunday morning, you didn't perform with the group. Perhaps that was why she was failing to connect, so that she wouldn't be kicked offstage. Frankly, Penelope, even with a missed practice, was the least of my musical worries. I was much more afraid that Barb and Walter would lead off the wrong words and confidently carry the rest of the group along.

I did notice that Penelope had a faint wet spot on one

side of her chest, at boob height. I saw Barb point it out, and Penelope flushed and grabbed at the shirt there, turning away to button her cardigan over it.

Barb didn't look abashed at having embarrassed a fellow singer, but, then, little shamed Barb into silence. "Gopher, huh?" I heard her say loudly. "Little sucker! I remember when my kids were that age." She laughed merrily, and Penelope continued to avert her gaze, now in a general fashion. Walter moved to the other side of the group, unwinding his mic cord from his fellow singers as he adjusted himself.

We could hear Pastor Chris Bakker's clear, calm tenor voice welcome the congregation to the service, then invite everyone into a word of prayer. It was strange for everything to continue as normal when a church member had just been murdered, but one problem of a big, newcomer-centric church is invariably a lack of community. Potentially only five percent of the congregation would even know who the victim was, much less care. I knew Chris Bakker was a professional, and the show must go on.

While eyes were presumably closed for his neutral opening prayer, which invited God's presence and didn't mention the murderer in our midst, the curtain soundlessly parted and the singers moved forward, mics in hands and heads respectfully downcast until the prayer had ended.

Hal counted off the beats with his sticks, and the keyboard and guitars came in right on cue. It sounded good, and loud. Maybe something about this horrible Sunday could be redeemed.

The whole of our opening set went smoothly. Even the funny face Rob made at me from the third row back just made me smile wider and look all the more genuine, although I made a note to bean him later, over mozzarella sticks.

The lights dimmed as the praise team filed off backstage, passing the incoming drama players on the way and losing Blaine as we passed and he filed into their ranks, quickly pulling a slouchy hat onto his head. I suppose his presence in the skit explained his outfit of suspenders and hideously wide tie—maybe. They were all dressed as the elderly, I supposed because we didn't have many actual senior citizens in our congregation, with the exception of Gretchen and Heidi and Potter's great-grandmother, who would follow her genius trumpeter progeny anywhere. I looked at Gretchen and Heidi to see if they found the costumes offensive, but they didn't bat an eye. They weren't very good costumes. Maybe the twins thought they were dressed as hobos.

The praise team silently picked our way through the dim backstage area, hearing the beginning lines of the skit spoken into the attentive auditorium. As soon as we hit the sunlit back hallway, the group broke into conversation about what had gone wrong and right with the music thus far, including a messed-up setting on the keys and a particularly good mix in the on-stage monitors that we used as feedback. We hoped that whatever had gone wrong with the sound earlier had been fixed as far as the congregation was concerned as well.

We had a circuitous path to take through the building to get back to the auditorium so we could enter it from the rear in a less disturbing manner. We were all supposed to sit toward the back or sides if possible, though I preferred sneaking up to Rob so I would have someone to scratch my back during the sermon. Chatting away, we passed the PB&J kids assembling in the hallway before marching off to their classrooms. They had been dismissed one song early today, so as not to disturb the dramatic opening moments of the skit with their clattering exit. PB&J was another peculiarly New Vision euphemism to make church seem less churchy, like Watchkeepers for elder board or, heck, praise team for choir. In this case, the acronym PB&J stood for Praise, Bible, & Jesus and in layman's terms meant Sunday School.

Kirsten was accosted by her oldest two, who wrapped around their mother's legs in a tight hug and were squeezed in return before being gently disentangled by a teacher. I assumed the youngest three kidlets were in the infant and toddler nursery. I exchanged a friendly wave with Melissa Hernandez, the children's ministry leader.

Dylan and Zachary were unexpectedly walking together ahead of me, talking low and intensely, their dark and light heads close together. They suddenly stalled to one side, voices vehement but too low to hear more than a handful of words that broke free. I caught "quiet" and "bag" as I passed them.

Walter and Jim were walking quickly in the lead and chatting animatedly. Walter was doing most of the talking. Penelope we'd lost somewhere along the way. I wondered if she'd sidetracked to the nursery to feed Gopher.

I caught up to Gretchen and Heidi, who had started out ahead of me but were necessarily a little slower. I heard them chattering away to each other in Dutch.

I was surprised to find Avery at my side, the blue streaks in her hair catching the sunlight and her outfit a mix of pieces I would have worn as a dork in junior high but that somehow looked stylish on her. I would have thought she'd have stuck with her fellow teens.

"Hey," I said congenially.

"Hey," she returned.

I was really, really going to try not to talk about Tammy. "It's funny to hear them speak Dutch, isn't it?" I said, gesturing toward the twins as we passed.

"What?" Avery said, turning toward me. Her hazel eyes were obscured behind the sun glinting off her eyeglasses. Apparently she hadn't sprung for the anti-glare coating for her fake lenses.

"Even though everyone here is supposedly Dutch, they're the only ones I ever hear speaking it," I said, inclining my head their way.

"That's not Dutch," Avery said. "That's German."

"Are you sure?" I said.

"I've been studying it with my dad and Wren," Avery said.

"Huh," I said. But there was no time to say more, because Dylan and Zachary had surged ahead to catch up with us again, only to duck down a side hallway for some unknown detour. Avery broke away to join them.

I slowed my pace and waited until the twins once more drew even with me. "You're speaking German?" I said.

Gretchen glared at me. Heidi looked nervous, but maybe it was just her watery pale blue eyes. "We speak Dutch with a German accent," Gretchen said.

"Oh?" I said, trying to be polite. "Where were you raised?"

"Ber—," started Heidi.

"Holland," Gretchen said flatly.

"Our mother was German," Heidi explained in gentler tones.

"Ah," I said.

Just then, Valerie the newsletter editor appeared in a whirl of red coat in front of us, as if she had apparated in.

"Gretchen, Heidi," she said smoothly, wedging her way in between the twins and me. "Don't forget about our interview."

"What interview?" Heidi said tremulously.

"Silly," Valerie said, patting her on one rounded shoulder with her red diary. "That's just what I mean. I've been after you for weeks to set one up. I can't wait to do a profile on our church's oldest members."

The tails of Valerie's red coat swirled as the diminutive woman spun out of our orbit. "Phone me," she called back gaily.

Heidi stumbled a bit, and Gretchen reached out a solicitous hand. I noticed Heidi's on her cane was white knuckled.

"When did you start going to New Vision?" I said, trying to steer the conversation somewhere neutral.

"A year ago," Gretchen said, but her voice was still heavy. Heidi shook her head almost imperceptibly.

Suddenly, commotion erupted ahead of us. I could see the doors to the back of the cafetorium open, and I was going to hush my praise team members for causing such a ruckus when they were supposed to be entering the service quietly when I realized—the racket was coming from inside the auditorium, and the open doors had merely let the noise emit into the hallway.

I ran forward to join the group at the door. I thought I even heard the tapping of Heidi's cane get more rapid.

Walter, Jim, Kirsten, and Hal all stood in the doorway, staring dumbfounded. The errant group of youth caught up with us. "What's going on?" Avery asked.

"Don't look," Kirsten called out, lunging toward Avery to push her away from the door. Walter tried to block her with his arm as Avery pushed forward.

I tried to get a view toward the stage through the cramping of bodies in my way. Gavin DeHaan was Avery's father, I was reminded, as I heard the scream beside me.

"Daddy!"

Apparently Kirsten and Walter hadn't been fast enough.

There were two bodies up on the stage, and they didn't look good. In a recognition that sparked horror down my spine, I realized that the upper person I could make out was Blaine, the slouchy hat covering his spiky white-blond hair apparently lost in the disturbance, and beneath him at an odd angle was Gavin. My eyes tried to

99

make sense of what I was seeing, but it took time to process the incongruities from the back of the cafetorium.

Only half of each man was visible, the rest apparently being actually under the stage, as if a trapdoor had sprung open and surprised them. Only I knew there were no trapdoors on the school's stage.

Blood ran down one side of Blaine's face, and he was silent but clearly conscious, one arm stuck out at a stiff angle to hang on so that he didn't slip further into the gaping hole and one arm gripping around Gavin's chest from behind. One of Gavin's legs was rucked at an odd angle across the wood, while the other leg and one arm had disappeared into the hole that had opened up to swallow him. Most disturbing were the keening bellows that Gavin was emitting, the sound of an animal in pain.

Avery was sprinting toward the front of the auditorium, meeting up with her mother and younger sister on the way.

Other drama team members and various men from the church were circling the stage uneasily, gesturing to each other and apparently trying to figure out how best to help without breaking the meager support that still held the victims up. Someone had located a rope and was trying to fling it around the men, while Blaine was talking wildly to his would-be rescuers, maybe giving them tips on how not to end up hurting both of them more.

"Has someone called 911?" Kirsten asked, pulling her cell phone out of her pocket. Why was she always so cool and collected, I wondered, and why couldn't I be?

I spotted Rob down near the front at the same time he happened to glance back and see me. I rushed toward him, my safe haven from the tumult.

The congregation was no longer held in thrall, and people started milling and talking in what turned into a loud roar. Just before the standing bodies covered up my view of the oddly ratcheted men, I saw what seemed like hopeful movement out of the hole—or maybe it was death throes.

I reached Rob and felt his arms close around me, warm and tight. I buried my head in his chest, feeling as small as a child.

The service unceremoniously ended, and eventually most of the congregants filed out, buzzing to each other, after EMTs had loaded up Blaine and Gavin and rushed them away in ambulances.

Leaning into each other, Rob and I had stood off to the side and about midway down the auditorium, watching the commotion from a distance and trying not to get in the way of the medical efforts.

Hal had been standing farther toward the front, but now he threaded his way back through the folding chairs, to where he had left his black leather jacket, adorned with metal studs. He saw us standing nearby and ran a hand over his ponytail.

"Horrible," he said.

I nodded. "How bad is it?" My voice came out hoarse, as if I'd inhaled something noxious.

"Blaine was conscious and seemed beaten up but not too bad. Gavin, though..." Hal's face contorted. "They got him sedated, at least."

"What happened?" Rob asked from beside me.

"The floorboards gave way somehow, and underneath the stage was some sort of acid."

"What?" I wasn't sure I'd heard right.

"Acid?" Rob echoed. "Just sitting under the stage?"

"In some sort of container," Hal confirmed, shaking his head. "Why would someone store a vat of acid under a stage?"

"Why indeed?" Rob said.

"Was it some sort of trap?"

Hal shrugged, then pulled on his jacket.

"Anyway, Gavin got the worst of the acid on his leg and one side of his body. They're taking him to Graybeal General Hospital."

I made a mental note to put in a visit for Avery's sake. I wasn't sure Gavin wanted my clodhopper shoes back in his vicinity now that his own stomping days might be over.

"Are you coming?" someone called. It was Hal's girlfriend, with the matching long gray ponytail, standing in the middle of the auditorium and clutching a Bible to her ample, denim jumper–clad bosom.

Hall moved away to join her, and Rob and I could see that things were clearing out in general. We gathered up our jackets and my music bag and headed toward a side door. The sunlight coming into the dim hall was bright enough to blind us, and I ran straight into a figure on my way out.

I caught a glimpse of no-nonsense dress suit and impeccable pumps and realized I had collided with the good Detective Madari.

"Christine Song—no, Randal," Detective Madari corrected herself.

I nodded and smiled.

"I was actually hoping to talk with you," I said.

Detective Madari turned her flint-gray eyes up to me from the tablet she was studying. "We will be talking with all the church service participants within the next week." Her eyes went back to her tablet, as if that should satisfy me.

"I mean about something else," I said insistently.

"We received a phone threat from the killer," Rob said.

Detective Madari looked slowly from one to the other of us, the skin on her face pulling even tighter than usual. "When was this?"

"We got it last night," I said. "It was on my voicemail. I don't remember when exactly it was left, but yesterday evening sometime."

"Do you still have it?" Detective Madari looked at best mildly interested.

"Yes," Rob told her as I nodded eagerly, trying to will her to be more intrigued.

"I have my phone right here," I said, pulling it out.

She didn't even glance at my phone. "I'll arrange a time to have someone listen to it," she said, turning back to her tablet and swiping in a note. When she didn't resume eye contact, we realized we'd been dismissed.

Rob and I trudged away. I kicked a smallish block of ice that was melting in the noon sun and felt some satisfaction when it hit another block and broke in two.

"She didn't seem concerned at all," I told Rob.

"No," he agreed, and took a turn kicking the next block of ice we came to.

Chapter 8

It fortunately turned out that Gavin DeHaan wasn't, so far at least, close to death, but the damage was of the sort that could turn serious. He was in the Intensive Care Unit at Graybeal General Hospital. He had literally broken a leg in his fall through the stage, and there was extensive damage to his left leg, as well as moderate damage to his left arm. He was having a series of surgeries to try to repair what could be repaired. Blaine had been admitted overnight for observation but was in a regular unit. Barb had called me with all this information almost at the same moment we walked in the door, after a little detour on the way home to get a boatload of mini White Castle burgers, and I thanked her for keeping me in the prayer loop. I thought that was a more tactful way to put it than "gossip hotline."

Out of habit while talking on the phone, I flipped open my laptop and refreshed my email inbox. There was an email from Blaine, which seemed ghostly since it had been sent early that morning, before the incident. I had been in too big a rush to check my email before church.

Rob looked over my shoulder and was as surprised as

I was to see how detailed the police information was that Blaine had gotten on Tammy's death.

"Is this legal?" he asked.

"I assume that it most definitely is not," I said. "That's why I'm glad it's Blaine who's doing it and not us."

In skimming, it didn't seem that so far there was much new. A condensed version of the autopsy report was fascinating to look at, but the findings only confirmed what we already knew. The rest of the email was abbreviated notes either Blaine or someone else had taken on points of interest in the investigation so far. The police hadn't found anyone who had made an unusual purchase of tobacco, which made me wonder idly if they had checked my financial records, and plenty of suspects didn't have alibis. I knew usually mine was just that I was hanging out with Rob, and I assumed something like that didn't hold much weight one way or the other. I would have to read the rest of Blaine's notes later when we didn't have burgers cooling out in the living room.

"Ready to eat?" Rob said.

"Let me just change first," I said, prescient in my knowledge that White Castle burgers wouldn't sit well inside my wool church pants. I didn't go to formal affairs often enough to justify buying more than one pair of good pants, and these ones were from high school. I admitted that maybe I needed the next size up, but I hated to get rid of a good pair.

I noticed on my way to hang them in the closet that two new messages had come in on my phone. I always muted and stowed it away for church and I'd turned it back on just before Barb had called, so I wasn't sure when these had been left. I set it to speaker mode on the dresser while I rummaged for jammies.

"Hey, Christine," said the first one. "It's Blaine. I'm in the hospital here, but I think I'm fine." His voice sounded more subdued than normal, but it was a relief to hear him speak. "I just wanted to make sure I had the right email address for that stuff I sent you earlier. If you didn't get it, let me know." He apparently had no qualms at sending confidential information to a random email. Maybe a partnership with him would be dangerous. He signed off with his cell phone number and an invitation to call if I wanted more information on the morning's events, and this time I managed to write the number down before the next message clicked on.

"Christine," said the robot voice. I froze. "I have given you a warning." I became dimly aware that Rob had appeared in the office door to listen. "Your friendship is not with the painted whore but with God."

That was it. I was so confused by the last line that I automatically hit replay to listen to it through again.

When the female voice came on to tell us that it had been left a scant thirty minutes previous, I turned to look at Rob.

"What did that mean? Who's the painted whore?"

"Well," Rob said, "normally I'd say you, but how can you be friends with yourself?"

I threw the pencil I had used to write down Blaine's number his way. It glanced ineffectually off his side and planted itself, nose down, in the beige carpet.

"'Your friendship is not with the painted whore,'" I repeated. "Is that a person? Or like the Whore of Babylon?"

"Didn't that refer to Rome?"

"Do you think our killer has something against the Roman Empire?" I said with one eyebrow raised.

"I think our killer is completely deranged, so anything's possible." Rob undid his own church pants, the better to relax in his boxers. "If only one woman had been targeted—"

"Like Tammy," I broke in.

"Yeah," Rob said, scratching his lean stomach in thought. "If just Tammy were the target, then maybe she could be the whore. But as it is, I'd assume it's something bigger."

"The church?" I raised my hands, palms up. "New Vision in particular?"

"It is interesting that both attacks have taken place in such churchly atmospheres," Rob said. "A praise team practice and a Sunday worship service."

"Let me call Blaine." I changed tacks. "He said he had more information on this morning."

Rob leaned against the dresser and waited while I dialed.

"Christine," Blaine said when I got through. I hit speakerphone again so Rob could eavesdrop. "I'm not supposed to use a cell phone in here, so I'll have to keep it short."

"What?" I said. "Why?"

"I don't know," Blaine said. "Hospital rules. Maybe they ignite oxygen tanks."

"Cool," Rob said from the side. Blaine and I ignored him.

"Did you get the stuff I sent you on Tammy?"

"Yeah," I said. "Thanks. I haven't had a chance to read it all yet, but I didn't see anything new offhand."

"Yeah," Blaine said. The sound became muffled suddenly. Rob and I could hear voices, but as if they were under a blanket. "Sorry about that," Blaine said clearly once again. "A nurse came in and I had to stick the phone under the blankets." Ah. "I'll hurry and finish up. Did you see any of the drama?"

"No," I said. "We arrived at the back of the auditorium just after the accident."

"Oh, it was no accident," Blaine said. "It was the stage-left floorboards under Gavin that gave way, and there were signs that someone had weakened them intentionally."

"And then acid under the stage?" I said, still incredulous. It sounded medieval, like pouring boiling oil down in reverse.

"In an industrial vat, yeah," Blaine said. "So Gavin fell through first and soaked his leg and then some of his arm in it, and I fell on top of him a little but managed to catch most of my weight on good floorboards. So I kind of helped hold him up until the other guys could pull us off the stage."

"You're a hero," I said in wonder.

"Aw," Blaine said, and I swore I could hear him blushing, "it wasn't anything like that."

There was the sound of a little scuffle and a loud but indistinct voice. "Gotta go," Blaine said, and the line clicked off.

"Those burgers are getting cold," Rob said, pointing out to the living room.

I docilely followed him out to our trays. "So there's a weak hole in the stage, and a vat of acid beneath the drop." I pulled out a couple of the miniature burgers and unwrapped one. "It's a strange way to kill someone."

"Very hit or miss," Rob agreed.

I shuddered. "I'm glad the praise team stuck to the middle of the stage," I said. "If we had been over farther... "

"Don't even think it," he said.

"The randomness of it does compel the question, though," I said. "Did the killer know it had a big chance of failing?"

"You mean, was it staged, pardon the pun?"

I yukked obediently. "Poisoning's a little more...thorough."

"Although the killer didn't necessarily know that Tammy would eat the poisoned cough drop right then," Rob pointed out.

"And there's once again the question of whether the killer had a particular victim in mind," I said.

"Unless the killer knew in advance about the play's

blocking and had planned out exactly how much weight and damage the floor could take before it gave in," Rob mused. "That seems kind of far-fetched."

"Is it possible that Gavin planned it himself?"

"That he's the killer or an accomplice?" Rob said. "It's possible, though he's certainly screwed up his own life if so."

"Avery's on the praise team," I said. "I'd hate to think she had anything to do with something that hurt her father."

"Do you suspect her?" Rob said, eyeing me thoughtfully.

"Not really," I said. "But maybe that's just my prejudice against thirteen-year-old criminal masterminds. I can't picture fourteen-year-old Potter in the role, either."

"Avery's a lot more mature than Potter."

"Yeah, she's thirteen going on twenty-five, all right." I shook my head. "She's deep into something with Zachary and Dylan, but I get the feeling it's just the usual girlish impulse to drive men to distraction."

"Like you do with me." Rob assumed a moonstruck face.

"You know it," I said.

I thought it might help to reason out motives and suspects. I saw Rob's church program from the service on the coffee table and flipped to the sermon notes section. As I had guessed: empty. I scrounged for a pen I remembered dropping under the futon and started taking notes as we talked.

With the death in the church sanctuary, we reasoned that the pool of suspects might be wider than the praise-team members, but they still seemed the most likely bunch. It was possible that the cough drop had been placed into Barb's jacket at some other opportunity, but the practice gave the best chance, and there was the mysterious business of the disappearance of her purse and the other cough drops.

"And all within a locked building," Rob said. "I love locked-room mysteries." He actually rubbed his hands together as he said this.

"Even if it's not someone in the praise team," I said, "we could eliminate them." Rob looked at me. "As suspects," I amended.

"Oh, good," Rob said. "I was afraid you were the killer after all."

I swatted at him with the church bulletin.

"Violent tendencies!" Rob cried. "This is what I'm talking about."

I stuck out my tongue.

Rob returned to being serious. "Those two old ladies we visited," he began.

"Gretchen Plantinga and Heidi Abbing."

"Yeah," Rob said. "They interest me. Why would ninety-something-year-olds join a church like New Vision? That survey the church did a couple months ago showed that the average age is 32, and if you just look around, you see mostly married couples with young children, some younger couples, a few older or college-age kids with their middle-aged parents, but very few people older than that."

I nodded. "That is a place to look," I agreed. "But what would they have to gain by killing people off? Just because they're out of place here? They want to remind all of us that we're near death?"

We laughed. It was black humor, but it was all we had.

"How long have they been going to New Vision?"

"About a year."

"Is that it?" Rob said. "So maybe they're disgruntled newcomers."

"Oh, come on," I said. "At New Vision, that makes them practically in line for the pastorship. We've been here a year, too, and I'm the worship leader now."

"But we aren't disgruntled, are we?" I wasn't sure if it

was a rhetorical question so didn't respond. "What about the twins' attitude?"

"They've been edgy lately for sure," I said.

"Edgy how? Just because there's been a death?"

"Specifically to do with private conversations they've been having in...well, I was going to say Dutch, but Avery said it was German. Gretchen swore it was Dutch, though."

"Are they Dutch or German?" Rob asked.

"Heidi said their mother was German but that they were raised in the Netherlands." I scratched my forehead. "But they were definitely hiding something there."

"They're in their nineties," Rob repeated. "So in World War II, they'd have been, how old?"

I tried to do the math in my head, but Rob beat me to it.

"In their twenties," he finished. "What were they doing during the war? With a German mother, whether they lived in Holland or not."

"Hmm," I said. "I guess I forgot they'd have been adults during the war. Maybe there's something they're concealing there." I snapped my fingers as another thought occurred to me. "Valerie was bugging them about doing a news piece on their transfer to New Vision."

"That newspaper person who was at the Bible study?" Rob said. "She's been in everybody's face lately."

"You've noticed, too," I said, nodding. "She was hounding Mora, Dylan's mom, to do a college-transfer piece."

"When I came in from the car to church this morning, I saw she had cornered Walter, and he didn't seem any too happy about it."

I pondered this and drew stars around Gretchen and Heidi's names. "But back to the twins," I said. "Would they be able to build such an elaborate booby trap, sawing through floorboards and such?"

"I don't want to count out those war ladies," Rob said.

"You know, Rosie the Riveter and all that." But then he laughed. "No, I can't really see them managing the handiwork necessary to do that. Would they hook the tools over one of their canes?"

Something he said reminded me of...what? "Tools," I said.

"Tools?"

"Albert had tools," I said. "Maybe he did it."

"Maybe." Rob sounded enthusiastic. "Who's Albert?"

"Their great-nephew," I said. "That blond guy who came in while we were there. He was fixing their shed or something."

"So they hire him as a killer? Close-knit family."

I shrugged and scribbled over my stars. "I'm discounting them as suspects, unless you think Albert looked suspicious."

"I don't even remember him."

"Well, then." I hadn't taken very many notes after all, and now I found myself doodling a baby with a curlicue on the top of his head. "Penelope," I thought aloud. "Did you know Penelope was a single mom?"

"No," Rob said. "Then again, I don't know who Penelope is."

"Red curls, always has a baby tied to her."

"Right. Soprano."

"Mm. She seems nice enough, but she's also one of the new ones at New Vision. And I'm not sure where the father of the baby's at. There might be something there."

"Has she expressed any murderous intentions toward the singles group or dramatic players?" Rob arched a brow.

"Ah, no. Maybe the father of the baby is the killer."

"Why would that be?" Rob asked.

"Because it sounds mysterious."

Rob didn't pursue my fanciful line of deductive reasoning. "Is it more or less likely that the murderer is an old-timer?" he began instead.

I looked down at the pig-like horse I'd drawn and embellished the mane a little more to emphasize the horsiness, then added a crown for no good reason. "For old-timers, you've got Walter and Barb. They've both been part of New Vision from the start," I said. "Walter's one of the original Watchkeepers, and Barb's husband is, too. I'm not sure what they'd have to gain from killing off church members."

"Well, being part of the church for longer gives them more opportunity to have created enemies," Rob said. "Maybe there are grudges and feuds we know nothing about. Like Walter and firing Tammy. Did you find out more about that?"

"Not yet," I said, jotting it in a new to-do section I started in the prayer requests column by first helpfully crossing out "Prayer Requests." To be serious about my new status of private investigator, I would have to compile and expand these notes into a text file later, I decided, maybe even something fancy in Evernote, but I didn't feel like moving from the futon to retrieve my laptop from the other room. "Plus, several of the kids go to Nederland Christian, where Walter's the principal, and apparently where Penelope works as well. Who knows what tensions lurk in those hallowed halls?" I raised and lowered my eyebrows dramatically and drew a boat for the horse to ride in, adding dramatic waves beneath the hull.

Rob shook his head. "Speaking of students, if Avery's off your list, who are the other young hoodlums who might have done it?"

"Um, Potter, Zachary, Dylan."

"And who are they again?"

I grinned. Rob's propensity for forgetting names was making me question his observational skills just a tad. "Potter's the little trumpeter. I don't really suspect him. He barely says boo."

"Sometimes it's the silent types that everyone says afterward, 'He seemed so nice,'" Rob warned.

I smiled. "Yeah, okay, I guess if he was being malicious but immature, he might have done the poisoned lozenge, but cutting through the floorboards and dragging in a vat of acid must have taken some serious tinkering, not to mention transportation to the school in the middle of the night. Potter's still in junior high, and I'm guessing he couldn't have gotten his mother to drive him out to murder someone."

"Maybe she's in on it," Rob said, spreading his hands and widening his deep brown eyes. "She can't stand her son not being the star of the praise team, so she hatches a plan to gain him instant notoriety." His gestures became more dramatic as his story did.

"That sounds more like Zachary's mom's line." I rolled my eyes. "She'd probably kill for her son to play the real drums versus the bongos."

"It's a thought," Rob said.

I pursed my lips in distaste at just thinking about the woman. "After the Texas cheerleader murders, anything's possible."

"And who was the other guy?" Rob said.

"Dylan Ruiz, the bassist. You met his parents at the Bible study—Alexander and Mora. He's in his first year at college, has his own band, really supa-cool. Or thinks he is."

"You don't like him."

"No." I sighed. "But that doesn't necessarily make him a murderer. He's slippery, though, hard to talk to. He has this story about transferring to Blanchard, but after overhearing Valerie's interrogation of Mora, I think maybe there's something fishy there."

"Like what?" Rob said.

"Like he never got in in the first place. The story they're putting about is that he likes community college or they can't afford Blanchard or whatever...kind of muddled."

"Wait, Alexander Ruiz? Does he own Alex Ruiz GM, and Ford, and Chevrolet, and...et cetera?"

I shrugged. "Yup. I know they don't look to be hurting."

"And they can't afford more than community college?"

I shrugged again. "Like I said, fishy. And I don't like Dylan. I'm not sure how that makes him murderous, except maybe against Valerie, who's alive and kicking. But he's the only one I wouldn't mind it being."

"He's on my short list," Rob said loyally. "Who else is on the praise team?"

"Blaine the web designer."

"And eager partner in murder investigation," Rob continued. "That was weird, how forward he was about that, and before this latest incident had even happened."

"Oh, my gosh," I said, "do you think he was targeted because he was poking his nose in, just like we've been getting threatening messages?"

Rob blew out a long breath. "It's scary to think, but I guess it's possible, assuming there was any targeting. As far as suspecting him goes, I've talked with him in passing about a few design projects for New Vision, and I didn't get the feeling he has any deep resentment toward the church."

"I think his parents go and brought him along," I said. "But you're right. He's never seemed resentful about being there. I think he wanted to be praise team leader instead of me, but is that reason to start attacking the church?"

"We should watch him around you."

"But, Rob, if he's the killer, why on earth did he spring the trap while he was on it?"

"Maybe he's a very inept killer," Rob said.

"Hal is new." I tried to remember how a babysitter

taught me to draw Garfield the cat in elementary school, but it came out like a doughy circle with ears and arms and stripes. Actually, I reconsidered, I think that was how I used to draw it.

"Hal, the guy with the ponytail?" Rob prompted.

I looked up from my roly-poly Garfield. "Yeah. I don't think he's a Christian at all."

"Ahh," Rob said thoughtfully.

"But I don't want to suspect him on that basis alone," I said. "I mean, we're a seeker church, right? That's exactly the person we're supposed to be attracting."

"But it's strange, isn't it?" Rob steepled his long tan fingers. "I mean, the whole idea of seekers. Who grows up unreligious and then suddenly decides that church is a good idea? I mean, outside of any religion looking in, it looks pretty ridiculous and unappetizing." Rob paused. "And boring."

I thought. "I heard sometime that he grew up Catholic. So that might explain it. Guilt at not going for so many years, but not wanting to choose a really churchy church to return to." I tilted my head. "Plus, he loves to play the drums. I think that more than anything influenced his decision—a church with a praise band that needed a drummer. And, well, you saw today—his girlfriend goes."

"Aha." Rob nodded meaningfully.

"As far as means go, though, I think he's an electrician."

"What does that mean?" Rob said.

"He works with his hands and seems pretty fit," I explained. "Unlike say, Potter, I could see Hal sawing floorboards and dragging in a vat and filling it with acid. And knowing where to procure such."

"Well, you certainly wouldn't know how to do those things," Rob conceded.

"Exactly." I wrote down the next name that came to mind. "Jim is an interesting one," I said. "He's new, too.

Get this"—I leaned forward to give the coffee table a drum beat—"he owns his own company that sends out home-improvement workers. I don't know what he was trained in himself, but he probably has some handy knowledge, maybe enough to rig a booby trap or two."

Rob peered over my shoulder to consider the list.

"Hal, Jim, and Blaine were all in One-on-One together with Tammy." I obediently circled their names on my marked-up bulletin and frowned at it as Rob continued. "Though now that Gavin and Blaine were attacked, I don't know that there's a connection to the group at all. Gavin is married."

I considered. "He wasn't recently, though. Wren told me that his current wife, Marjorie, is only 28. I don't know if there's any scandal there with the divorce."

"What connection might there be between Tammy and Gavin?" Rob said. "If they were targeted, that is."

"Wouldn't we both like to know."

"Something's been niggling at the back of my brain." Rob changed the subject. "About the first incident. Tammy asked for a cough drop, right?"

"Right," I said.

"And then Barb found one, and gave it to her. Did the murderer know to give Barb the poisoned drop before or after Tammy asked?"

I thought about the night in question. "Wait. Walter asked for one, too."

Rob cocked his head to one side. "Did he ask before or after Tammy?"

"Before," I said immediately. "Wait. I think so. I don't remember. I know they both asked, and Barb could only find the one, so Walter said Tammy could have it."

"Whoa," Rob breathed. "That means Walter might have known it was poisoned. Didn't you say he was helping sort the coats?"

"Yeah," I said. "But wasn't he taking kind of a risk, asking for a cough drop, not knowing if anyone else would want one? If he was given the poisoned one, what then?"

"Well, obviously, he wouldn't take it, unless he was really determined to frame Barb." We both thought this was funny. "But I see what you mean. Unless Tammy asked first, and he knew he could then safely ask and then let Tammy have the single drop that was left."

"N-o-o-o," I said, thinking hard. "I really think Walter asked first. But then he definitely volunteered Tammy for the drop when Barb found it. Then he and Jim got water instead."

"Jim, too?"

"Yeah," I said, trying to remember. "Jim asked for one, too." I tapped my pencil against Garfield and tried to crystallize the memories of that night, which seemed so far away now. "I think it was after Barb had found her purse, though. Then he and Walter went out for water when Barb realized the rest of her stash was gone."

"Well," Rob said. "I'm not sure how that helps one way or the other."

"I wish being a detective was like doing a logic puzzle," I said, waving my hand, "where you know every clue will help solve it and there's nothing extraneous. I feel like I'm picking up a lot of useless information and maybe nothing helpful at all, but how can we know?"

"Did we go over everyone on the team?" Rob said.

I looked down at my list of suspects and racked my brain some more.

"Kirsten," I finished triumphantly. "And I think that's it. And, frankly, I don't see where you'd have time to murder someone if you have infant triplets and two toddlers at home."

Rob gave a low whistle. "I can't imagine."

"Let's pray we never have to," I said fervently.

Chapter 9

On Monday morning, I resolutely refused to succumb to the wiles of the snooze button. Well, much. I got up only a couple hours after Rob left, showered and dressed, and checked my messages.

Sure enough, there was a new obscene one sandwiched between the usual telemarketing clicks and static.

"The body is God's temple, Christine," said the robot voice. "Do not defile the body."

Could he see me? I wondered, looking around guiltily while licking breakfast Ding Dong crème off my fingers. Noting the tightly closed blinds in the office, I reconsidered, but it still felt creepy even to listen to these messages when Rob wasn't around.

With the whore and the body reference, I thought it was pretty certain that he meant the Church as a whole, called the Body of Christ in Christianese. But was New Vision the whore or the temple? Or both?

I looked up the nonemergency number for the Murphy Police and dialed. A bored receptionist patched me through to Detective Madari, but all I got was her voicemail.

"This is Detective Adeela Madari. Leave a message," it told me in no uncertain terms.

I told the detective that I'd received two more threatening phone messages and reminded her that she had promised to send someone to listen to them.

I was feeling more than a little annoyed that the police weren't taking threats against me seriously, considering there was a would-be two-time killer on the loose.

Rob had our car, so I tried navigating the county bus schedule online. Setting my phone's GPS to navigate me to the bus stop, I hit the streets, letting the wintry air clear my head.

Despite having a reputation for being rural, Indiana, at least the northwest corner, was not made for pedestrians. I ended up skirting my way through drainage ditches most of the journey to my bus stop, avoiding icy patches and ignoring the stares from passing motorists on the busy street, and there was no direct route to the hospital.

After a very cold hour and a half waiting for a transfer, I eventually made it to Graybeal General, where Gavin De-Haan was recuperating, lovingly surrounded by family. His young wife, Marjorie, and daughters, Avery and Wren, were in his room when I walked in, after being directed the right way by a helpful nurse.

"Gavin," I said. "You look great."

Gavin laughed hoarsely. But he did, all in all. Half his head was covered in bandages, and his brown hair was sticking up at odd angles as if part of it had been shaved and the rest tousled beyond repair. His left arm and leg were so swollen, either just by the bandages or by actual trauma, that I couldn't tell what if anything had been removed. He looked groggy and leaned against the pillows, but despite all that, he was grinning, and his color was not the death white of the last time I'd seen him.

I noticed that his thumb was on a button that led to his IV drip and wondered if narcotics were the cause of his unexpected cheeriness.

Marjorie smiled shyly, her pallor matching her locks, and gestured to a stiff visitor's chair. This incident had clearly taken its toll. I handed over the get-well card I'd unearthed from a stack deep inside one of my desk drawers, part of a short-lived resolve to send cards to people for every occasion and in a timely manner.

"How are you feeling?" I asked Gavin, smiling around at the assembled family members as well.

"He's doing much better," Marjorie whispered. "His throat's still sore from the tubes they put in for the surgeries, but he's recovering very well, considering." Considering that someone had tried to kill him.

"That's great," I said. "How are the rest of you holding up?"

Avery and Wren weren't making eye contact. I wasn't surprised by Wren's reticence, since she barely knew me and was engrossed in another of her workbooks, but I couldn't figure out why Avery was avoiding me.

Marjorie answered again for the bunch, and I had to strain to hear. "Tired. But grateful."

That about summed it up.

A nurse entered then, to do mysterious nursely things involving tubes and who knew what. She gave me a look and started to pull the curtain around the bed, sectioning the girls and me off from Gavin and Marjorie inside. I hurriedly said my goodbyes and good wishes to Gavin and Marjorie.

It gave me the opportunity to cull the calf from the herd.

"Avery," I said. She looked at me finally. "Can I talk to you out in the hallway about praise team? I don't want to disturb your father." I smiled to soften any sense she might have of being called to the principal's office.

She stood up silently and slouched her way in front of me out into the hall. We narrowly avoided an empty wheelchair being pushed quickly past by an orderly and found a safe place along the other side of the corridor. She twirled one blue-toned lock and ignored me.

"I'm looking into this thing that's going on at church," I said without preamble.

That got her attention.

"Who do you think's behind this?"

Avery blinked behind the clear lenses of her nerd-chic glasses. I stared her down from the thick, nearsighted-ness- and astigmatism-correcting lenses of my quite-pragmatic ones.

"I don't know," she whispered. "Is it you?"

It was my turn to blink. "Are you scared of me?" I asked in disbelief.

She paused, then shook her head.

"What are you scared of, then?" I said.

She stared at a loaded gurney being rolled past, apparently considering what or whether to answer.

"Zachary and Dylan," she whispered at last.

"You think they're behind this?" My voice lowered of its own accord. Could this really be solved so quickly?

"I don't know," she said. "They won't tell me. They're not talking to each other. They're not telling me what's going on. But something is."

"Have you told your parents?"

"No!" she yelled. A passing nurse stared. "No," she said again, more quietly this time. "Don't you think I feel awful?" she said. "What if I had said something and my father hadn't been hurt?"

"Why do you suspect Zachary and Dylan of something?" I said, wanting to get to the meat of the matter but not sure what it was. I had never suspected Zachary and Dylan being in cahoots for anything, much less murder—they hated each other, right?

"They haven't been friendly to each other lately." She took off her glasses and wiped her hazel eyes. Instead of putting them back on, she folded them and tucked them in a pocket. That was the difference between her glasses wearing and mine.

As to the lack of friendship between the boys—well, no duh, I thought, and then said as much.

"What do you mean?" she said.

"They're jealous of each other."

"What?" She stared at me blankly.

"They're jealous of each other," I repeated, leaning toward her for emphasis, as if that would help her understand.

"But why?" She seemed honestly mystified.

"Because they both like you."

"What?" She recoiled.

Suddenly I remembered. She was thirteen years old. When I was thirteen, boys were just changing from icky to intriguing. Maybe I'd credited her with too much maturity.

"They like me? Me?" She pointed to her flat chest to illustrate what the word meant. Yup, I needed to remember her real age, not her apparent one.

"Sweetie," I said, "of course they do. Why do you think they follow you around everywhere?"

Her eyes remained wide as she took it all in. "I thought they must be mad about something they were in on together, like a drug deal or something. And then when the accidents started happening..."

"Is there any other reason to suspect them?" I asked, trying for businesslike. "For instance, what were you all doing together when you left rehearsal the night Tammy was killed?"

She looked sheepish.

"What?" I demanded.

She stared at one foot, the toe of her purple flats scuffing the gleaming surface of the hallway. "We took Barb's purse," she said quietly.

"You?" I said, incredulous.

"All three of us," she said. "And her cough drops."

"Where are they now?"

"At home," she said. "In my underwear drawer."

"You haven't eaten any, have you?" I said, horrified.

"No, of course not."

"You need to hand them over to the police," I insisted.

"But won't we get in trouble for stealing?"

I kept myself from rolling my eyes. "I doubt it. It doesn't matter. It's evidence. If they're poisoned, too, it suggests one thing, and if they're not, it suggests another. You have to turn them over."

Avery did roll her eyes. "Fine."

"Whose idea was it?" I asked. "To steal the purse and the cough drops?"

"I think it was Dylan's. We were just hiding her purse," she clarified, "not stealing it, just messing with her." She thought. "I think Zachary suggested taking the lozenges, when we were going through it. It was before you'd gotten to practice. We were bored."

Another mark against my tardiness. Fine, okay, I got it.

"Why did Zachary suggest taking the drops?"

She shrugged. "I don't know. Just for fun, I guess. I'm not sure it was Zachary, but maybe."

It was hard to imagine the lackadaisical Zachary coming up with such an ambitious scheme. It was strange, too, how convincing his blank-faced lie at the Bible study, that he had just been using the restroom, had been to me. "Not you, though."

"Not me." She kicked at the floor with the same toe of her shoe. "Are you going to tell my parents?"

"Aren't you?" I said. "Take the lozenges to the police. It will be fine. Just get it over with. It's a lot better to catch a murderer than keep from admitting some pointless prank."

"All right." She sighed.

I impulsively reached out to hug her. "I'm glad your dad's okay."

"Me, too," she said in a small voice.

If the murderer was going to accuse me of investigating, I might as well investigate, I thought. A real detective would start interviewing all the suspects. I decided to start with another person I didn't suspect overly much, to ease into things.

I was serious when I said that I couldn't imagine Kirsten finagling childcare for five children while she committed mayhem, but I didn't want to rule her out on that alone. Besides, she had been a little distant toward me lately, and I wasn't sure what that meant. My phone helpfully told me which return bus would drop me off a mere half-mile from her split-level. I turned into her subdivision and walked along Oak Lane to Willow Drive, hanging a left finally on Maple Court. I figured these were all named after the trees they'd cut down to build the houses.

Here it was: 1332 Maple Court. Kirsten was always hinting around that she could use help babysitting her spawn. Well, babysitter she wanted, babysitter she would get. I couldn't imagine a better cover.

"Kirsten!" I exclaimed when she opened the door. I had determined that enthusiasm would help cover the inanity of dropping in uninvited.

But it wasn't Kirsten who stood in the door. No one was standing in the door. I heard a squawking sound near my knees. I looked down.

"Grace?" I said tentatively. I couldn't quite remember her kids' names. The child there let out another squawk and then twirled in place.

"I'm a kanina!" she told me, dancing off into the living room that was level with the entryway.

Whatever that was, she seemed happy about it.

"Kirsten," I called. I didn't want to cross the threshold without her permission, and it felt wrong to encourage her children to let strangers into the house.

"Coming!" she called from somewhere deep inside the split-level. "Who is it?" she asked belatedly.

"It's Christine," I yelled back. "From praise team."

Suddenly, she was right by the door, and I felt rude for yelling.

"Christine," she said, looking puzzled. "Just a minute," she said to the screeching kid clinging to one leg. Unlike the squawking kanina I could see romping cheerfully through the living room, this one was not making happy sounds. "What are you doing here?" She had turned back to me but was almost immediately distracted by something she detected behind her and up the stairs. I could almost see her ears prick up like a watchdog's.

"What is it?" I said.

"The babies," she moaned, turning in one fluid motion to pick up the screeching barnacle, say "I love your dance, honey" to the kanina, and head up the stairs before I even caught the first whimpering sounds emanating from a closed door beyond. By the time she'd opened the door, the whimpering had turned to wails in stereo. Or in triplicate, I supposed.

Kirsten was dressed in pajama bottoms and a hoodie, her feet in fuzzy slippers, her blond hair mussed. In fact, she looked like I looked most days, and I didn't even have five babies to justify it.

I decided to let myself in, and I closed the door behind me to keep out the chill, rubbing my raw hands in the heated warmth inside as I trudged up the stairs after Kirsten and followed her into the babies' room.

"Can I help?" I asked. Kirsten had one baby in mid-diapering at a changing table while two others screamed in the largest crib I had ever seen. The unhappy toddler clung again to one leg and seemed about to burst a lung.

Kirsten looked at me, and even in the dim light, I thought I could see her rolling her blue eyes.

I shrugged out of my winter jacket, pushed up my sleeves, and got to work.

Chapter 10

After all that, I was quite annoyed to find a flurry of emails waiting for me in my inbox when I got home—in one piece, despite the lack of sidewalks and crosswalks. They were all from paying clients, and in good conscience I had to accept them all.

When Rob came home, plopping his laptop bag down at the desk, he widened his mouth in feigned shock to find me assiduously tip-typing away in a real-live paying client's Word document. I held up one finger, since another word for "respective" was just on the tip of my brain, and I was afraid Rob would derail my train of thought.

"Chris!" Rob said. "I can't believe you're doing actual work."

Choo choo choo—aaaa! Off the tracks.

I looked up and glared. "What does holding up a finger mean these days?" I groused.

"German safety researcher?" He ignored my complaint.

"Yes." I sighed. "This time I'm learning about extended rear facing of toddlers and the decrease in internal decapitation."

Rob whistled. "That sounds like a laugh."

"But this woman has used the word 'respective' five times this page. I either need a new synonym, or I'm going to have to do some serious rewriting."

"Corresponding," Rob offered.

I typed it in. "Okay." I looked up again. "How was your day?"

"Boring." Rob sighed and plopped into his seat, winter jacket still on and rustling as he sat.

"It always is," I said.

"I wish I had your job," Rob said wistfully.

"But then who would make any money?" I countered.

"You're so practical," Rob said. A pause. "When are you going to get your P.I. license, open an agency, and keep me in the style I so richly deserve?"

I saved the document and closed it down to read it over again later. "After I solve my first case." I gestured at my screen. "But I have to do this annoying real work instead," I groused. "I'll have barely any time to sleuth."

"Maybe I can help out when I get home," he suggested, "and we can save some bigger tasks for Saturday."

"Let's just hope the killer isn't caught by then," I said, and then wrinkled my forehead when I realized what I'd said.

Rob laughed but then grew serious. "I hope no one else is killed by then."

"I know," I said. "That's why I shouldn't be editing all week."

"We'll just have to hope the killer is busy with work, too," Rob said.

"Well, I did manage to visit with Avery at the hospital and with Kirsten at home."

"You went to a suspect's house?" Rob's generously wide eyebrows nearly disappeared into his equally dark hairline.

"I don't really suspect Kirsten," I said, defending what in hindsight did look rather foolhardy. "Do you want the day's findings or not?"

"Sure, I do," Rob said, apparently forgiving my indiscretion. "Right after dinner. 'Rogies?"

"Yum!" I agreed, and followed Rob out to the kitchen to watch him start preparing the meal. I had to stand in the little dining room so as not to bump into him in the galley kitchen, but that didn't bother me. It meant I was farther away from the onions he was chopping.

With pierogies, mushroom gravy, and sautéed onions on plates, and a dollop of fermented sour cream on top, we made our way to the futon, where we stretched out side by side and watched a recorded show we'd been meaning to catch up on.

"So what did you find out?" Rob asked me later that evening over a glass of wine that was quickly going to turn into a whole bottle.

"I found out that we should never reproduce," I said.

"No, I meant about the murders."

"Rob." I looked him in the eye. "It was absolutely nonstop chaos. There was always, always someone crying. Those kids are intense. I was diapering, I was feeding, I was playing kaninas…"

"Kaninas?" Rob said.

"Don't ask."

"So you didn't accomplish anything?"

"Hey," I protested, "I accomplished plenty. Kirsten got a shower for the first time in a week, for one."

"She left you alone with them?" Rob said in surprise.

"I'm not the murderer!" I said.

"Well, she doesn't know that." Rob sipped his wine.

"Maybe she does," I returned, raising my eyebrows meaningfully.

Rob swirled his glass. "That's not funny, considering you were there alone. Do you really think she could be the one?"

"No," I said. "Definitely no possibility of sneaking out to set those traps, not with her husband working such long hours to support the seven of them."

"She had two more children since the last time I saw her?" Rob gasped.

"I meant the children plus the adults, numbskull," I said affectionately. "Look, if you're going to make any detective calls tonight, you'd better do it now before you've had any more wine."

"Calls? Why do I have to make calls?" Rob groused.

"Because someone should, and I went to the hospital and to Kirsten's," I answered.

"I went to work," Rob said importantly.

"Anyway, I think you should be the one to call the guys we're interested in, to get the male perspective."

"And you're calling the girls?"

"Yeah, sure. But you go first: Zachary, Jim, and Dylan."

"And Hal and Blaine." Rob sighed.

"Well, pick a couple for tonight, and then we'll call it a day."

"Who are you calling tonight?" Rob said, suspicious.

"I just said you'll call a couple tonight, and then we'll call it a day." I gestured toward the bottle. "I have wine to drink."

Rob rolled his eyes and headed for the office. He emerged a few moments later carrying his phone and my laptop, where the church directory was still open.

"I'll call one," he said, "and then the wine will have kicked in but good. What do you think—Dylan?"

"Oo," I said, "ask him about the thing with him and Avery and Zachary."

Rob stared at me blankly. "What thing with him and Avery and Zachary?"

"Oh, right," I said, "I didn't tell you my whole conversation with Avery at the hospital." I gestured for his phone. "All right, let me call him."

Rob handed it over gratefully and poured himself some more wine.

"Dylan," I said when his mom handed over the phone. "It's Christine from praise team."

"Christine," he said unenthusiastically.

"I hate to bother you on a school night," I said, wondering belatedly if that sounded condescending. "I just had a talk with Avery today and wanted to ask you a few questions."

"Ever consider minding your own business?" he said.

I could hardly believe my ears. "Excuse me?"

"I wish I could," he snarled.

I wondered if his was the voice I heard disguised on my voicemail every day.

"I just want to know why you stole Barb's purse and cough drops."

"Oh, that," Dylan said, blowing out his breath in what sounded like relief. What had he thought I was going to say? "That was Zachary's terrible idea."

"Did you tell the police what you did?"

"Are you kidding me?" Dylan said.

I left a pregnant silence. "Um, no, Dylan. Someone was killed by those cough drops. The police need to analyze that bag."

"Whatever," Dylan said. "Avery has them. She can turn them in if she wants."

"What's with you and Avery anyway?"

"What's that supposed to mean?" His voice had grown guarded again.

"It's obvious you like her," I said. "Are you jealous of Zachary or something? Is she more interested in him than you?"

Dylan laughed, a little too loudly. "Look, Avery's a little young for me, wouldn't you think? It'd be, like, a felony or something. I'm in college, and she's barely in junior high."

"It is weird," I agreed, then kicked myself.

"It would be weird," he said loudly. "It's not weird, because there's nothing going on."

"Right," I said. "That's what I meant." I decided to continue on my ambushing tactics, since slick and smooth apparently wasn't going to work on Dylan. "Anyway, just wondering if you or Zachary or Avery had switched out the cough drop in her coat for the poisoned one."

Dylan coughed. "Yeah, Christine. I did it. You got me." He muttered something unflattering about my mental state, which I pretended not to hear.

"Fine," I said, trying to remain reasonable. "Did you see Avery or Zachary do anything suspicious?"

"It was just a prank," he said. "We were bored. You were late."

Yes, yes, I got it. I needed to work on getting to things on time. I wished people would stop harping on it.

Dylan was continuing. "It didn't mean anything. But, afterwards, we were scared. Obviously." He said this loudly so that even my dim wits could get it. "So we didn't say anything about it."

"But you are going to now," I said, not making it a question. If I had any authority at all over this praise team, maybe my insistence would bear fruit.

"Yeah, okay," Dylan said.

"So they can catch the killer," I continued.

"I said, okay!"

I backed off. On that topic. "Were you really accepted into Blanchard?"

Silence, and then an angry, "What? Of course."

"Valerie hinted to me that you didn't get in." I decided to phrase it that way, the lying way, in hopes that it might affect him more.

There was a big sigh on the other end. "What difference does it make," Dylan said heavily. "Yeah, she's been kind of annoying to me about it, hinting around. The thing is—I don't really care so much, where I go to school or who knows, but I think my mom wants to keep it quiet." He sounded like he was telling the truth—without any arm twisting for once.

"Yeah," I said.

"Where were you Saturday night?" I asked him.

"Setting up some acid under the stage," he said, flipping automatically back to sarcasm. I thought.

I gave it up. "Thanks for your help and your honesty," I told him, in as much sincerity as I could muster. "I'll see you on Thursday."

"Yeah, okay," he said. "See you." He clicked off. I wondered how much he was already regretting sharing with me.

I had only been in the detecting biz for a day, and I was already surprised what people were willing to spill. Apparently most people can't pass up an opportunity to talk about their favorite subject—themselves. It would presumably come in handy.

Rob put down the library book he was reading and waited for an account of the conversation. Why hadn't he just one-sided eavesdropped the way I always did? Then I'd have half as much to fill him in on.

I dutifully recited what I remembered, including Avery's revelations at the hospital, and finished with, "I don't think Dylan's in on it. It's possible one of the other three, say, Zachary, had a more nefarious purpose to stealing the cough drops, but I don't think Dylan thinks so. And Zachary just seems too...dim, for lack of a kinder word, to be any sort of mastermind. But that's just my gut reaction."

"Well," Rob said, "going on your gut reaction, I agree. Should I call someone else, then? Oo—" He broke off as his channel flipping earned him an old and slapstick Miss Marple with Margaret Rutherford and her real-life husband

Stringer Davis, who played the role of her investigatory partner, just like my ever helpful Rob. I realized that I could probably start deducting the cost of cable from my taxes. That was assuming, of course, that I became a paid detective, since right now I was earning nothing from all my hard work.

That reminded me that I really needed to finish up the editing before I went to bed. Reluctantly, I left my colleague to Miss Marple and hauled myself and my laptop off the futon and back into the office. I called up the Word document and stared at the cross-outs and underlines of red that marked my corrections. This particular researcher's English was really quite good, but I had to do a lot of reformatting to fit the APA guidelines for references. It was a boring job, I thought as I scanned the commas and colons in the works-cited list, but somebody had to do it. I retrieved my wine glass, refilling it and Rob's, too, for good measure.

Rob had fallen asleep with the TV on when I emerged a few hours later. I switched it off, turned down our halogen lamp, and went to brush my teeth before snuggling up beside him.

Chapter 11

Tuesday morning was always a difficult one for me, because I had to subvert my normal routine and get up with the sun to go to the worship planning meeting. Rob always dropped me off on his way to work, and Barb drove me home afterward.

The committee consisted of Chris Bakker, the pastor, and several eager laypeople. Barb was the most eager of them all, loving to have her fingers in any church pie. Melissa Hernandez, the children's director, attended to give any input on ministry toward the short members of the congregation. I was required to put in my appearance as the interim worship leader. Zachary's mother, Debbie Brown, rounded out the last of the small group.

"Christine," Debbie greeted me. "I wanted to talk with you about Sunday." Debbie's hair was as bright blond as her son's, but I suspected the fluffy curls and the light color were less naturally occurring.

"Terrible thing," I murmured.

"Yes," she said, looking puzzled. "Hal played drums on all of the songs in the opening set."

I stared back at her blankly before I regained enough

of my voice and composure to answer. "Yes," I said. "Zachary was slated to play in the closing set, but that was prevented by...circumstances," I said euphemistically.

Barb clucked her tongue sympathetically.

"But the closing set usually has only two songs," Debbie persisted.

I took my time removing my jacket so that I didn't say the first thing that landed on my tongue. "Zachary was playing the congas for the opening set," I reminded her.

Debbie's expression showed what she thought of that attempt at a palliative.

"Let's get started," Pastor Chris said, his narrow face sober under its sandy-red beard and his voice firm.

The next forty minutes were the same as any meeting anywhere: a detailed and generally dull rehashing of a long list of minutiae, almost none of which applied directly to me.

"We'll look into pricing then," Pastor Chris said of ordering new floodlights.

"And I'll download the Birch drama skit we need," Barb said, jotting down a note to herself.

"Anything happening with you and the music ministry, Christine?"

I smiled, but grimly. "Besides the recent incidents..." I consulted my scrawled note to myself. "Penelope and Heidi wanted to suggest a new song, but unfortunately I don't have it with me to run by you yet. I take it it's some sort of new version of an old hymn."

"A hymn," Barb said, distastefully.

As a seeker church, New Vision tried to avoid turning people off with language that was too churchy or required a lot of thought. God and Jesus were okay to say, but Jehovah Jireh was right out. The Sunday-morning services in general were meant to be more of a production the congregants could enjoy rather than feel compelled to participate in, featuring dramatic skits, special musical solos, and a worship band with several singers and a loud sound system, the better to drown out the congregation, so they wouldn't feel awkward for not singing along. But if they did want to join in, the worship planning committee made sure the songs were easy enough to pick up in a hurry.

"The lyrics might be too complicated," Pastor Chris expanded. "Too theological."

"No, I know," I said. "That's why I thought we could judge it together. I was hoping to have a copy today."

"Can anyone even play drums on hymns?" Debbie broke in.

I ignored her. "I'll try to stop by Penelope's today and get the sheet music from her. Maybe I could email out the lyrics." I tried for a conciliatory smile at Debbie and Barb. "Some of those old hymns are really meaningful, and Penelope seemed really excited about the possibility of singing it here."

Barb looked skeptical. Pastor Chris agreed that I send out the lyrics.

"Any luck on finding a full-time worship leader?" I found myself saying.

Pastor Chris looked somewhat surprised. "It hasn't been top of our agenda, no," he admitted.

"What would you pay a full-time leader, anyway?"

He looked down at his notes. "That's negotiable." He turned unceremoniously toward Melissa. "How are people liking the new Sunday school name of PB&J?"

"They love it," she said.

"Hey," Barb said, "The praise team should get a catchy name, too!"

I waited with suppressed horror.

"Like...Echoes of Love!"

"Yuck," I said. I couldn't help myself.

Barb wasn't one to be abashed. "I'm going to think of something great." She gave herself a full one and a half seconds. "Angelic Melodies!"

"I think we're going to have to leave that for another day," Pastor Chris said. "I have to get back to the office for an appointment."

Barb was still tapping her pencil against her open notebook, deep in thought. "And this group could use a title, too. Worship planning committee is way too literal."

I scrunched my piece of paper into a pocket and pulled on my jacket. "Hey, Barb," I said, "would you mind stopping by Penelope's on the way? I think she lives near here, right?"

"Sure!" Barb was nothing if not agreeable.

It was only as I was strapping myself into her passenger seat that I spared a moment's thought that I was once again alone with a suspect, and at the mercy of her winter driving skills. She could toss me in the back of her hilariously oversize SUV, and it would take a week for sniffer dogs to cover all the ground back there.

The worship planning committee met at Debbie's house in Nederland, Illinois, and Penelope's mobile home park was in Yakey, both towns just across the border from Rob and me in Indiana.

"So you don't like Echoes of Love?" Barb started the conversational track. "What did you think about Angelic Melodies?"

My brain spun its gears. Did I agree to an idiotic name, or did I risk ticking off a potential murderer?

"It will be interesting to see what else you come up with." I tried for vague and diplomatic.

To my relief, it seemed to work. "Just think," Barb said, still chipper, "we could get matching polos with the name embroidered on the chest."

"Wow." It was all I could think to respond to that.

"Did you hear that Tammy's memorial service will be in Kentucky?" Barb switched topics to the one occupying most of my mindspace as well.

"Yeah, I think Kirsten told me. I guess that's for the

best."

"I have a copy of the obituary if you want to see," she offered, reaching an arm down to pat her voluminous orange handbag. "And I have the family's address if you want to send a note of condolence."

"That would be good," I said. How did Barb become such a dispenser of information about everyone in the congregation? Was it good connections, extreme nosiness, or just constant friendly chatter?

"I found out who stole your cough drops," I suddenly said. I hadn't meant to, but it occurred to me that I had one piece of information she hadn't yet ferreted out.

"What? Really? Who was it?" Barb didn't sound upset with the theft, just pleasantly interested to have a mystery solved.

"The kids were fooling around and thought they'd hide them," I said, belatedly adopting some discretion by not naming them directly.

"Huh," Barb said. "Isn't that the darndest thing."

"They didn't put the poison one in, though," I added hastily.

"Oh, I know," Barb returned cheerfully.

I declined to investigate further what her certainty could mean. At any rate, we had arrived at Penelope's trailer park and it took both of us to read numbers and signs along the circuitous routes through the mobile homes.

Penelope lived in a pink single-wide that had seen better days but whose outer appearance had been maintained well enough. Barb's monster vehicle stuck out into the street when she tried to maneuver it into the half-space behind Penelope's subcompact, but Barb didn't seem concerned about creating a road hazard. She turned off the ignition and gathered up her purse.

"Oh, you don't need to come in," I said. "I'm just going to run in and grab the sheet music and then run back out."

Barb was not deterred. "I love to see where people live." So it was some mix of friendliness and nosiness, I determined, but unlike Valerie's, it didn't seem malicious. I could learn a thing or two from Barb about how to gather information.

Gopher was in his purple-batik sling on Penelope's broad front, wailing as usual, when Penelope opened the door to her trailer. Her copper ringlets were disheveled. Penelope rhythmically bounced up and down for a few beats as she stared at her unexpected guests.

"Come in," she said finally.

I took in the squalor of clothes dropped on the floor, unwashed dishes in the sink, and crumbs ground into the carpet. It looked like home.

"Can I hold him?" Barb gestured toward the writhing bundle, looking pleasantly anticipatory rather than horrified at the thought of trying to calm the banshee.

Penelope gestured to a rocker. "I was just going to feed him."

"All right," Barb said equitably. Without fanfare, and without asking Penelope's permission, Barb began to pick up the floor of the trailer, piling discarded clothing in a heap and finding two plastic bags to fill with any trash and recycling that littered the hand-me-down furniture, or that had gathered in the spaces underneath.

At a loss, I moved toward Penelope's RV-sized kitchen, which would give Rob's and my one-butt space a challenge for least ergonomic, and started filling up the sink with hot water.

I actually found dishwashing by hand soothing. I had a system of soaking and washing in turn that made my job easy and satisfying. Penelope had a small sink and small drying rack and a lot of dishes, so I did the washing and drying in stages and found appropriate places to put things away. I didn't want to bother her to ask for direction as the baby slurped away at her breast. He seemed contented, and she probably liked him that way. Barb appeared halfway through my efforts and took over the drying and putting away.

During our final sink full, Penelope appeared at the entry to the tiny kitchen, purple sling still wrapped loosely around her but empty. "He's down." She gestured behind her. "Thanks for cleaning."

"Glad to help," Barb said cheerfully. "I remember those days."

Oh, crap, I thought. Did that mean our home would get messier once we'd had a kid? I tried to picture it while I put the final measuring cup in the rack and wiped my hands on a dingy towel that had a picture of a hot dog on it and the inspiring statement to "Get it here." I didn't want to ask what it meant. Perhaps it had been a parting gift from Penelope's lover.

Penelope had tucked herself behind a folding table at the edge of the kitchen that apparently served as the extent of the dining room. Barb and I joined her.

"Did you know Tammy?" Barb asked.

I looked at her. Was Barb also playing the role of amateur detective, or just unabashed gossipmonger?

"I wasn't in One-on-One," Penelope said, picking at a scratch in the laminated surface of the table.

I could sense Barb gearing up to ask why not, so I broke in with the reason for our visit.

"I was wondering if you had that sheet music," I said. "That's why we stopped by. I had wanted the worship planning committee to take a look."

Penelope nodded and extricated herself to go retrieve the music.

"We've got to get a better name for the worship planning committee," Barb said, and I could see her putting on her thinking cap. At least that might keep her occupied for a few minutes, I thought. "Sunday Makers!" she exclaimed. So much for a break. I didn't respond to her suggestion, because I couldn't figure out what it meant.

Penelope returned and handed me two photocopied sheets.

"Who's the father of your baby?" Barb asked.

If I had been drinking, I would have had to do a spit take. As it was, I kept my wide eyes glued to the sheet music.

"Someone who couldn't support us," Penelope said smoothly. "But I have a promotion now, so that will help."

"That's nice," I said. "What is it?"

"Was the dad someone at your old church?" Barb persisted.

I raised the sheet music to obscure my expression and looked at Barb to tell her to can it, but she wasn't seeking social cues.

"You're a lot like Valerie," Penelope said, avoiding the question. To me, she said, "I'm working in the administrative office at Nederland Christian School."

"What's going on with Valerie?" Barb didn't seem to be following our side of the conversation. "Running a church newsletter doesn't make you a real reporter." Barb actually looked miffed. I wondered what Valerie could have been bothering her about.

"She's persistent," Penelope agreed, smiling a seemingly beatific smile that didn't reach her eyes.

"It's the weirdest thing," Barb said, lost in thought. "I saw her in the parking lot of the school on Saturday night."

I flopped the sheet music onto the laminated table. "What? Did you tell the police that?"

"And what were you doing there?" Penelope added, looking rightfully suspicious.

"I thought I'd left my keys in the lot," Barb said. "So I went back to look for them, and I'm sure I saw Valerie's red coat."

"Was it dark?" I said. "It's hard to see color in the

dark."

Barb screwed up her face into its thinking pose. "I think it was more like twilight."

"Were there cars in the parking lot?"

"A couple," Barb said after a pause. "I don't remember." Apparently her compulsive need to know everything about everyone didn't extend to inanimate objects.

"You have to tell the police what you saw," I told Barb. "And steer clear of Valerie," I said to both of them.

"You don't need to tell me twice," Penelope said, folding her arms across her milk-expanded chest.

"Why?" Barb said.

It took a minute for me to realize Barb really couldn't connect any dots on her own. "Because Valerie might be the killer."

"Oh, I don't think so," Barb said. "Besides, I think there was someone else with her."

"Oh, my gosh, Barb, call the police," I said. "Like, now."

"Okay," Barb said amenably. "I'll call them when I get home."

"Did you find your keys?" Penelope asked.

"Oh," Barb said, "it turns out they were in the ignition."

Penelope's reply was lost under her breath.

I had finally had the presence to focus on the music in front of me, an update of "Come, Ye Fount of Every Blessing." "Can't do it," I said.

Penelope looked at me, her rusty brows lowering. "The song? Why?"

"Wording like 'Here I fix my Ebenezer.'" I pointed to the offending line.

Barb took the papers from my grasp. "I'm not a fan of hymns," she said cheerfully. She studied the pages for a space. "I don't even know what this means."

Penelope reached for the pages back with one faintly freckled hand. She looked genuinely hurt at my refusal.

144

"It's not me," I said, trying to backpedal. "I love this hymn. It's a great hymn, very meaningful. It's just—New Vision's the sort of place where we try to make things accessible."

"Dumb them down," Penelope muttered.

"Really easy words," Barb volunteered happily.

"Wouldn't it be nice to sing something 'very meaningful' every once in a while?" Penelope looked at me, throwing my words back in my face.

"We might be able to do a verse or two," I said. I gently tugged on the sheets in her hand until she released them. "Let me run it by the worship planning committee next week and see what they say."

Penelope grumbled a thank you.

"The Spirit Movers!" Barb shouted.

"What?" I said, before realizing she was once again naming our committee. She might just have done a worse job than Penelope at naming Gopher, I thought.

As if prompted, a wail pierced the mid-morning silence of the trailer park. Penelope gave a deep sigh, then rose from the folding table.

I took it as Barb's and my sign to exit. "Good luck," I said. I meant it.

Penelope moved in the direction of the screaming, and I coaxed Barb out the opposite way.

Chapter 12

When I went to turn my phone's ringer back on upon arriving home, I discovered another nasty phone message. It went against my instincts to save it, but I wanted it available to hand over to the police.

Feeling pretty spooked to hear that evil, icy voice on my own, I called the police station, and the receptionist, sounding unenthusiastic as usual, patched me through to Adeela Madari, where once more her voicemail picked up instead of the detective herself.

I told her about my latest phone message and reiterated my willingness to have someone listen. I offered to bring myself and my phone to the station at any time convenient to them. I had started telling her about Barb's revelation that she had seen Valerie and a couple cars in the middle school parking lot when a mechanical voice cut in and gave me message options, letting me know there was no more space left to continue rambling. I guess the good detective must have thought everyone was as concise as she was.

I considered calling back but decided I would give her the news if and when the police ever got around to contacting me about the threats, or interviewing me about the latest attacks.

Blaine also had texted, saying he was fully recovered and back at work, and also that he had some information, so I called him back. I wondered if his employers minded that he worked on extraneous projects during the day. Fortunately, my employer didn't care what I did.

"Hey," Blaine said when we connected. "I found out that the police have analyzed some of the new cough drops."

"The cough drops from the bag?" I said.

"Yeah, apparently someone turned them in."

"Avery," I said.

"Oh?" Blaine returned. "I hadn't heard about that."

Despite his promise of partnering with us, I really wasn't sure how much I wanted to share back. I didn't have good reason to suspect him of killing anyone, but I didn't have good reason to rule him out, either.

"I talked with her yesterday," I said, trying to sidestep the issue. "That was fast, if they've already analyzed them. She must have turned it in right after she talked with me."

"I guess they haven't gone through the whole bag yet," Blaine said, sounding mollified enough. "But so far they've found no traces of poison."

"Huh," I said, taking in this newest information. "So, if that remains the case, then only the lozenge in Barb's pocket was affected."

"And it might not have even come from that bag," Blaine confirmed.

"At least it looks less suspicious for Avery," I said, leaving Dylan and Zachary's role out of it for now. "Hey," I said, finding myself unable to keep from asking, "how do you find out all this stuff?"

"It's better if you don't know, don't you think?"

Curiosity and prudence warred internally. "Yeah, you're probably right. Thanks for the info."

"Have you learned anything else?" Blaine asked, as I was about to ring off.

"Oh, uh," I said, my mind racing. I thought about everything I'd learned: Penelope's affair, perhaps with someone at her old church, Barb's being present at the church on Saturday night and purportedly seeing Valerie along with someone else, and the little intrigue between Avery and her cohorts. "No."

"Well, keep me posted," Blaine said. I felt paranoid and wasn't sure if I really heard suspicion in his tone or just disappointment.

"Will do. Thanks for all your work. We really appreciate it. So glad you're feeling better." I was overcompensating, I knew.

I changed into my work uniform of pajama pants and hoodie but didn't actually do any work. I found a string of court shows to watch on TV, wondering what sort of judge the suspect would face once I caught him or her.

When Rob got home a couple hours later, I told him about the new message but didn't get a chance to fill him in on everything else until he'd checked it out for himself. He took my phone, shut the office door behind him, and listened to the voicemail at a low volume, so I didn't have to participate. He came back out to the living room, his face grim.

"This creep's not messing around," he said. "'There'll be consequences' if you don't stop? I don't like that you're still being targeted, and I'm not around most of the day."

"What do you want me to do?" I said. "I called the police again."

"And?"

"And nothing. Detective Madari is never in, and she never calls back. She's supposed to be investigating me as a suspect for the Sunday attack."

"Maybe you've been ruled out," Rob said. "Maybe she has someone else in her sights."

"Yeah, maybe," I said, wondering why I felt a little regret at the thought that they might wrap up this case before I could solve it.

"Well, seeing as we can't count on police protection, make sure you don't take any unnecessary risks," Rob said.

"Like what?" I said, hugging my arms around myself.

"Like make sure someone always knows where you are, preferably me, and we could check in off and on during the day. And don't meet with suspects in private."

"Like driving with Barb?" I said.

"I forgot she gives you a ride home from worship planning committee."

"You mean The Spirit Movers," I said.

"The what now?"

"Never mind. We stopped at Penelope's on our way home," I said, hoping to turn the conversation from how foolhardy I'd possibly been. I did wonder how much of my detecting was hubris versus actual aptitude. Maybe the only reason I hadn't been killed yet was pure luck. Maybe there was a trap that had sprung just after I'd passed. I envisioned myself blithely walking on while a spear thudded into the wall where my head had just been.

At any rate, the distraction worked. I told Rob about Penelope's background and her reasons for leaving the church.

"It's interesting that Valerie is bothering her, too," Rob said.

"Very. And—here's the best part." I added a dramatic pause. "Barb saw Valerie at the school the night before the Sunday incident."

Rob's mouth dropped, then closed as he chewed on this clue. "So maybe Valerie's the killer, which would mean it's not someone in the praise team after all."

"Well, she does seem to be omnipresent," I pointed out. "We don't know when the cough drop was slipped into Barb's jacket."

I told Rob Blaine's report that the other cough drops so far had not been poisonous.

"Did you tell Blaine anything else?"

I shook my head.

"Probably best," Rob said.

"I feel guilty, though."

"The other possibility," he said, moving past my guilt, "is that Barb is lying about seeing Valerie, trying to pin the blame on her."

"No offense to Barb," I said, about to say something incredibly offensive toward her, "but I think she's too dim to be the killer."

"Maybe she's faking it," Rob said, "so she can be annoying with impunity."

"You should have heard her today," I sighed. "She was in rare form. Oh, but I forgot, she also said that someone else might have been with Valerie."

"Huh," Rob continued his train of thought. "Then it's also possible that Valerie..."

But he broke off at an insistent knock at our door. I wondered who was coming to visit. It might be the police finally, I thought.

Rob shrugged in silent acknowledgment of this mystery and crept to the door. We didn't want to give away our presence in case it was anyone unappealing, like Box Boy.

He turned back toward me, the lines between his eyes furrowed. "Nothing," he whispered.

I shook my head.

"There's no one there," he stage whispered, louder.

I shrugged, and he cautiously pulled back the chain. He peeked around the opening and I could see from my position the same thing he said: nothing.

I remembered little Grace's answering the door earlier and looked down. My heart had already been racing, but now it felt like it was going to keel over inside my chest. I pointed to the floor.

Rob eyed the brown paper bag sitting there. He reached out one hand, when I suddenly snapped out of my paralysis.

"Don't touch it," I screeched. "Close the door." Rob began to swing it shut. "Carefully!" He gently closed it to.

After he relatched the deadbolt and chain, I picked up the phone and tugged on his shirt to pull him with me toward the back room. If that thing was going to explode, I wanted to be well away when it did.

"911, what's your emergency?" said the professional voice on the other end.

"Someone dropped off a package at our door," I said, my voice shaking as I recited our address right off, since I wasn't sure they could get a fix on my cell's location.

"There's a package at your door?" The operator sounded incredulous, and I realized how inane my opening line had sounded.

"I think it might be a bomb, or a threat, or a body part or something."

"Why would you think that, ma'am?" The operator sounded only mildly interested.

"Someone's been threatening me," I said, my voice rising. "There have been murders at my church, and we're trying to solve them, and someone doesn't like it."

"Are you a police officer, ma'am?"

"No." Even to my ears, I sounded petulant.

"It sounds like you should leave solving crimes to the police, ma'am."

"Uh-huh," I said, "thanks for your help. Look, are you going to send the police or what?"

"They're already on their way, ma'am." She remained unflappable.

"Oh," I said. "All right, then."

"Please stay on the line until they arrive. Have you

moved away from the suspicious item?"

Shouldn't she have asked that right away? "Yes, we're in the back room."

"All right, then," she said. "Let me verify your address."

I told her she had it right, and we kept an uneasy silence until we heard more knocking at the door.

"They're here," I told her. Rob left the office to walk to the door and peer out the peephole. I stood in the hall just outside the office door to watch.

Rob turned back to me, perplexed.

"What?" I mouthed.

"It's Dylan," he whispered.

I could feel my eyebrows scrunching. "Dylan?" I mouthed back.

"Are you still there, ma'am?"

"Yes," I told the operator. "It's not the police after all. It's a friend." Or maybe not. I gestured wildly at Rob and continued to mouth at him. "Get away from the door! Come back here!"

He got the message and retreated to the office doorway with me.

The knock came again, and there was a rustling of paper outside.

"Dylan!" I screamed. "Put that down!"

"What?" he yelled back through the door. "The bag?"

"Don't touch it!" I screamed. Rob put a finger in his ear and took a step away. "Go away! The police are coming!"

I figured the reference to the police would deter him if he had planted it there himself, and otherwise I was helping keep him safe.

I braced myself to hear a "kaboom," and jumped when I heard the outer door slam open. We lived down a half-story of steps from the main entrance to our apartment building, in what was either the ground-floor or the basement apartment, depending on your perspective. I could hear boots thundering down the short flight of steps and then shuffling around outside our door.

"I believe they are here," I said to the operator.

"Yes," she said, omnisciently. "They are." She disconnected before I could say thanks.

I left the phone on the dresser, and Rob and I huddled together in the small hallway between the office and bathroom, waiting for the verdict from the corridor.

"Boom, boom, boom!" went a fist on our door. We both jumped.

"Yes?" I called, my voice quavering.

Rob strode forward. "Yes?" he called more manfully. My hero, I thought.

"Police," came a forceful voice.

They didn't even have to say "open up" for us to obey.

Outside our apartment door stood six flak-jacketed, face-shielded cops, along with a dog on a leash, taking it easy after a hard five minutes' work.

One officer, shield pushed up on top of his head, was holding the open brown bag in black-gloved hands. "Our dog sniffed it," he said, gesturing behind him. "There's no bomb."

He tipped it forward so we could see, then pulled out the contents to hand to us.

"Just these photos," he said, holding them up so we could see them.

The top one was of us.

"What are those?" I asked, reaching out to take them.

"Fingerprints, ma'am," the officer barked, drawing them out of reach. Then he apparently relented. "All right," he said, "here, I'll hold them out and you look at them."

He turned his back to us, and Rob and I peered over his shoulder to look as he flipped through.

There was Rob talking to a coworker outside his office

building. There I was looking bored on the side of the road while waiting for the bus. There were the two of us getting into our car in the apartment complex's parking lot. I was telling some joke, my mouth wide and smiling.

I met Rob's eyes.

We both turned to look at the waiting police officer, who had tapped the photos back into a neat stack against his palm.

"Thank you," I said in a small voice.

Another officer came forward with plastic bags, and the photos were dropped inside one. Then a bigger one was flapped open to encase the brown paper bag. This bag-in-bag action seemed funny to me somehow, despite the circumstances.

"Ms. Randal." The curt tone cut through my random thoughts and the conversation that had started among the relaxed bomb squad. I looked toward the door, and sure enough, there were Detective Adeela Madari's immaculate legs descending the steps, no-nonsense black trench flapping around them, pantyhose with no runs showing, and shining black pumps.

"Christine," another voice said. I turned toward the other end of the hall and saw Dylan, leaning in a corner, looking completely unruffled. He took a few steps closer. "I just came to talk, but I can see this is a bad time."

"Dylan," I said. "Do you want to come in and wait?"

"No, no," he said. "I'll just see you Thursday."

"Okay," I called, since I could hardly insist he stay with the bomb-squadded lady and the detective hot on her trail.

"Detective Madari," I greeted the woman as she cut through the departing officers and arrived at our door. I gestured to my right. "This is Rob Song, my husband."

"Yes," she said. "I know."

Well, she would.

"Please come in," I said.

"May I see these?" She reached out an unobtrusively

154

manicured hand, and the officer with the photographs obediently slapped the bag into her palm. She waited with her other hand up until someone produced a pair of latex gloves. As she pulled them on in her efficient manner, I marveled at the authority that produced instant results without speaking. She removed the photos from their bag once more and flicked through them quickly, still standing with her coat on in our entranceway.

"Who took these?" She looked up at us, and it was all I could do not to say something sarcastic back.

"The murderer, I imagine," I said. "At any rate, someone following us. Sorry it wasn't a bomb, by the way. I was worried."

She waved that off. "How many threats have you gotten since the last time we spoke?"

"Well, they've all been voicemail messages until this one." I gestured toward the office. "I have them saved on my phone if you want to listen."

Detective Madari sat in my desk chair and took notes as I played each rasping, horrible message on speakerphone. She showed no sign of emotion and thanked me afterward for playing them.

"I'll talk with you later," she said. "Thank you for your help." She started to walk swiftly toward the front door.

Surprised, I raced after her. "Do you know who did it?" I asked. "Do you know who's been taking those pictures?"

"If we did," she said, "he or she would be in custody." She shot me a look with her steel-colored eyes that must make suspects quiver. Well, of course, it did. I was a suspect, after all.

"All right," I said in a small voice. "Thanks."

She was almost out the door when I had a thought. "Do we get police protection or anything?"

She gave the first sign of emotion, a small smile of regret. "I'm sorry, but we don't have the personnel to spare. Be careful. What you did tonight was just right." And, with that, she was out the door.

At least she made me feel a little better for having called in the bomb squad for some photographs.

When I had closed and locked the door behind her, the room seemed eerily silent. I unconsciously backed away from it toward the center of the room, as if I didn't want a shotgun blast through the back from unseen predators lurking outside.

Rob was sitting on the unmade futon, staring at the darkened television screen. I sat next to him.

"Those pictures," Rob began.

I swallowed. They had been so innocuous, no awareness in our expressions of the danger watching us nearby.

"I wonder where they were taken from," Rob said reasonably. "I'm thinking the one of me at the office must have been taken from a car. At least he can't get inside the building without a keycard."

I nodded. That was something, at least.

"And the one of us in the parking lot here." Rob shook his head. "I wish we had copies of them. But I think it was focused on your side of the car, so the photographer must have been—where?"

"Behind another car?" I suggested. "Or taking it out the window, maybe?"

"Kind of a risk," Rob said. "And other cars would get in the way, you'd think."

"Wait," I said, "was that the day we parked around the corner because our usual spot was taken?" I considered the lot's layout. "He could have been in the Dumpster shelter."

Rob snapped his fingers. "You're right."

Talking about the photographs wasn't doing anything all that useful, but it was diminishing the creepiness of them. It helped to remain outwardly unfazed by the terrorizing tactics.

"And there was one of you on the side of the road,"

Rob said.

"I was waiting for the bus," I said. I didn't want to sound like a streetwalker.

Rob nodded. "It was from pretty far away. Maybe a telephoto lens?"

I thought about where that particular bus stop was situated. "There's a strip mall across the street. Maybe he could have been in a parked car there."

"I wish we could have had another look through them."

"Do you think Blaine could get us copies?" I said in a small voice.

"Do you trust him enough to ask?"

I shrugged.

"Well." Rob rubbed his hands on his jeans, as if cleaning them off. "Do you want to go out to the Dumpster and see if the guy left any clues there?"

I considered it, then shook my head. "I don't really want to leave," I said in a quiet voice. So much for not giving in to terrorists.

Rob squeezed my arm. "How about we stay in and watch Mystery Science Theater?"

"Sounds good to me," I said. I needed a laugh to take my mind off it all.

It was halfway through the B-movie that I interrupted the sarcastic robots by sitting bolt upright out of my lounging position in Rob's arms. "What was Dylan doing here?"

Rob paused the movie and looked at me. "I don't know."

"Strange," I said, relaxing back onto Rob's chest and waiting for him to resume the movie. "I'll have to call him tomorrow."

"Don't visit him alone," Rob reminded me, ominously.

"You think he dropped off the prints?" I asked, twisting around in his arms to look at him.

"I don't know what to think," he said grimly. "But we can't afford to trust anyone now. I don't know why that package tonight wasn't a bomb, to be honest."

I had wondered that myself.

"But we can't take any chances," Rob concluded. "So be double careful."

"I'm thinking this newest threat might have an upside," I said, hoping to avoid further discussion of my vulnerability.

"Do tell," Rob said.

"The killer obviously thinks we're getting close."

Rob nodded slowly.

"Shoot," I burst out. "I forgot to tell Detective Madari what Barb said." I considered our brief conversations. "Not that she'd care."

"She'd tell you to leave the policing to the police." Rob did a fine impression of the emotionless detective.

"You got that right. I guess I'll call her again tomorrow anyway." I sighed.

Rob switched tacks. "Are you hungry?"

I consulted my stomach. Despite the stress of the last few hours, I was indeed. Mystery Science Theater had calmed my insides down enough to want to eat.

Rob went out to the kitchen to throw together a stir fry with some frozen veggies. I could hear him futzing with his state-of-the-art rice cooker, a wedding gift from his parents and among his most prized possessions. An Asian needs good rice, he told me whenever I kidded him about its incongruity among the rest of our thrift-store-sourced appliances.

While I waited, I switched from the paused DVD to the TV so I could flip channels to keep my brain from thinking too hard.

I happened upon a true-crime show about a church where several parishioners were poisoned by tainted coffee at a potluck.

"Rob!" I called. "Are you hearing this?"

But he had already poked his head around the corner of our dining nook to see. During a commercial, he quickly finished up the food and brought it out on two paper plates. Apparently we hadn't remembered to run the dishwasher yet. Then we settled in to watch the uncanny similarities.

When the program switched to profile a different murder, Rob switched off the set and turned toward me.

"Why would you start killing off people at church?"

"Gee, Rob, I don't know. Why would I?"

"No, seriously," he said. "What would be the point?"

I stared at the ceiling to help me think, though that just reminded me of our upstairs neighbors' distractingly pounding bass. I sighed and looked off toward our unused dining nook instead.

"To settle a score," I suggested. "To make a point."

"What point?" He narrowed his eyes in thought.

"To protest a certain church? Or certain decisions?"

"If the deaths are this random," Rob said, "it really does imply an untargeted crime spree, in the sense that no particular victims were chosen. That makes the church itself the likeliest target."

"What makes this church in particular a target?" I said, hopping on Rob's train of thought.

"And who in the church is most likely to disagree with this particular church, so vehemently that murder becomes the way of expressing an opinion?"

"Well, as to the first," I said, "New Vision is an innovative style of church."

"It's a seeker church," Rob said. "Traditional churches might disagree with its philosophy, and so might churches who are unconventional but in a different way, like emergent churches."

"Aren't emergent churches too po-mo to send out hit men?"

"It certainly seems like more of a conservative thing to do," Rob agreed.

"Well, then, maybe we can kill two birds with one stone, no killing reference intended," I hastily amended. "Who in our pool of suspects came from a background or a church radically different from New Vision?"

"Who would be most likely to hate New Vision's guts?" Rob clarified.

"Exactly."

Rob emerged from the walk-in closet in the office some time later. Since the office was really the apartment's bedroom and we slept in the living room, the office closet was our closet. But it was big enough to hold our clothes and some extra storage besides, whatever random things didn't fit elsewhere.

For instance, the great big easel and whiteboard Rob was hauling into the living room.

"Oh, Rob," I said, "we don't have time for Pictionary right now."

"Ha ha," he said, wrestling the easel into submission in an easy line of sight from the futon.

"Can you see?" he asked me, since I was still cozily reclining against the wooden armrest.

"Absolutely," I said.

He flourished an assorted pack of erasable markers and began to write suspects' names across the top of the board with a bright blue.

"Hey," I said, "those are my markers. Don't use up all the ink for one color. That's going to be my productivity board." The pack of twenty-one markers had been next to the whiteboards at the office store. I had chosen it because it normally had only twenty, but this one had a bonus color, which made it that much better.

"When did you buy it?" Rob said evenly, continuing to

write names.

"Six months ago, I think." I paused. "I'm still figuring out how to assign each color. What if I need bright blue a lot?"

Rob capped the bright blue and switched to a strange off-red that wasn't quite pink.

"Well, now, that looks terrible," I said. "And like you're emphasizing those names over the blue ones. Stick with one color per topic."

Rob sighed and picked up the white-board eraser. He continued writing suspects' names in the blue, asking me for everyone's last names and some of the firsts as well. While scrawling the final one, he said under his breath, "If you ever use this whiteboard for anything useful, Eggs..."

"What then?" I challenged.

"I will have to copy your system," he hurriedly finished. Apparently Rob wanted some tonight.

"Anyway, you're using it for something useful," I complimented. Apparently I wanted some, too. "Okay, are we going suspect by suspect?"

"Yes," Rob said, "looking specifically for what each might have against New Vision."

"Wait," I said, "shouldn't I be a suspect?"

"Sorry," Rob said, uncapping Big Blue again and scribbling me in in the last available slot.

"That's better." I stared at the board, overwhelmed by how many suspects we had to eliminate or accuse. Besides the praise-team members, we had added Valerie Dejong, the newsletter editor, and the pastor, Chris Bakker.

"Would Pastor Chris have had any way of making the first murder happen?" I asked.

"Well," Rob said, "he's the pastor. He can make things happen, right?"

"He hates the church so much that he became the pastor of it so he could cause its downfall from within?" I tried to get the hang of it.

"Stranger things have happened," Rob said philosophically.

"In fiction," I said.

"Maybe I'll write Chris in the weird red," Rob said. So he had noticed what a crappy color assortment I'd gotten. "To show that he's not a prime suspect."

"Or maybe just underline the ones that are."

"All right," Rob said. "Right now, or after we've gone through them?"

"I don't know," I said. I threw up my hands. "This is why I've never used this stinking whiteboard. I don't know how to make it work. And all the colors..."

"Calm down," Rob said gently. "I know, it all seems overwhelming right now. First, let's throw out some of these markers." He chose Big Blue, Weird Red, and a plain, honest black, and tossed the rest unceremoniously into the office by just leaning into the hallway and chucking the packet.

"All right," he said. "For now, I'll just put parentheses around people we don't suspect as much." He added blue parentheses around Chris. "Anyone else?"

"How about me?" I said in a small voice.

Rob tapped the blue marker to his lips. "Maybe we should talk that one through first."

I reached for the eraser so I could throw it at him. It bounced off his heinie while he was belatedly drawing the parentheses around my name.

"I've decided you couldn't have done it," Rob said, "because you were with me on the night before the second incident."

"Maybe I sneaked out," I said.

"Hmm," Rob said. "And you definitely had opportunity for the first attack."

"Just think, Rob," I said, "you might be married to a mass-murderess."

"Spicy," Rob said. He crossed my name off for good

measure. "I'm still counting you out. As much as you like to complain about New Vision, I just don't think you have it in you to commit murder."

"Well, thank you," I said.

"You're much too lazy," he continued.

I picked up the eraser again, but this time I missed and it thwocked off the board.

"Careful," Rob admonished, retouching the "er" where it had nicked "Potter."

"I'm bored already," I said. "I could never stand meetings."

"That's why you could never have a real job," Rob said.

"Amen and amen," I said. "Let's just concentrate on the people we think coulda done it."

"Who first?"

"Walter."

"Walter, the gentle and kind principal of a Christian school?"

"For Christian school, read conservative with a capital C. And," I said, "he fired Tammy, and he works with Penelope, and he has connections with a lot of the kids on the praise team. Maybe their hoolinanigans riled him up so much he decided to come down and teach their church a lesson."

"Huh?" Rob said. "And, also, hoolinanigans is not a word. I'm not putting it on the board."

"Well, put the other stuff," I said.

Rob carefully printed, using True Black, "principal of Nederland Christian, fired Tammy, works with Penelope, knows youth."

"Has he ever expressed any dissatisfaction with New Vision?" Rob asked.

"No," I said, catching myself sighing in disappointment. "He's a founding member, and a Watchkeeper, and usually never seems anything but jovial. Oh, well."

"I'll make a 'con' category," Rob said, switching to off-red and writing "jolly and positive" under Walter's pro-murder list. "But what do you mean by 'usually'?"

"Lately, he's seemed a little stressed. Maybe because his kids are going off to college? I get the sense he and Belinda are growing apart or something."

Rob wrote "usually" next to "jolly" and underlined the descriptive. "That's good." He caught my expression. "I mean, for our purposes."

"Do you think we'll ever grow apart?" I asked wistfully.

"Not a chance, babe." Rob blew me a kiss from orange-dusted lips.

I caught it in one hand, slapped my palm against my own cheek, and continued. "Hal," I said. "He's a non-Christian."

"Non-Christian," Rob wrote in an echo, making the switch back to Deadly Nightshade. "Drummer."

"Why does that make him a murderer?"

"You tell me." Rob waggled his thick eyebrows at me meaningfully, or as it turned out, meaninglessly, because he then reached around and drew his palm over "drummer" to expunge it.

"That's about all I can think of," I said. "Oh, he was in the singles' group with Tammy, though that's not a reason to hate New Vision specifically."

"Unless the group really sucks," Rob said.

"Yes," I said. "Should we include general suspect-y items, or just anti-New Vision agendas?"

"Maybe just anti-New Vision," Rob said, "since we've already done the other thing before. This is to clear our minds, get us thinking—"

"Please don't say 'outside the box,'" I interrupted.

"I didn't," Rob said. "You did."

"It's too meeting-like," I insisted.

"To get us thinking along different lines," Rob finished.

"All right." I nodded my head. "Then, non-Christian,

so maybe he hates Christians in general."

"I can't really think of anything to add there," Rob said. "Moving on. Barb." He tapped the marker emphatically beside her name.

"What about her?"

"Oh, crap," he said, visibly disappointed. "I can't think of anything."

"I agree," I said, grimacing at him sympathetically. "She's a founding member, too, and she's always all idolizing Birch Park, which she calls Birch like it's her best friend."

"Yeah," Rob said sadly. "On this chart, Barb's got nothing." He sighed. "Parentheses?"

I nodded. "Parentheses."

"For now," Rob added with a frown, making the required symbols.

"That's the beautiful thing about these markers," I consoled him. "They erase with a flick of the finger."

"Good," he said, folding his arms.

We considered the next victims, er, suspects.

"Gretchen and Heidi," I said, pondering. "Funny how we think of them as a set. Wouldn't it be funny if one had committed murder under the other's nose?"

"Hilarious," Rob agreed. "Well, they're old-school for sure." Rob wrote down "traditional church background." "We don't know why they left their old church."

"They definitely seem squirrelly about something in their past," I said. "And they're frightened of Valerie poking into it."

"What if they left their old church because the truth had come out there?" Rob speculated.

"Like with Penelope and her baby daddy?"

"And Valerie's deep in that, too," Rob pointed out.

"So they leave their old church, start at a completely different type of church, and then...what? The gossip follows them here, say."

"And then they get so murderously angry that they start killing everybody," Rob finished. "Yeah, it doesn't sound too plausible, particularly considering the physical work involved in the last attack."

"Just picturing it makes me think of Arsenic and Old Lace," I said. "I can't quite imagine Gretchen or Heidi lying down under the stage to saw through the floor boards. How would they get back up again?"

"Well, there are two of them, so one can help the other up. Isn't that a verse in Proverbs?"

"Very biblical of you," I said.

"So to move on to Penelope, she also presumably left a church because of a situation that happened there."

"That situation being Gopher," I said.

"But why would someone whose only beef with New Vision was the fact that Valerie might have found out some gossip bother to kill a couple random people?" Rob suddenly said, making a face of exasperation.

I realized the logic and couldn't suggest a reason that didn't sound flawed even in my head.

"Well, anyway," Rob said, "let's not strain our brains trying to figure out both incidents at once. Maybe a person who'd been offended by one person at New Vision had been offended by others."

"But our whole point of making this chart," I said, gesturing at the board, "was to ferret out who hated New Vision as a whole. I mean, the booby traps have been random, right? Even if, say, Gavin or Tammy had offended a boatload of people at church, it doesn't mean the deaths were related to their actions at all."

Rob sighed. "Only if the killer also had grudges against the church as a whole. All right, back to square one." He picked up the eraser and swiped it through what we'd written under Gretchen and Heidi and Penelope. "I'm leaving Walter up. I think it's more significant when a suspect had an issue with the first victim, Tammy. Because maybe, after Tammy's death, you might decide to kill off some other people who've offended you."

"But anyone might have a secret grudge against Tammy and Gavin," I said. "That's not going to get us far."

"Urgh," Rob said.

"My thinker hurts," I said.

Rob rewrote his information about the twins and Penelope. "I'm just putting it up, anyway," Rob said. "Let's still think along New Vision-hating lines and for now ignore the order of the incidents or the salience of the motives."

"Mo-kay," I said. "But I need something." I stood up off the futon, stretching out the kinks in my legs from sitting so long.

Rob looked after me as I walked from the room. "What?"

"These," I said, bringing back Cheetos from the kitchen and pulling open the bag, letting out the cheesy scent.

"Brain food," Rob said, reaching his hand toward the crinkling sack.

"Hang on," I said, trying to pull the bag away. "You'll be farting up a storm tonight if you eat these."

"Doesn't bother me." Rob shrugged.

I gave in and let him at the Cheetos. I hoped we could finish this up and get down to sexy business before the gas cloud arose.

"These puffy kind are even better than the regular ones," I said through the crunching, determined to enjoy them while I could.

Rob nodded at my reasoned review of cheese snacks. Then he dusted off his hands and uncapped the marker once more.

"All right—Jim." He paused, marker to chin. "What do we know about Jim's church background?"

I looked down at the Cheetos bag in thought. "Not a

whole heck of a lot," I said. "You met him. He's really shy."

"And he was practically crying at the Bible study," Rob confirmed. "Have you talked to him since?"

"No," I said. "I've been nervous about dealing with male suspects alone."

Rob raised his eyebrows. "But handling a female murderer would be fine?"

"I'm pretty buff. I could take 'em. Especially the ninety-somethings." I flexed my biceps and looked closely to see if I could discern any bulge in my upper arm.

Rob shook his head.

"All right, anyway," I said, "I should definitely give Jim a call." Rob put a little star by his name. "Here's what I do know: He used to attend Nederland Christian Reformed. We actually have quite a few people at New Vision who used to go there, because it's kind of dying out."

"Is that a motive, or is that a motive?" Rob said, underlining Jim's name.

"Depends whether he came to New Vision because he was upset with Nederland Christian Reformed, or because he was upset with New Vision."

"Still," Rob said, "that's the kind of person we're looking for." He used one finger to carefully erase the line under Jim's name. "It doesn't necessarily have to be Jim, but that's exactly the kind of situation that would lead a person to start killing off other church members. Here's an old, established, respected church that's sinking into nonexistence because the new, flashy church is stealing members away. Who else in this list came from a traditional church?"

I scrutinized the list. "Everyone."

"Really?" Rob asked.

"Everyone but Hal," I said, "since he didn't come from a church at all. Everyone else had been attending a traditional church when New Vision started up five years ago. Obviously, Potter and Avery were quite young then, but everyone else had grown up in a traditional service. Although I think Barb had tried out attending Birch Park before New Vision started, even though it was such a long drive. She's committed to the philosophy."

"Yeah, in this scenario, we're going to have to discount Barb as a suspect," Rob said sadly, staring at those parentheses. "Unless she's just a total weirdo, why would she pretend for so well and so long to adore New Vision, but then start killing off people who are involved in it?"

"Unless she's dissatisfied with the direction New Vision is heading?" I suggested. "Maybe she sees it diverging from the precious Birch."

"Any hint of that?" Rob asked.

"None at all."

"All right," Rob said. "That's a line of inquiry to pursue, but for now we'll move along."

"Oh, great," I said. "Pursuing inquiries with her is like reasoning with a Chihuahua. Maybe she is on a long con."

"Wouldn't surprise me at all," Rob said, perking up a little.

Glad to have comforted him, I continued. "Kirsten. With five young kids, who has time to murder?"

"But does she hate New Vision?" Rob said.

"I know she's annoyed sometimes that more people don't help her babysit," I said. "She always gives that as her prayer request at practice."

"That God will make her less annoyed?"

"Ha ha," I said. "That God will send her veritable angels to volunteer to watch her hellions. She never does offer to pay anyone for the privilege of helping her out, which is maybe why God isn't attending more closely to that particular request."

"So, in this scenario, Kirsten is so murderously angry that New Vision forced her to accept fertility treatments when she already had two preschoolers that she starts killing off people who refuse to babysit."

"Yeah," I said, "it's not much. All I'm saying now is, I'm glad I helped her out that day."

Rob chortled.

I gestured with a Cheeto puff reflectively. "I have suspicions not based in this line of thought, though. She was the first one to reach Tammy, and she's a nurse. Maybe she helped her; maybe she intentionally didn't. Maybe she made things worse. I'm not saying she did, but it would be a good opportunity to look like you're above suspicion while at the same time crafting the situation you want."

"How does that square with the other attack?" Rob said.

"Don't people say poisons and booby traps and such are more women's methods?" I made a face. "None of the methods required any brute strength in the moment, just opportunity and preparation beforehand."

"Which required time, which Kirsten probably doesn't have."

"Agreed," I said. "Well, put parentheses around her for now."

Rob did. "I don't think we should discount the male gender just because these are sneaky crimes," he said.

"Thank you."

"It's a more clever way to kill, hands off and out of the area when the trap is sprung. It gives you an alibi."

"Are you suggesting, then, that it's more male than female, because it takes brains?" I gestured a new Cheeto even more dramatically. "What's left for us poor women, if brains and brawn are both denied us?"

"No," Rob said, "I was suggesting that such methods might appeal to men and women equally, or at least a certain kind of either gender."

"It's strange, isn't it?" I mused. "The person has to be passionate enough to kill, but cold-blooded and analytical enough to plan it out in advance and then sit back to watch whoever gets caught in the trap."

"Yuck," Rob said. He shook himself. "Who's left?"

We looked up at the board. "Blaine and the kids."

"Do you have anything on Blaine?" Rob asked.

"Well, that he's a little intense and has way too many shady connections to law enforcement. But nothing along the church-hating line. I know he started coming to New Vision because his family did."

"I guess we could ferret out whether he was pleased with the switch."

"Weird to offer to help us out, though, if he did it," I said. "And, I mean, he's done more than offer. He really truly shanghaied that police info."

"Does that show a criminal background?" Rob said.

I shrugged.

"I guess we'll have to talk with him further," Rob said. "At least we have a good excuse now, under the guise of being partners."

"The other big strike against Blaine, of course," I said, "is that he was caught in the second trap himself, and only through grace was saved from an acid bath."

"That is cutting it a little close," Rob said. "But that second attack was inept in so many ways that it's possible that was only part of what went awry. Let's say he was trying to lead Gavin to step on a particular weakened board but misjudged the size of the hole that would open up and got swallowed in it."

"But he had the benefit of not being surprised," I continued. "So he was able to grab hold and keep himself from falling in."

"And he knew he needed to," Rob summed up.

"Wow," I said. "Now I'm getting really creeped out about talking with him about the case. What if he's just laughing behind his hand at us scurrying around like ants, trying to figure out his moves? And then, when we're least expecting it, he'll squash us."

"If he hadn't sent us the autopsy report," Rob said, "I'd

wonder if he knew all that police info just because he already had the facts without their assistance."

"Maybe he didn't happen to meet us at the theater," I said. "Maybe he's the one following us." I made a moue of distaste.

"Back to the whiteboard?" Rob suggested.

"Back to the whiteboard," I agreed. "The kids. Avery, Dylan, Zachary, Potter."

"Should we take them one at a time?"

"Well, let's look at Dylan, at least. He's not really a kid anymore."

"Does he have reason to hate New Vision?" Rob asked.

"He seems dissociated from it, at least," I said.

"What do you mean?"

"Just, not interested. He shows up, plays the bass, goes home. I've never known him to get involved in a small group Bible study, that sort of thing."

"So he's using New Vision for what he can get out of it?" Rob said.

"Maybe." I shrugged. "Then again, I can't stand the guy, so I just avoid talking to him. I don't know much about what he thinks about the philosophy of the church or anything. All I know is he doesn't pay attention when I do the devotional in practice, and he keeps his eyes open when we pray."

"How do you know that?" Rob accused me.

"I have to keep an eye on my flock," I said piously.

"So do you think Dylan has enough passion in him to be a killer?"

"Not against New Vision, not as far as I know. Maybe against people who know that he didn't get into the college he said he did. Of course, that's us now, too." I widened my eyes at the thought. "And Valerie, obviously. And he implied that his mom would be more upset than he was if the truth came out. Maybe the patrician Mora isn't so cool when crossed. It might be worth having you talk with him again, since you're a guy. He doesn't give me the time of day. Or maybe I could ask Avery more about him."

Rob considered the empty space under Dylan's name and sighed. "I'll put a star by his name, too, then, to indicate that he warrants another conversation."

"Agreed. Avery."

"Daughter of one of the victims. Maybe she secretly hates Daddy and was building up to that final moment."

"Assuming it is the final one," I said ominously.

"Yuck," Rob said again, as we contemplated yet another attack on a church member.

"I can't think of why Avery would hate the church. She fits in like she was born to it. She sings, she has friends, she has boys following her. I don't see her being discontented, much less homicidal."

"What about her mom?"

"Her stepmom," I clarified.

"Or her mom mom," Rob said. "Maybe Gavin was the real target, and either the cough drop went astray, or the poisoning was intended to throw us off the scent."

I sat and thought. "There is no way on earth to figure that out from staring at a whiteboard," I said finally.

Rob sighed and nodded. "Potter or Zachary?" He gestured toward the last white end of the board.

"Nope, and nope," I said. "Maybe they'd want to get out from under their mothers' thumbs, but what good does killing church members do for that?"

"You get to go to prison, where Mommy can't reach you."

"You're really dark about families tonight," I said. "I guess under Zachary, you could put that he lied to me at the Bible study without blinking."

"What about?" Rob said.

"He told me he'd gone to the bathroom the night they'd stolen Barb's purse, but Avery and Dylan remembered that taking the cough drops at least had been his idea."

"Lying about a prank isn't the same as murder," Rob said reasonably.

"But the fact that he is a good liar surprises me," I said. "I wouldn't have thought he had it in him. So maybe I'm underestimating him in general."

"I'll put a star by his name, to remind us to talk with him again," Rob said. "And if we're discounting Pastor Chris, then only Valerie's left."

"Valerie," I said heavily. "She's definitely ruffling feathers. But maybe she's just investigating, too."

"Or blackmailing," Rob said ominously.

"You think?"

"She sure does seem like it," he returned.

"Maybe she just likes holding bad secrets over people," I suggested.

"Emotional blackmail?"

"Or spiritual," I said. "An 'I know your sin, and I'm going to tell everybody' kind of thing."

"Does that make her more or less likely to kill everyone in the church?" Rob said.

"Could go either way, I suppose. Is she happy to have such a juicy herd of imperfect people to prey on, or is she so fed up with the deceptions and shortcomings of the congregation that she's ready to take her revenge?"

"Or God's revenge," Rob said. "Like the messages have been saying."

"I guess we need to talk with her directly," I said. "Although she seems like the kind of person it's preferable to keep your distance from."

Rob starred her name and then stared at the board for a long moment.

"It looks like we've gotten...hmmm...nowhere." Rob plopped down on the futon, discouraged. He capped the black marker and threw it on the carpeted floor.

"Don't lose that," I warned. "I'm excluding Potter. I just don't think he has it in him."

Rob shrugged. "Whatever."

"Who are our prime suspects at this point?" I said.

Rob sighed and studied the board. "I guess Walter, Penelope, Jim, um...Gretchen and Heidi, Hal, Valerie...and talk with Dylan and Zachary again?"

"Yeah," I said. "That sounds about right. Let's talk with all of them again, if we can."

"I guess I should notate those," Rob said, searching for True Black where it had rolled under the futon.

"Here, wait," I said, lunging off the futon and toward the office. "You need one more color," I said, retrieving the pack and pulling out a fiery orange that matched our fingertip stains. "Here, circle the prime-os with this."

Rob uncapped Orange Surprise and drew a nice big circle around Walter, Penelope, Jim, Gretchen, Heidi, Hal, and Valerie, and then underlined Dylan and Zachary. "They're potentials," he explained, "depending how my interrogation of them pans out."

"I love it when you talk tough," I growled, on all fours on the futon.

Rob capped the orange and tossed the marker over one shoulder, where it cleared the whiteboard and landed with a barely audible plop on the wall-to-wall beige. He advanced toward me with a look in his eye. I twisted over to turn down the halogen lamp.

Chapter 13

The next day I heard the door shut behind Rob as my eyes cracked open.

I leaped out of bed and hurriedly got ready. I was too edgy even to shower.

If the killer thought I was getting close, I had better keep pushing through. I felt the adrenaline rush through my system. I felt like I was bluffing my way through a game, only it was a game with a known killer.

I checked my email to see if fate or anything like it could deter me from becoming an amateur detective, but no editing clients needed my assistance. I was on my own.

I made myself breakfast and picked at it until I felt it was a decent hour. Then I retrieved my phone and pulled up the church directory, then dialed Dylan Ruiz's number at home. I waited nervously through the rings, planning what to say when he picked up. Only, it was Mora who did.

"Oh, um, hi," I said. "Is Dylan there?" I felt like a teenager talking to my friend's mom.

"He's at school," Mora said.

Well, dang, now I really felt like a teenager. I thanked Mora. I guess I shouldn't have waited till a decent hour after all. Upon reflection, I realized I should have asked Mora if Dylan had a cell phone number I could have. I was going to feel ridiculous to have to keep calling his parents to get in touch with him.

I shook off the disappointment and dialed the next victim.

Jim Vegter answered on the fifth ring, past the time I was expecting it to go to voicemail. Caught unprepared for a live human, I floundered for an opening.

"Ah, Jim!" I said. "Christine here. From praise team."

"Hello, Christine." Cautious.

"Um, I was wondering, uh..." Apparently I should have written out a script, just like a telemarketer. "Are you free today to meet somewhere? A coffee shop or something? For lunch or just, you know, for a...a meeting," I finished pathetically.

"Um." Jim left a silence that I would have called awkward if I hadn't already perfected awkwardness in this conversation. "Sure, okay, how about Fazoli's. I go there for lunch. At one?"

"Yeah," I said enthusiastically. That was unexpectedly easy, and safely public to boot. "Okay, see you there. At one."

I looked up the bus schedules to the Fazoli's in Murphy, where Jim had said to meet after he had met with a client about an electrical problem. I still had an hour and a half to kill before I had to leave. Oh, fine, I decided. I would shower after all, even though I kind of liked my second-day hair. Oh, wait. I felt the roots. No, it was third-day hair. Best to shower.

I deep conditioned and shaved to kill time. After drying off, I put on some makeup and considered leaving my hair to dry wavy. Then I thought about the frigid wind outside and how my hair would freeze even under a knit cap, and I blew it dry and even unearthed my straightening iron.

I made sure my cell was charged in case I needed to call in another emergency, and I was on my way. As I walked toward the bus stop, I kept edgily looking around like a gazelle sensing lions in the underbrush, wondering if each person in a parked car was the killer or someone he or she had hired, keeping an eye on me.

But I didn't spot anyone, and I made it to the Fazoli's without incident. Jim was already there, hunkered down at a table with his pasta and still wearing his puffy black jacket, I supposed the better to show off his company's logo at all times. Maybe he could deduct this as a business lunch if he continued to advertise all through it. I waved, and his sleeve's shiny surface caught the light as he lifted one arm to acknowledge me. I ordered my spaghetti at the counter, then brought it over when it was ready and sat down across from him.

"Breadstick?" said a passing waitress, tongs poised.

I hadn't taken even a bite of the one already on my plate yet, but what the heck?

"Sure," I said.

"Sure," Jim said.

Duly breadsticked, I greeted Jim, and tried for some pleasantries.

They didn't work.

"Christine," Jim said, solemnly chewing his Alfredo-doused breadstick while looking me in the eye, "I'm glad you called. I had been wanting to speak with you."

"Really?" I raised my eyebrows. Was this going to be a big confession, or at least a big break in the case?

"What do you think about hymns?" he asked.

Right. That wasn't where I thought the conversation was headed.

"Hymns?" I said. "Um..." I wasn't sure what he was looking for. "I like them."

He nodded, so I continued.

"The good ones have intricate lyrics with Biblical backing, and interesting melodic lines with complex harmonies." I laughed. "Of course, there are some real stinkers out there, too."

He didn't laugh. "I miss hymns," he said. "At my old church, all we sang were hymns."

"Yeah," I said, "too much of anything can be too much."

"Exactly," he said. "I was wondering if we could include a few in the praise team's rotation."

I hesitated. "I'd have to bring it up with the worship planning committee," I said. I considered telling Jim the joke about Barb's renaming prowess but thought better of it. He looked far too earnest. "We've been looking into doing one or two, but the problem is, we're a seeker church, and it's hard to find hymns that are appropriate for unchurched people."

"What does that even mean?" he exploded, his tray becoming dotted with Alfredo spittle. "What's inappropriate about giving the word of God to unchurched people? Isn't that exactly what they need? Why are we spoon feeding them pap when they could be supping on the bounty of God's table?" He had half-risen, and his paper napkin, politely placed in his lap, had dropped to the carpeted floor. "Sorry," he muttered, retrieving it and resuming his seat.

"I totally agree with you," I said.

"What?" He looked up at me, surprised.

"It frustrates me, the way the planning team rejects songs for being too...too Christian." I screwed up my face. "It's church! I know we're trying to be open and unintimidating, but come on, people know they're going to church! They have to expect some songs about theology."

"Yes!" Jim's face lit up. "So why couldn't we sing, say, 'Come, Thou Fount of Every Blessing'? That's one of my favorites."

"Mine, too." I sighed in pleasure as I ran the lyrics through my head. "And it's one that Penelope and Heidi

179

just suggested. But," I said, "you get lines like 'Here I raise mine Ebenezer.'" I shook my head ruefully. "And even raised-in-the-church Christians generally have no idea what that means."

"Well, they should." Jim pursed his lips. "If they hear lines like that, they might ask questions. They might seek out the answers. Like the Bereans in Acts."

"I hear you."

"Better than these insipid lines we have in our choruses all the time," he said. "What's the chorus to that new one we're doing, 'I Give My All'? 'I praise you with my heart, with my heart, my heart.' It's all I, I, I. It's all self-focused...drivel." He spat a little more sauce.

I nodded. "I wish that there was more of a drive for excellence in Christian music," I agreed. "But, there are a lot of praise choruses I really love. And I think they offer a different kind of worship. A meditative worship."

Jim looked disappointed and twirled his fork viciously into his spaghetti.

"I know it's not everyone's cup of tea—just ask my mother." I laughed, and Jim gave a small smile, his attention on his Alfredo-drenched noodles. "But when you repeat a line like 'I praise you with my heart' a gazillion times, it gives people a chance to stop thinking so analytically and start...just...connecting. Opening their spirits, tuning in to the presence of God. Sometimes the lyrics like hymns have, ones that change syllables with every note and offer a bunch of theology to chew on, can distract people from that emotional connection."

Jim stabbed the air with his fork. "Emotional. See, you said it."

I must have looked perplexed.

"Religion's not supposed to be emotional," he said. "That's self-centeredness again. We're supposed to be focused on how good God is, not on how good he makes us feel."

I sucked in my top lip and tried to answer his reasoning. "I don't know," I finally said. "I guess I'll have to think about it more. But I guess I don't see how we're fully human without our emotions, and God's the one who made us human. I definitely need both sides to my relationship with him—the logical, and the emotional. When I concentrate too long on just the logical, reasonable side of my personality, I start feeling like Spock." I laughed.

Jim smiled sadly, not laughing along. "You sound like my wife," he said.

I must have looked startled or confused, or both.

"I'm not married now," he laughed. "They wouldn't have let me stay in One-on-One if I were."

I laughed along with him. "I didn't know you were married."

"Yeah," he said quietly, idly giving his remaining noodles a twirl but not bringing any to his lips. "She wasn't connecting with the church in Nederland, didn't think our kids were, either. They all moved to California, started up with Saddleback."

My eyes were wide as I took in this untapped back story.

"I had to try out a seeker church myself just to see what all the fuss was about."

"I'm sorry about your...parting," I said finally. What was the correct term here? "That must be tough."

Jim smiled tightly. I remembered that he'd become close to Tammy and now had lost her as well, and presumably he didn't see his children all that often.

"For what it's worth, we're glad to have you at New Vision, even if it's a little out of the norm for you."

Jim nodded and turned brisk, as if shrugging off the emotions. "Well, sorry to take up so much of your time. I have to get back to work, and probably this wasn't at all what you were going to talk with me about."

"No," I said, "no, this has been good. Thanks for meeting me here. I'll definitely try to think of some hymns that might fit in well with the New Vision model, and you let me know if any come to your mind."

Jim smiled slightly again but made no verbal reply.

"I was just wondering." I thought I'd take a stab at getting some answers before he ran off. "Why don't you go back to your old church if New Vision bothers you so much?"

"New Vision doesn't bother me," he said quickly. "I think people here are doing great work, God's work. I understand now what my wife and children found so appealing in the new styles. There are just some things I miss."

"You went to Nederland Christian Reformed, right?"

"Um-hm."

"Is it very old-school? Hymns and liturgy and so on?"

"It's very traditional, yes," Jim said. He looked at his watch. "I really have to run, or I'll be late for my next appointment."

"Sorry," I said, waving my fork apologetically. "Thanks again for meeting me. Have a good rest of the day."

He waved as he rushed toward the exit.

I scooped up the rest of my noodles, trying to soak them in as much marinara as possible. The waitress appeared again, basket over her arm and tongs at the ready. "Breadstick?" she asked.

Oh, why the heck not, I thought. Wouldn't like to waste all that extra sauce.

A couple additional breadsticks later, I bundled up and prepared to walk back to the bus. It had warmed up just enough today to start an unpleasant drizzling, so I tried to wrap my scarf around my head and pull it out like a little brim to keep my glasses from getting rain-specked. I was fiddling with it outside when I swore I heard the whirring of a camera shutter.

I whipped my head around, peering through the landscaped trees at the edges of the strip mall and around the cars in the parking lot. I turned fully around to see if someone was behind me. I couldn't see anybody else walking, except a woman a couple blocks away waiting for her dog to finish pooping on the sidewalk verge. She walked away without scooping, but that was the only misdemeanor I saw her commit.

Maybe I'd imagined it, I told myself. I was just spooked.

I speed walked to the bus stop and was fortunate to catch one that was just pulling up. Entering between a woman with kelly green earmuffs and mittens you could go seal hunting in and a high school student insouciant in short sleeves, with a heavy backpack and skateboard, I felt the safety in numbers. I paid and swayed unsteadily to an empty seat as the bus pulled away. I watched out the window and thought I caught a glimpse of a dark jacket beside a car in the side lot, but that was all before shrubbery robbed me of my view. I half-stood in my seat, but a billboard ran into my line of vision, and then we were around a corner.

I tried to remember. Who wore a dark jacket? When we went through the jackets at praise team that fateful night, what colors were people wearing?

I remembered Jim's company jacket today—that was black. But besides the one I'd just seen, what else was there? Barb had a cheerful purple suede, and Avery had a striking puffy silver, and Valerie's was bright red. But for other dark jackets, I couldn't remember a single one. That was the problem with jackets. Most were boring.

I really sucked at being a detective. Last bus ride, I had tried training my brain to be observant by memorizing fellow bus passengers and making up little quizzes about them to test myself, like naming from memory each piece and color of clothing a particular person was wearing. But today I slouched down in my seat, too discouraged to bother.

Chapter 14

Once I arrived home, soaked and shivering from the icy drizzle, there was more discouragement in store.

I passed our little green car in the parking lot, but Rob shouldn't have been home for a couple hours yet.

He was sitting in the living room on the edge of the futon when I arrived, morosely watching an old rerun of Oprah.

"Get used to this sight," he said when he saw me. "This is all I'll be doing from now on."

"What are you talking about?" I asked, pulling off my rain-sodden scarf and ruffling my drowned-rat hairdo. So much for blowing it straight today.

"I'm out of work."

I gasped. "They fired you? Why?" I shucked off my wet jacket and shoes as quickly as I could and ran to sit beside him.

"Not fired. Not yet. I've been suspended with pay—for now—pending the results of an investigation into professional misconduct."

I gasped again and put my arms around him. Then, distracted by the sincerity on the set, I pulled the remote out of his limp fingers and made Oprah go away.

"What on earth?" I said, once I could concentrate.

"Someone called my boss and accused me of sharing proprietary information with another firm. You know we work with these big companies all the time who are intensely secretive about their new product lines and whatever." He turned to me. "I don't even know what secret I'm supposed to have leaked. They wouldn't tell me anything."

"That's ridiculous." I thought about it. "Maybe you were just talking with someone else, and it got back to them?" I suggested

"You're saying I did it." Rob's eyes flashed.

"Not on purpose!" I exclaimed. "But do you ever meet designers from other firms and talk shop? Maybe they misinterpreted something you said. I mean, I agree it's totally unfair regard—"

He cut me off. "I don't know any other designers!"

"Except Blaine."

He quieted. "I forgot about Blaine. He wouldn't have ratted me out, would he?"

"I never heard you talk about anything specific with him, anyway," I said. "Unless you talked with him when I wasn't around."

"A long time ago," Rob said. "When we were discussing some New Vision projects a couple times. But, no, I never talk about the clients' projects. Never. Not even to you, usually. I mean, mostly just because it's so boring. But I don't do it."

"No," I said, "you wouldn't. It must be a mistake. Did they tell you who called, or from what firm?"

"No. They wouldn't say. They wouldn't say anything, just that they would be following up the accusation, and then they kicked me out. Seriously, security escorted me out of the building. They took my key card, confiscated my laptop and all my files."

"That's major," I breathed.

"And now I'm stuck here at home. In a meaningless existence."

"Like me," I confirmed. "We'll be meaningless together."

"What will we live on?" Rob wailed.

"You said you're being paid for now," I said.

"For now," he echoed sullenly.

"Plus, I've been researching how to get my P.I. license. And then there's always my astonishingly high-paying worship team director salary. So, really, we're set."

Rob finally allowed himself a half-smile. "I guess I'll get to help you investigate at least," he managed.

"That's the spirit!" I said.

"Eggs, please."

Undeterred, I continued my cheerleading. "And in no time, they'll call and say it was all a big mistake. Or fire you, and you'll get a better job."

Rob groaned and keeled over to bury his face in the comforter. I needed to work on my pep talks.

"I know," I said. "We'll start calling people, like we said. How about you sniff around Blaine, see if he's the jerk who framed you?"

"I don't want to," a voice moaned from the comforter.

"Okay," I said. "I'll do it. I was thinking, since we're not actually sharing anything with him, it might be good to give the appearance of being candid by calling a lot. You think it's a good idea?"

Rob waved a hand back behind him. I wasn't sure if it signified "go ahead" or "go away."

I went into the office and out of habit clicked around on my laptop after I'd dialed and was waiting for Blaine to pick up. His phone was ringing an awfully long time, so I refreshed my email inbox. There was an email from Blaine at the top, with an attachment.

I reached his voicemail at the same time I clicked on the email. "Blaine, it's Christine, checking in. I was wondering if you had any new information. Give me a call."

The email had finally loaded, along with the attachment—several photo files. I dimly recognized an odd clicking in my ear and realized it was the call waiting feature. I remembered hearing it once or twice while speaking with our parents, but I'd never dared click over while on the phone with a loved one. I broke off staring at the photos to fumble with my cell phone until I figured out what to push to switch lines.

"Christine, it's Blaine," said the voice on the other end. "I saw that you called. Sorry I couldn't get to the phone."

"Oh, that's fine," I said. My voice sounded hollow.

"Did you get my email?"

"Y—" I cleared my throat and tried again. "Yes."

"Why didn't you tell me you were being threatened?"

I paused. "Excuse me?"

"Those photos taken of you guys, and there were several threatening messages on your voicemail? Isn't that something you should have shared with your partner?" He emphasized the last word.

"Um...," I faltered. "We didn't want to scare you." I swallowed hard again. "Have you gotten anything like this?"

"No. It's really creepy, isn't it? You didn't notice someone taking pictures of you all those times you were out?"

I shook my head, then remembered I was on the phone. "No. Today, I thought..."

"What?"

"Never mind."

Rob had emerged from his dead man's float on the futon and was standing in the doorway, watching me with a furrowed brow and quizzical gaze. I waved him over and pointed to my laptop screen.

"Well, anyway," Blaine said, "there were no fingerprints found on the prints. Dylan's were on the bag, though—does that mean anything?"

"No," I said on a sigh. "Dylan was here last night to talk to me and picked it up."

"Oh." Blaine continued his report. "No suspicious vehicles seen in the area. Neighbors didn't see anything." There was a ringing noise in the background. "Sorry, Christine, I'm going to have to cut this short. The boss is staging a conference call."

He rang off.

"That was an abrupt ending," Rob observed.

"Conference call," I explained.

"I remember when I had conference calls," he lamented.

"I remember when you complained about having conference calls."

"He sent you the photos from the bag," Rob said.

"Yeah," I said flatly.

"What does that mean?"

I exhaled. "I have no idea."

"Let me look at them up close," Rob said. We switched places, and he downloaded the attachments, then opened them to full size.

"They don't necessarily look scanned, but I guess they might be. They were taken from so far away and were a little blurry to begin with that they're not the best quality, anyway."

"What are you looking for?" I asked.

"Indications that he doesn't have the original jpgs but has sent us the images as scanned by the police. That smudge there, for instance"—Rob pointed—"that looks like a fingerprint, but it can't be if the perp really did wear gloves. But it could be a fingerprint on the scanner, or on the camera lens. I wish I could compare these files to the original prints." Rob scrutinized the images further. "There's no obvious bowing of straight lines, as if a print had curled slightly under the scanner cover. But maybe they just did a good job scanning." He pushed away from my desk and leaned back in my chair. "There's no way to tell," he said, disappointed.

"Was that the e-news?"

"Was what the what?" Rob said.

I gestured him out of my seat and, once I'd situated myself, clicked back into my inbox to check. Sure enough, I'd seen the New Vision e-news under Blaine's missive.

"I want to see if it says anything about what's going on," I said.

"Come to the men's prayer breakfast, and, oh, there's a killer on the loose," Rob suggested.

"Nothing," I said, mystified, skimming it all again. "There's even a blurb for One-on-One, but nothing about having one of their own killed off."

"The church doesn't always deal well with grief," Rob said.

I clicked on the One-on-One link and was directed to the church website's page dedicated to the singles group, filled mostly with photo albums of outings. I clicked on a camping trip from the past summer.

"Oh, man," I said, "there's Tammy. She's in a lot of these photos."

"And there's Hal." Rob pointed to the drummer, his ponytail disheveled from roughing it. Tammy looked demure as usual, her smile showing she was genuinely enjoying herself out in the wild. Better her than me, I thought.

"And there's Blaine." Rob earned points for spotting all our praise team members.

"Is that Jim?" I said, squinting at my monitor.

Rob studied the blurry figure behind a campfire. "No, whoever that is has a mustache."

"Oh, I thought it was camping grime."

I clicked back to the albums page and selected the most recent, a fall retreat near the Indiana Dunes.

"There sure are a lot of Tammy," I said. "It's kind of

eerie, almost like someone was stalking her."

"I guess she was just photogenic," Rob said.

I clicked on another album, but it was more of the same, and I wasn't sure what I was looking for anyway.

"What if these aren't random crimes at all?" I asked. "What if they just seem that way from the methods, and really Tammy and Gavin, or Blaine, had done something terrible to someone?"

Rob looked thoughtful. "I hate to say it," he said, "but we almost need a third attack to help us figure it out."

Chapter 15

That night Rob spent moping over his lost job, so I stayed up to mope with him, which in my case meant eating chocolate chip cookie dough straight from the tube and watching the rest of the DVD we were in the middle of.

Finally, at 2 a.m., we were out of snacks and I was bored. I had a hankering for frosted cookies, and, completely incidentally, needed new white socks, so I suggested a run to Meijer.

"What difference does it make how late I stay up?" Rob said, bleary-eyed. "I have nowhere important to be tomorrow."

And so we rushed off in the frigid night air to the superstore.

I had my cookies, plus some chocolate donuts and Fritos for Rob, who informed me he was not under any circumstances done with his wallowing. I was cutting through the children's clothes to get to women's hosiery when I bumped my unsteerable cart straight into someone else's as I was rounding a corner.

"Christine!" exclaimed the owner of the cart before I

had a chance to apologize.

"Kirsten," I said, blinking in surprise and feeling a little awkward to be caught in the ratty hoodie I hadn't bothered to change out of to make a late-night snack run. I had at least put on jeans instead of chancing it with my jammy pants.

I looked more closely at Kirsten, though, and stopped feeling bad. Her normal smooth mom bob was half up in a tousled mess—not an artful mess, but one that suggested a lack of mirror and time. She was wearing sweatpants and a paint-splattered, oversize sweatshirt that looked to have come out of her husband's drawer.

"Fancy meeting you here," she said, nervously cheerful.

Maybe she was becoming aware of her state of appearance just as I was.

"You're up late," I observed. "Where are the kids?"

Kirsten laughed. "In bed. I hope. Back with Stefan. I just needed some air. And some socks." She gestured with a pack of children's ankle socks.

"Hey, me, too," I said.

"You're up late yourself," she said. "Is Rob here?"

"Oh, yeah, we both are. I always stay up late." I smiled. "I pretty sure I'm part vampire."

"I'm just used to shift work. From being a nurse." She smiled ruefully. "And a mom. Are you thinking of having kids?"

The question caught me by surprise but shouldn't have. It was a question we were asked quite a bit. People—Kirsten especially—were probably wondering how we could have been married two whole years and not be frantically hopping on the baby train.

"Oh, sometime," I said. "We're young yet."

"How old are you?" She coughed. "If you don't mind my asking."

"Twenty-six."

"Yeah," she laughed. "You have time. Of course, I had five kids by your age."

"What? Really?"

Kirsten looked a little offended. "I'm twenty-seven."

"I'm sorry. I just figured, to have five kids..." I trailed off. "Wow. Well, no. I mean, you're welcome to them. But I...no."

"Oh, you might change your mind," Kirsten said. "They're a lot of fun when they're your own."

"And yet here you've escaped to Meijer," I said, laughing.

Kirsten chuckled slightly. "Yeah."

"We're enjoying our time just being married right now," I said. "It's fun, to be able to travel and sleep in and take late-night trips to fabulous places—." I gestured at the racks of discount clothing that surrounded us.

"Oh, sure," Kirsten said. "There are things I miss about being carefree. But I figure I have time in the future to do those things again. And that's why I'm trying to get all the child-raising down quickly."

I nodded, biting my tongue so I didn't comment on what her haste to reproduce had wrought.

"I miss leading the praise team," she said.

I blinked again. "You led the praise team?"

"You didn't know that?" Kirsten cocked her messy blond head to one side. "Before Paul."

Paul had been the interim leader before my tenure had started. When he married and transferred to his new wife's church six months previously was when the search for a new interim praise team leader had begun and I had been elevated to the role.

"Paul's all I knew," I said.

"When did you join New Vision?" Kirsten asked.

"A little over a year. I didn't join the praise team till a couple months after that."

"Yeah," said Kirsten, and I could see her eyes rise as

she did math in her head. "That would have been right after I took time off to go on bed rest with the triplets."

"So was Paul part of the praise team in your time?"

"He played keys."

"Huh. And you?"

"I mostly sang," Kirsten said pleasantly.

"Oh." I looked into her cart and counted five packs of socks. That must have been a good sale. "Did you want to sing now? Or not play keys? I can play if I have to."

"Oh, I like playing keys," Kirsten said. "I wouldn't mind singing if you want to put a mic back by me."

"Sure," I said, feeling sheepish that I never knew how multi-talented Kirsten was. I had accepted her at face value as one of many instrumental volunteers.

"The only problem is," she continued, "there are so many singers as it is. It's going to start sounding like a choir."

"Yeah." I paused. "I had an idea, but I wasn't sure how it would go over."

"What's that?"

"Maybe we could split into two teams."

Kirsten mulled this over. "I think that could work. You'd have to figure out the logistics, of course. A nice side effect is that it might actually help attract new volunteers. Right now it looks full up, like there are no holes for people to fit into."

I nodded slowly. "That makes so much sense." As long as I was using her consulting abilities, I figured I'd continue. "Do you think we have enough instruments to split, though? Drummers, yes." I thought of Zachary's mother and her leap of joy when she saw her son be the star of a whole service. "But not so much the other things."

"You could start off just splitting singers, I guess. And keys." She smiled.

I smiled back.

"It might be nice, though," she said, "if the practices

were still combined. So that people could still feel like they're part of a bigger team."

"I was just thinking that."

We smiled at each other again. In my head was the niggling thought that she must have been a better leader than I was—and probably got paid accordingly. Maybe the worship planning committee was just waiting and hoping that Kirsten would come back into power and stalling with interim leaders in the meantime.

I shook my head slightly to clear it. "Thanks for thinking it through with me. I'll have to bring it up with worship planning and see what they think."

Rob rounded the same corner and smacked into my cart. "There you are. Oh, hi, Kirsten."

Kirsten waved, then looked at her watch. "Yowza. I'd better get back home before one or all of them wake up." She pushed her cart off toward the checkout.

"Kirsten shops at Meijer in the middle of the night?" Rob asked. "How'd she get away from Baby Central?"

"I asked the same thing. Funny how we assumed she'd be tied down at night, and here she is wandering free."

"You ready?" Rob said, pouring a new armful of junk into the cart.

"Yes. No. Socks." I wrenched the horrible cart into the right direction and led him on.

I paused in my discouraging perusal of fabric content labels, looking in vain for something with more cotton percentage. "Do you think Kirsten's jealous of me?"

"Because of your nice socks?" Rob asked. "Or because of your fine man?"

"Uh-huh," I said. "And my lack of five babies. Did you know she's twenty-seven?"

"No!" Rob breathed. "We could have five babies by next year?"

"We'd better not," I warned. "Speaking of which, do we need condoms?"

Rob pointed into the cart. "Done."

"Heh, heh," I said.

"Why jealous?" Rob said.

I stopped my fantasizing. "It turns out Kirsten was praise team director before we moved here."

"Huh," Rob said. "So she might want it back?"

"And I know there were several people who probably felt passed over when I was picked for interim leader. I know Avery wanted the post, and I heard Blaine did, though he hasn't said anything. I think someone said Dylan did, too."

"Are you suggesting this as a motive for murder?"

"I'm not suggesting anything. I'm just thinking it's difficult to be on the receiving end of that much frustration. Especially since they all probably think they could do a better job."

Rob shook his head.

"And they're right," I finished.

Rob shook his head harder. "Not even."

I returned to Rob's supposition. "Do you think it could be a motive for murder?"

"How? Like, they're so mad that you're the interim leader that they start killing off praise team members to show you who's boss?"

I raised my eyebrows. "Well, it would take a madman. But I'm not sure that's not who we're dealing with."

"Whom," Rob said.

I accidentally threw the socks I'd chosen at him instead of directly into the cart.

Chapter 16

Rob spent the morning continuing his wallow while I puttered, getting used to having a man around the house. He had no laptop, so he kept borrowing mine to check his work email, in case there was some news about his suspension. In between stalking his account, he sat on the futon and ate his junk haul from the night before. Soon there were a Fritos bag, a melting half-pint of sorbet, an empty sleeve of graham crackers, and an opened jar of strawberry jam on his tray. I noticed that his wallowing looked a lot like my working.

I had come out of the office to clean it up and tempt him with some detecting work.

"I guess," Rob said. "I have nothing better to do."

That was enthusiasm enough for me.

I found the number for Nederland Christian School and asked to be connected to Walter Kappas. When he answered, he said he'd be available to meet with me after all the kids had gotten off into their buses and carpools for the day. Rob and I got ready and managed to arrive at Nederland Christian School a half-hour after the final period let out. The place was eerily silent, but I imagined that we had just missed all the pandemonium of students pouring into idling vehicles in the circular driveway and side lots.

We followed signs that directed us in no uncertain terms to the office, since that's where we wanted to be anyway. Our footsteps echoed through the empty hallways, past all the closed lockers.

The other administrative staff had already gone home for the day, but Walter somehow sensed our presence and opened the door to his inner sanctum to see us standing at the office counter, like students waiting for a late slip.

"Christine, Rob," he said heartily. His omnipresent suit today was dark gray with a widely spaced pinstripe and an improbable lime-green tie. I'd never seen him wear any color so flamboyant and wondered if it was a present from a student. "Come on in." He stood in the door of his office and gestured inside.

We padded around the counter into the carpeted sanctuary. I had never been on the other side of the counter before, or indeed in a principal's office. I couldn't now decide if that was a good thing or just meant that I was boring.

"I'm surprised to see you, Rob," Walter began. Rob looked at him sharply. "I thought you'd be at work right now."

"Rob has the day off," I inserted, giving Rob a tactful out.

"I've been suspended," Rob said flatly. Apparently he didn't want my offering.

"Oh, no!" Walter exclaimed. "What happened?"

"Someone falsely accused me of intellectual theft," Rob said, still wooden.

"That's terrible." Walter clucked. "Truly terrible. Who would do such a thing?" He shook his head gravely, his meager supply of brown hair bobbing slightly with the movement. "I will certainly be praying for you. I will pray that the truth comes out and that God will restore everything you deserve."

Rob said nothing. "Thank you," I supplied for him.

"That's terrible," Walter said again.

"Yes, well," I cut in. "We just had a quick question."

"Certainly," Walter said, folding his hands on his desk next to his half-full #1 Principal mug and a plaque that read "Principals are PALS." "Ask away."

"We're just checking on some things." I cleared my throat, astonished at how tactless being a detective made me feel. "I heard Tammy was fired from here just before she died." My voice squeaked a little at the end.

"Oh, that." Walter sighed heavily and ran a hand over his bald spot. "The police made a lot of that as well. I wasn't the one who did the firing."

"Who did?" Rob broke in.

"There's an office manager in charge of hiring and firing staff. Tammy had taken too many sick days, and there was a more qualified applicant available within the department, so it was..." He cleared his throat. "Uh...I just...it made more sense to promote the more qualified applicant." He cleared his throat again. I had an intense urge to offer him a cough drop. "It made it very awkward to face her in praise team, you can imagine."

"Yes," I said.

"Didn't Tammy work in procuring donations for the school?" Rob said. At least the detecting was bringing him out of his sulk for a while.

"That's right," Walter said, nodding gravely. "She wrote letters and made phone calls to alumni, and we need someone who's dedicated to the job.. I'd like to pretend that a Christian school is completely altruistic, that we survive on manna dropped from above." He chuckled, and I gave a polite smile in return. "But the truth is, we need donations badly. We have a lot of scholarship students— pastors' kids and missionaries' kids and the like. And we have expenses just like any school. Well, actually we don't have nearly the resources that your average public school would have, like fancy computer labs or what have you, because we don't get all the local and state funding."

I nodded, letting him go through his spiel, but at this point he seemed to run out of steam.

"Who was the more qualified applicant?"

Walter loosened his tie, as if it felt tight all of a sudden. "Uh...well, actually, you know her!" He tried for a bright smile and overshot it. "It's...uh...Penelope!"

"Penelope? She told us she had a new promotion. I hadn't realized she'd ousted Tammy." I rounded my eyes. "Talk about awkward."

"Well, it wasn't Penelope's fault," Walter said sharply. "I feel bad that we fired Tammy, but it was a tough decision that had to be made." He eyed both of us in turn. "It had nothing to do with her death, though."

"No," I said, and my voice squeaked again.

"No," Rob agreed.

I was suddenly aware that we were closeted in an inner office with a murder suspect, with no one else in or near the building as far as I knew, and with no one else aware of our location. In my relief at having Rob investigate alongside me, I'd forgotten that prudence would still behoove us. We had just corporately broken all the rules Rob had prescribed for me. I could tell from the fact that Rob scooted his chair back and half rose that he had become aware of the situation as well.

"There was no ill will between us personally," Walter emphasized. "And Penelope deserved the promotion."

Rob and I nodded along. I panicked a little when I tried to push my chair back and found it stuck on the thick carpeting, but I pushed harder and freed myself to stand beside Rob. I found myself straining to hear any footsteps in the corridors outside, but whether the carpeted office was too insulated or whether we were the only souls in the building, I couldn't hear anything besides Walter's voice and my own breathing.

"Yes," I said, adding hoarse into the mix. I seriously sounded like Minnie Mouse with a cold. "Just checking up on loose ends." Rob edged backwards toward the door. I tripped over his chair a little in my haste to join him.

"Thank you for your candor," I said. Rob wrenched at the doorknob. I could taste the freedom of the empty office beyond.

But Walter followed us out and waved us through the outer door into the echoing corridor. He pointed a finger at me. I jumped. "See you tonight," he said, cocking his finger like a gun.

"What? Where?"

Walter looked puzzled. "At praise team."

"Right!" I tried to inhale. "See you."

Rob and I turned in unison and race-walked through the hall. I could feel my back burn as if it had a target on it. I breathed in the icy air with relief and then started giggling.

Rob paused a moment and then joined in.

"Yea, we're alive," he said.

I laughed a little more. "This is so embarrassing," I said. "He's probably not even the murderer."

"He hid the thing with Tammy," Rob pointed out.

"Yeah," I agreed. "And he's much more pragmatic than his jolly front suggests, and there is something going on with Penelope. But still—"

"Yeah," Rob said. "If he is the killer, he really wasted his chance back there. And we're safe now, out here in public."

I looked back at the front of the school building. "Still and all," I said, "let's get out of here, just in case."

We cheesed it.

When we got home, I tried to reach Dylan again to see

what he had wanted the night before last, but this time no one at all answered. It was strange that he showed up the night the photos were delivered to my door. If he hadn't put them there, I hoped he hadn't seen something that had gotten him in trouble. I expected to see him at praise team practice tonight, so maybe that mystery would be put to rest.

A sound dinged on my laptop. I swiveled my finger over the mouse area to get rid of the screensaver.

"Blaine Grotenhouse wants to chat with you," my email program told me. "Accept or deny?"

I clicked "Accept."

"christiine, its blaine," came the message.

"Hey, Blaine," I typed into the box and hit "return."

"Blaine Grotenhouse is typing," the box told me.

"find out anthing? cough drops bag definately not poisnous. just the one in the pocket."

Apparently Blaine Grotenhouse was typing too fast for accuracy. It occurred to me that this might only appear to be Blaine, so I should be careful not to reveal anything secret. Or maybe I could test him.

"What do you think of the new church E-boards?" I typed.

"you mean aboards?" came the response. "barf."

It was Blaine. "So the drops weren't meant to poison the whole team, then," I typed. "Just one person."

"thats what i thot," typed Blaine, for whom speed apparently counted more than correct English. "and threats to you were from;acelll." Blaine started a new line and started over. "from a disposable cell phone."

"So they can't trace them?" I typed.

"yup. i mean nope. nothing usefull sofar."

"Question for you." It occurred to me that now was a good time to figure out some more puzzles. "You are typing," my screen helpfully told me. I hoped Blaine was patient so I could get it all out before he started typing on top of my message. "On the night of the poisoning, why were you and Hal moving boxes in the office?"

"boxes? dont know. hal was so i joined."

I wanted to clarify. "Hal was moving the boxes? So you just thought it would be a good idea to do your own searching in the same area?"

"sounds silly now you say it"

There was a pause, and then "Blaine Grotenhouse is typing."

"what does it mean"

"I don't know," I typed back.

"Can I check my work email?" Rob asked from the office doorway.

"I'm chatting with Blaine," I said.

"What?" Rob's face looked like I'd just revealed gross infidelity. "Has he admitted to framing me?"

"You think he did it?" I asked Rob. "Should I ask him?" My hands were poised over the keyboard.

"No!" Rob said. "Yes! I don't know. Should we?"

"Maybe just hint at it?" I said.

Rob wedged himself between the back of my office chair and the wall so he could peer over my shoulder.

"Okay, say, 'Have you heard anything about Rob's job?'"

I started typing. "You are typing," my screen told me.

"No, no," Rob said.

I backspaced through it all. My screen wasn't sure now whether I was typing or not so was silent on the matter.

"No, that should work," Rob said.

"u there?" Blaine asked.

I tried to remember the phrasing and started typing it in again.

"'Have you heard about Rob's job?'" Rob prompted me. "No, wait, 'anything about Rob's job.'"

I corrected my line and then waited, finger hovering over the return button. "Send?" I asked.

"Send," Rob said. He grimaced.

I pushed the button.

We waited for Blaine to start typing again.

"what aboot robs job?"

"He's Canadian," I laughed. Rob wasn't laughing. I wiped the grin off my face.

"What do we say now?" Rob said, eyes riveted to the chat screen. "What do we say now? Um... 'Interesting things happening...' No..."

"Oh, forget it," I said. "I'll just ask him outright."

"Rob was suspended because someone called in an accusation that he'd been leaking proprietary information."

"False accusation," Rob amended.

I had already hit return, so I added that as a separate line.

A little yellow head appeared in Blaine's box. Rob and I watched as the head's mouth dropped open and the eyes bugged out.

"thats awful," Blaine typed. "who wold do that? think itts the killer?"

"We don't know," I said. "Keep your ears open."

"righto. have to go. confrence call." "Blaine Grotenhouse has signed off," the screen told me.

Again?

"Again?" Rob said. "Is he just running away from us?"

"I don't know," I said. "His emoji said he was shocked to hear the news."

Rob glowered at me.

"Well, what do you want me to do? It's hard to interrogate a suspect over instant messaging."

"Particularly if said suspect buggers off," Rob grumbled.

"I'll see him tonight," I said, hoping to perk him up. "Speaking of which, I should really get ready."

"And you'll probably want some dinner, too." Rob sighed. "Now that I'm a house husband, I guess I'll start

205

being taken advantage of for all my domestic skills."

"Oh, honey," I said, heading for the bathroom to repair my makeup, "I've always taken advantage of you."

Chapter 17

Thursday evening was our first praise team practice after the two attacks. The room was buzzing with conversation when I entered, late as usual. The group was divided into older and younger contingents, with the exception of Hal, who was standing off near the boxes observing the commotion. I busied myself putting down my belongings and arranging my music, but finally I had to say something.

"Everyone," I called, and for once they heard and obeyed. "If you could take your seats, please." There was a subdued clatter as people settled. I saw no one absent, save poor Tammy, and all eyes were on me.

"This has been a tough week. We're all missing Tammy, and now with the recent attacks on Avery's dad and Blaine"—I gestured toward the two team members in turn—"this is a terrible time for our church body."

"How's your dad, honey?" Barb cut in. It was the right thing to ask, though, so I lapsed into silence and let Avery talk.

"He's okay," Avery said, rubbing her eyes beneath her faux lenses. "They're talking about sending him home on the weekend. He lost most of his left foot."

There was a collective indrawn breath.

"And he had to have a lot of skin grafts. But fortunately the surgeries were able to preserve most of the function in his left hand. He's starting physical therapy now."

"And how are you, Blaine?" Kirsten called from over at the piano. "Any ill effects?"

"No," Blaine said. "Fortunately." He looked a little sheepish about his luck.

I regained control. "I'd like to spend some time in prayer before we begin practice."

It was the right way to start. Everyone seemed in the mood to quiet down and request help from Someone who could do something. All of the members offered a personal petition, with the unsurprising exceptions of Potter, whom I had never heard speak out in a group setting, and Dylan, who as usual had his eyes opened, I discovered as I slitted mine during a lull. Dylan was staring at Avery while leaning back in his chair with his arms crossed, whereas I was just making sure it wasn't time for me to close out the prayer.

Hal's contribution was oddly phrased but heartfelt, directed more to the universe than to anyone in particular and without any of the "Father God" and other Christianese terms that peppered the established church members' prayers. I could tell Jim, Barb, and Walter were champion group pray-ers, beseeching God for complete healing for Gavin and that God's name be glorified by having the perpetrator brought to justice. Penelope whispered her grief at the death and her hope that a resolution would come soon. Avery's message was short and emotion-packed, and I detected no hint that she was aware of Dylan's scrutiny. I slanted my half-closed eyes over to her to make sure, but hers were shut tight and she was nodding along to the other prayers, tears seeping beneath her lids. I belatedly realized that Hal had his eyes opened, too, and from the angle of his head, I thought he was looking in my direction. I hurriedly bowed my head further and played pious.

After the final "Amens" echoed around the circle, the group seemed to perk up a bit. I was able to get us all off and singing the opening song with minimal persuasion. It helped that it was a familiar one, and a favorite of many. I had intentionally chosen what I termed comfort songs that week, so the group might feel cozy, even if there was a killer in our midst. I shuddered as I looked around at the earnest singers and intent instrumentalists, realizing that in all likelihood one of them was hiding a dreadful secret and a murderous nature, all the while pretending to praise God and commune with other like-minded people.

After the rehearsal, I saw Potter pick up his trumpet and, not even bothering to stash it back in its case but merely tucking the case under one arm and holding the trumpet in the other hand, start hauling butt toward the door. I raced after.

"Potter!" I wasn't sure I'd reach him before he took off down the stairs. He turned at the door to the stairwell, eyes wide.

"Got a minute?" I asked.

He darted his brown eyes from side to side, apparently seeking rescue. "My mom's waiting downstairs," he whispered.

"This will just take a sec." I tried to keep my voice jovial and nonthreatening. It wasn't having any noticeable effect on his comfort level, in terms of the stiffness with which one dark-brown arm remained awkwardly jutting out over the case.

"Want me to help you put that away?" I asked, gently reaching for the trumpet. I had to abandon gentleness and pry it loose from his grasp, but finally he gave way and held up the case for me to help him properly cache his instrument.

"I'm just asking everyone in the group," I said as I worked with him, so that neither of us had to make uncomfortable eye contact. "Did you know Tammy, or are you friends with Gavin?"

"Tammy, no." Potter's voice was so low as to be almost inaudible. I had to make some facial contact just to read his lips. "Gavin's wife is my godmother."

"Marjorie?"

Potter looked down at his lace-up shoes. "No, his first wife." Some of the other praise team members crossed behind us and chose the elevator, presumably since Potter and I were blocking the stairs.

"Okay," I said. "Thanks for talking with me. And I'm glad you've recovered from your cold."

As if to belie my last statement, Potter sniffled.

"See you Sunday," I said, as eager as he was to end the awkwardness.

Potter nodded and backed away, then turned and ran down the stairs. I held the door open until he had disappeared around the first bend.

I didn't think that kid could possibly be the murderer, but dang it if I was going to break both our hearts interrogating him to find out. If it was Potter, the police were going to have to handle it, because I was officially crossing the wide-eyed fourteen-year-old off my list.

I turned around to reenter the practice room. I still had to straighten it up and gather my belongings before I could leave.

Only Dylan was left. I looked around, willing some other people to just be hiding around the corner, but eventually I couldn't avoid the fact that we were alone. I knew all the offices below us were closed for the night.

I smiled at Dylan and busied myself putting my music back into its binder. "Hi, Dylan," I said. "Did you want to talk about something the other night?"

"Mm-hm," he said. I looked up and saw his smile that always looked to me like a smirk. "But you looked a little busy."

"Yeah," I said, rapping my music straight on a table, maybe a little more sharply than was warranted. "So what was it?"

"Oh, I was just in the neighborhood and thought I'd drop by something."

"Mm-hm," I said, imitating his reticence. I bent down to pick up a pencil someone had dropped.

He had been sitting on a desk against the wall of windows, but now I caught movement as he slid off and walked toward me.

I straightened, holding the pencil in front of my chest, pointy end out.

But all Dylan had in his hand was a sheet of paper. He held it out halfway toward me. I reached across the distance and took it from his grasp.

"What's this?" I said, examining the title. "'Pure Gaze'?"

Dylan rocked back and forth on his heels. "It's...a praise song I wrote."

I looked up, but his eyes were studying the industrial office carpeting.

I quickly scanned the lyrics in front of me. On first glance, they sounded actually...good. Worshipful, no less.

Dylan's other hand, which had been ensconced in a jacket pocket, started drawing something out. I couldn't help the cold slither of fear that ran through me, but it turned out to be only a flash drive. "Here's a recording of it," Dylan said, handing it over. "I don't really know how to write down music, so I thought I'd just...you know, sing it. It's not a very good recording," he finished hurriedly.

"Thanks, Dylan," I said. "Did you want the team to sing it?"

"Um, you know, if it's decent." He ran a hand through

his perfectly messy black hair but continued to avoid eye contact.

"I'll have a listen and run it by the worship planning committee. It looks good so far." I didn't see any tricky theological terms, which meant the lyrics wouldn't prove a burden for the seekers in our congregation, and yet the lyrics were intriguingly complex. I wanted to get home and read them through a few more times to think about them. It had imagery that made perfect sense and yet that I hadn't heard a million times before, and the message was both inspiring and challenging. If the music ended up being just as promising, I was looking forward to singing this in church.

"Yeah, okay," he said, sauntering toward the exit. He called over his shoulder as he left. "Thanks."

I quickly finished up collecting my things and rearranging the chairs, then turned off the lights to leave. I was acutely conscious as I rode the elevator down that I had no idea who might be on the other side of the doors when they opened. I reached in my pocket for my cell phone to call Rob for reassurance. It wasn't there. I patted my other jacket pocket, then frantically around my jeans to hit all possible storage spots. Nothing. My mind flashed on a vision of it resting in its charging dock on my desk at home. I'd decided to leave it there till the last possible moment to have it as full of juice as possible for practice. Curse my phone's deteriorating battery!

The elevator doors slid open, and I looked cautiously out into the darkened corridor. Nothing, at least that I could see from my vantage point.

I poked my head around the door to look, and the doors started sliding shut. Not wishing to be decapitated, I leaped forward into the entranceway.

I whipped my head in both directions. Still nothing.

I pulled my keys from my pocket, holding them rigidly as my only potential weapon. I walked cautiously to the door and peered through the glass. The parking lot lights pooled in scattered spots, leaving the rest of the lot in darkness.

Everyone else had left already, leaving me feeling like a minor character in a horror movie.

I opened the door, bracing myself for the cold to enter my lungs, and for whatever else might be out there.

My car was two-thirds of the way across the lot from the door. I race walked over, keys in hand, breath bursting in icy puffs into the still black air. I jammed my key into the car's door, wishing more fervently than usual that my key fob still worked.

I peered in the windows as my iced fingers fumbled with the lock but couldn't see anything but soda cans that had rolled out of our backseat recycling bag, an extra cardigan, and store fliers that had collected in the corners.

It was as the lock finally clicked that unknown headlights entered the lot.

I tore open the door and launched myself into the driver's seat, hitting my thigh on the steering wheel on my way in. There was no time to rub the impending bruise in self-pity, though. I smashed on the lock button and heard the reassuring chunk of all four doors being secured.

I also heard the roar of the other car coming up behind mine, the bright lights searing my retinas in my rearview mirror.

With my numb, gloveless fingers, I fumbled to fit the key into the ignition. I took a deep breath and told myself I would manage it if I just concentrated. The mind game worked, and I started the car.

The other car had pulled behind me and was a menacing, rumbling tiger trying to block my path out.

Forget that, I thought. I floored the gas and peeled forward and around. It was as I caromed past that I recognized the gigantic white form of Barb's SUV.

And, more than that, I recognized Barb's face peering

out at me from the driver's window.

I screeched my car to a halt several yards away, then reversed it slowly till I was even with Barb's window.

"Hey," I said casually.

"Hey, Christine," Barb said cheerfully. "I realized we'd all left you behind alone, and I thought I should just make sure you got off all right."

"Thanks, Barb," I said. "I appreciate it. I'm fine." I unclenched my hands from the steering wheel and flexed the knuckles.

"Okay then. Brrr, it's cold out tonight," she said, and rolled her window back up. Giving a jaunty wave, she pulled around my little green car and headed out of the lot.

I followed her monster vehicle until it was time for me to turn toward Mansardville and the poorer side of the tracks.

"Oh, thank God." Rob yanked open the door while I was trying to unlock it and enveloped me in a tight squeeze.

Then he dragged me in with him and shut and locked the door behind me.

"Are you okay?"

He looked at me with red-rimmed eyes. "He called your phone while you were gone. The killer."

I gasped. "You picked up?"

"I thought it might be you calling in from someone else's phone since you forgot yours," Rob said. "He told me that you were in grave danger. I almost thought it was a ransom demand at first." He gave a sound like a half-hiccup, half-sob.

I sat down beside him and put my arm around him.

"But then he asked, was I enjoying my time off from work."

I bit a knuckle. "He did it."

"I know he did," Rob wailed. "He set me up. And I have no proof whatsoever."

I let my head tip back to look up at the ceiling, shaking with our neighbors' bass. It was true. "It's not on the voice-mail," I said.

"Bastard," Rob said feelingly.

"Are you going to tell your company about it?"

"What good would it do?" Rob said morosely. "Hey, Mr. Wheeler, I had a mysterious phone call that told me a madman faked the tip to keep my wife from investigating a murder."

"It's worth a shot," I said.

Rob shrugged, his cheeks bunching up as he rested his face on his upturned palms. It was actually pretty cute.

"I'm calling the police, at least," I said, heading for the phone I'd forgotten earlier. I considered tossing in a complaint of noise disturbance for our upstairs neighbors while I was at it but decided to take one fight at a time.

Either the number was catchy, or I had dialed it often enough recently, but I didn't need to look it up. The police receptionist informed me in a voice that made a monotone sound jazzy that Detective Madari had left for the day, that in fact she was taking a couple days off due to a personal emergency. Maybe the receptionist's depressiveness was due to an inability to do the same.

"Is there someone else I could talk to about the Tammy Dykstra case?" I asked.

"Just a moment," the receptionist intoned, and put me on hold. As I listened to bad jazz, I wandered into the kitchen to find Rob boiling water on the stove.

"Cocoa?" he mouthed. He was turning to comfort chocolate, I saw.

I nodded.

After an excruciating seven and a half minutes, the music clicked off. I waited, but there was no voice forthcoming. "Hello?" I ventured. Silence.

In disgust, I stared at the screen to confirm. "They cut me off!"

"Bummer," Rob said sullenly, rummaging in the cupboards. "Do you want marshmallows?"

"Of course I want marshmallows," I said. "What do I do now?"

"About the marshmallows?"

"About the cops!"

"Call back?"

I made a growling sound. "I'm sick of them. You call back."

Rob made a face. "It'll keep. They don't seem to care about us, anyway."

"Yeah, okay." I was feeling just as hopeless as he was. I watched him rip open packets of chocolate powder and shake them into the waiting mugs.

"I want the Grover one," I said, pointing.

"You got it," he said.

Chapter 18

On Friday morning, I checked my email while Rob slept in. In the midst of the usual newsletters and chain forwards from my father-in-law, I spotted an email with an attachment. I sighed and clicked it open. Sure enough, there was a job to do. I had forgotten that the world didn't know to stop spinning while I solved the mysteries surrounding me.

The new client was a student enrolled in postgraduate business study who was required to take a class on effective writing and turn in five essays by Monday showcasing his work.

I opened up the first of the essays and by the first paragraph could see how badly he needed me. I wasn't sure what the ethics were of editing writing class assignments, but I figured this guy, as a future businessman, was at least learning how to delegate. And, hey, money was money, particularly if the investigation into Rob's accusation went badly.

I didn't want to dwell on that possibility.

I tiptoed into the kitchen for some breakfast to fortify me for the work ahead. I stood in front of the fridge for five minutes before my stocking feet got too cold and I was forced to choose. There was leftover pico de gallo, so I grabbed some lime tortilla chips and tried not to rustle the bag too loudly on my way back into the office.

Some while later, Rob appeared in the doorway, his thick hair sleep tousled and eyes blinking against the halogen glow, as well as what meager sunlight crept through the closed blinds.

"Hey," I said. A breeze smelling of raw onions and cilantro passed my own nose, and I wondered if Rob could smell it from where he stood. It was hard to tell through his sleep grimace and puffy eyes.

He grunted something in reply, then turned around to head into the bathroom. After a few minutes, I heard the shower start up.

I continued to bleed virtual red ink all over the business student's documents while I waited for Rob to reappear.

"You're working?" he said, sounding at least eighty percent more conscious.

"Yup, go figure."

"I guess someone has to bring home the bacon now," Rob said, flopping into his office chair and staring at the empty spot on his desk where his laptop used to sit when he was home.

"I hope this seventy-four dollars keeps you in the style to which you are accustomed," I said, excising an entire irrelevant paragraph from one of the essays and adding a note to the student with several leading questions that I hoped would help him construct a better one in its place. He wasn't paying me enough to rewrite it all from scratch myself.

"I don't think you charge enough," Rob said from his side of the room.

"Don't worry. I don't work very hard to make up for it."

"Can I check my email?"

"Yup," I said, getting up and stretching. "I need to pee, anyhow."

When I came back, Rob was sitting in my desk chair but just staring into the distance.

"What is it?"

"Should I call them?"

"Of course," I said. "They should know that the killer admitted to framing you."

"It sounds so far-fetched," Rob said. "Maybe I should tell the police first and let them tell my company."

"Sure."

He reached for his phone from my seat, and I waved him out of my chair so I could get back to the painful editing I was doing. It was like watching a surgery on television—it made me queasy, but it was too compelling to look away. I wanted to know what other nauseous thing I was going to witness next.

I heard Rob go through the same process with the receptionist as I had, but he was eventually connected to some sort of person.

"No, I know we've already reported the threats, but this is different."

Rob listened to the other person, but whatever was said didn't appease him.

"The guy who called me practically admitted that he influenced my company to suspend me. I'm out of work here!"

Another pause.

"No, I don't have it on tape." This was said grudgingly. Rob's voice had descended into grumbling range. "All right. All right. Thanks." After he clicked off, he added, "For nothing."

"They wouldn't take a new report?" I had been sufficiently distracted from my editing.

"It was some guy this time, and he was looking at the

report that they'd already made about us, and didn't seem to think this was anything new." His voice was small. "They're not going to tell my company."

"You should call your boss, though, at least let him know what the situation is."

Rob swayed his body from side to side as he considered. "All right," he said finally, dialing his company's 800 number from heart.

"Mr. Wheeler," he said when he was patched through. "This is Rob Song....Fine, fine, thanks."

I raised my eyebrows at that optimistic description of Rob's mood.

"I received an anonymous phone call yesterday, where the person sort of took credit for accusing me."

There was a pause.

"No, unfortunately I don't have it recorded, since I answered the phone and talked to the person directly."

My breath stuck high in my chest as I waited.

"Um, he asked how being off work was going for me... Well, no, no name... But there have been some incidents at my church... Uh-huh... Right. Well, it could be, I suppose... All right, I understand."

He didn't say goodbye.

He tossed his phone onto the carpet and threw himself into his seat. I bit back a reprimand for combining technology and violence, particularly when our finances were shaky. Rob wasn't in a mood to hear a lecture.

"Now they either think I'm a nutcase, a liar, or guilty as accused. Mr. Wheeler suggested that, even if the person who called is the person who called in the tip, they might just be making sure I know I should feel bad."

"That's ridiculous," I said. "Did you tell them about the voice modulator, and how it's the same person who's called us about a fricking murder at our church, and how the police..."

Rob cut me off angrily. "You heard my end of the conversation, Chris. You know I could barely get a word in edgewise."

I sighed. "Maybe you should write them an email or something. Explain your side of it, but thoroughly, and in writing."

Rob looked pained, but he nodded. "It's a thought."

"Want to do some investigating in the meantime, call a few suspects?" I tried to inject my voice with cheer.

"Nah," he said. "I'll just hang out until your computer's free and I can write the email."

I stood up. "You can go ahead. I'll just go take a shower."

I figured he'd stew about it if he couldn't start right away. Rob ambled over from his side of the room, and I left him typing up a draft.

Since he was still working at it when I was ready for the day, I poked through my rediscovered stash of little-used stationery and found a pastel-flowered note card that was subdued enough to serve condolence purposes. I had been meaning to send Tammy's parents an honest, hand-written letter, but I never seemed to find the chance to write letters anymore. Maybe if Rob would steal my laptop at least once a week, I could become a famed correspondent.

I wasn't sure exactly what to say about a woman I hardly knew, so I kept it brief and was generically positive about their daughter. Remembering all the pictures of her on the One-on-One site, I mentioned that she obviously had a place in the hearts of the singles community at New Vision. I also said that she had a very lovely voice, which we would miss.

I had never lost someone close to me. I wasn't sure if receiving cards from someone you didn't know who didn't much know your loved one was any comfort or not, but it felt like the thing to do. Besides, I didn't have anything else to do, minus a laptop.

Rob asked me to proof his email before he sent it. I did, and refrained from charging him for the privilege. It was a good presentation of the facts, and I didn't think it made him sound paranoid, although the whole situation was definitely unreal. "Maybe you could include Detective Madari's number, for verification that we've been receiving these threats."

"That's a good idea," Rob said.

I added the line and typed in the number of the police station from memory.

I traded places with Rob again, and he carefully copied and pasted his missive into his email window, added his boss's address, hesitated, then clicked send.

He looked up at me. "We need salami."

"Pardon?"

"Let's go to Strack's."

"All right."

I got out of Rob's way so he could pick out some clothes from the debris on the floor, and in minutes we were on our way to our neighborhood grocery store, a branch of Strack & Van Til's.

We had strayed from the deli aisles and were contemplating the baked pastries when two ladies hove into view, one tall and gray-haired, and one stooped and white-haired leaning heavily on the cart as she pushed it.

"Gretchen! Heidi!" I called. It did no good. I tried it a couple more times, but it wasn't until I was directly in their line of vision, blocking the bread aisle, that they noticed me there.

"Christine," Gretchen said.

Rob had joined me. "Hello."

Heidi nodded pleasantly.

"We're looking into the incidents at New Vision," Rob announced.

I was surprised by his forcefulness but tried to be a good partner and not show it. Maybe he was the bad cop, and I was the good one. Maybe we should have talked this out before I accosted the twins.

"Let the police handle it," Gretchen said gruffly. In her no-nonsense way, she reminded me a lot of Detective Madari, or maybe her mother.

"They're not willing to hear all the information," Rob said.

"And the lead detective's even gone on vacation," I said.

They looked surprised. "Well, that doesn't sound right at all," Heidi said.

"So we're doing what we can," I continued, "and then we'll pass it all on to them later."

For no good reason, this seemed to satisfy them.

"We're trying to figure out who might have a grudge against the church," Rob said authoritatively, "since the attacks seem to be primarily against New Vision."

He was doing a good impression of an officer of the law, I thought.

"Why did you start going to New Vision?" I said, not sure if that made me the good or the bad cop.

Heidi leaned more heavily onto her cart. Gretchen dropped the wheat bread she had been considering back onto the shelf.

"There was...unpleasant gossip at our old church."

"And have you found New Vision welcoming?" I said.

They hesitated. "Most of the people are very nice," Heidi said in a quavering voice. She brought a crumpled tissue out of one cardigan sleeve and brought it up to dab at her watery pale blue eyes.

"Who's not nice?" Rob said. His tone let me know that he was the bad cop. "Valerie?"

Heidi shuddered, and Gretchen glared. "She has been most inconwenient," Gretchen said.

Another customer came up to reach for some bread, but Gretchen's poison stare kept him at bay. He wandered off as if stunned.

"You're not really Dutch at all, are you?" Rob said. Yup, definitely bad cop. "You're faking being Dutch to keep people from finding out your real history."

"Stop," Heidi pleaded, her blue eyes watering more heavily.

Gretchen shook her head angrily. "Ve are Dutch. On my fah-zer's side." She took a deep breath, and when she started again, her accent had diminished. "My father left us before we were born. We were raised by our mother in Berlin."

"So you were there during the war," Rob said.

"Valerie has told you, has she not?" Heidi wailed. "She promised she wouldn't tell anything we didn't want her to."

"We haven't spoken with Valerie," I said honestly. "We just did the math."

Gretchen still looked mad. "She is too curious, that one. It will get her in trouble."

"Are you angry with the church that you are being made so uncomfortable?" Rob persisted, trying to get the interrogation back in focus.

"Not with the church, no," Gretchen said. "No one else at New Wision knows our past, except you." She gave Rob and me a gimlet stare. Apparently our authoritative stance was wearing off.

"Thank you for your time and honesty," I said, wrapping up my good cop routine.

Gretchen glared at us as she put a heavily veined hand on Heidi's back and helped steer her further down the bread aisle and away from her tormentors.

Rob watched them go and turned back to me. "What did you learn at praise team practice this week?" he demanded. "Spill."

Oh, so now he was playing bad cop with me, was he? Clearly his zest for investigation had come back, all the frustration with his work situation channeling into it.

I tipped my head, the better to let the memories slide out. "Let's see," I started, refusing to be rushed despite Rob's intensity. He shifted his weight impatiently. "Oh!" Rob jumped. "Dylan gave me a song he wrote. We could look it over for clues."

Rob lifted an eyebrow.

"Yeah," I admitted. "It's not much. Oh!" Rob was better steeled this time and merely waited. "Potter told me his godmother was Gavin's first wife."

"What's her name?"

I shook my head. "I have no idea."

"What does that mean?"

I shrugged.

"Is that a clue, or is it not?" Rob asked, but mostly to the bread aisle.

"That's the problem with real life as opposed to mysteries on TV," I said philosophically. "There could be thousands of red herrings, because that's just how life is."

"Just think," Rob said, his ire now settled, "it could be this mysterious first Mrs. DeHaan. You've got to imagine she's nearby, probably sharing custody of Avery and Wren. The murderer could be this total stranger we've never met."

I took that in. "How disappointing."

"Yeah." Rob shook his head.

"Oo!" I pointed. Rob followed my gaze. "Little Debbie's!"

We continued our shopping for the essentials.

Chapter 19

Friday night meant it was time to return to the Bible study at Walter Kappas's house. Rob and I debated skipping but decided it would be a good chance to interrogate some suspects, if nothing else. Plus, if Walter were the killer, I didn't want him to suspect we were on to him from our absence.

I had misjudged what time I needed to start getting ready and was finally set to go when we realized that we didn't have our Bible study booklets.

"Where did we put them when we came in last week?" I shrieked to Rob as I tore through piles of clothing that had accumulated in the corners.

Rob wandered around, ineffectually shifting a shoe or a bag of chips here and there, reminding me of that night of inept searching for Barb's cough drops.

I spied the teetering stack of junk mail on top of the TV and reached out to sort through it. The whole stack tipped over and scattered coupons and fliers every which way. The good news was, our books had been in the middle somewhere, so I grabbed them out of the detritus in front of the entertainment stand and called to Rob to hurry and put his coat on.

The study had started in earnest by the time we arrived. Belinda greeted us at the door and offered me an armchair, sliding into a position on the floor. I realized that she must have given up her seat. Rob settled in on the carpet in front of my legs. Walter nodded our way from his position across the room, but he seemed guarded tonight and barely smiled. I hoped the stress wasn't affecting his heart condition.

Zachary occupied the same matching flowered easy chair as last time. I nodded to him, and he gave me his typical blank look of perplexed surprise.

Walter broke in to tell us what page we were on, and Rob and I studiously flipped through until we could follow along with the group.

Since Walter was reading the passage aloud, I had time to glance around and see who else had come. Alexander and Mora had taken Gavin and Marjorie's former position on the couch. I wasn't particularly surprised to see that, with Gavin still hospitalized, Marjorie and her stepdaughters had given tonight a miss.

Jim sat in a straight chair near Walter's seat on the floor, and Valerie, wearing a fire-engine red sweater, had snagged the third sofa spot next to Mora, who was a snow queen by contrast with her icy white sweater and sleek black hair. Instead of moving close to the arm, as most people would when sharing a couch with mere acquaintances, Valerie crowded close to Mora, who in turn continually shifted her weight uncomfortably, trying to edge toward her husband, who for his part seemed oblivious to the couch-sharing dynamics.

"We'll have the men go into the kitchen tonight," Walter announced perfunctorily after reading the lesson. "The women can stay here."

I looked around in surprise, and Rob got up from his position only after several beats had gone by and most of the men had already filed into the kitchen after Walter. His reluctance might have had something to do with the fact that I had been scratching his back as he sat in front of me.

"Do you often split men and women?" I asked Belinda when we ladies had been left behind. Belinda rose and settled into Zachary's vacated easy chair.

"Every other time," she said comfortably. "It gives us a chance to talk about issues that are particular to our experiences as men or women."

As it so happened, the issues that the women ended up talking about, once the Bible study questions had run out, were children and shopping. I didn't have much to contribute to either topic.

"How is your son doing?" Valerie asked Mora solicitously at one point. "It can be so trying to have a college-age son, I know."

"How is your dear Jeffrey?" Mora asked back, sidestepping Valerie's question.

"Oh, he's doing just lovely." Valerie beamed and noted something in her diary. I couldn't imagine what. Her diary tonight was canary yellow and formed a nice counterpoint to her bright red top. I wondered if she'd filled up her red book. I hadn't thought she was that far in to her last one, but maybe she'd worked overnight.

Finally Walter poked his head in to inform us that the men, too, were finished discussing for the night, and the ladies joined the men in the kitchen for refreshments. Belinda busied herself setting snacks out, and Mora lent a hand arranging the napkins and paper plates. I noticed the dishwasher had been filled in since last time. Its gleaming silver surface matched the other new appliances.

"Avery's not here again," Zachary said.

I turned to him. He wasn't looking at me, but I was the only one close enough to hear him. His fluffy blond head swiveled as he seemingly looked around the kitchen for any possible hiding places.

"No," I confirmed.

Rob walked up and put a hand at my back. "Hey."

"Hey," I said, reaching behind me to squeeze his hand. "Missed you."

He smiled.

"I thought she'd be here this week," Zachary said.

"Well," I said, "probably she's with her father, who's still recuperating."

"Oh, that makes sense."

"Hey," I said, striving for conversational, "Avery said it was your idea to hide Barb's purse and cough drops. What was that about?"

Zachary blinked up at me with his big blue eyes, blank-faced. "It wasn't my idea."

"Really?" I said. "Because Avery seemed to remember that it was you, and so did Dylan."

He blinked some more. I couldn't tell if he was thinking or stalling, or if he had just run out of brain juice and blinking helped pump some more out. "I went to the bathroom," he said. "When I came out, they were messing with the purse."

It was my turn to blink. "Huh."

Rob gave me a slight shrug when I looked at him.

"Zachary," I continued, "did you know Tammy at all?"

"Nah."

"You didn't go to One-on-One with her?"

"What?"

"The singles ministry?"

"Nah," he said. "That was just for old people like you."

Rob started snickering. I squeezed his hand harder, and he stopped.

"Well, thank you for your time."

But Zachary had already moved off, drawn by the fudge brownies Belinda was spreading out on a plate.

I was about to follow the siren call when Rob tugged

me back.

"What did the girls talk about?" he whispered.

"Periods," I whispered back. "Training bras."

"All we talked about was porn," he said.

I realized that he wasn't kidding.

"For or against?" I whispered.

He smiled and tugged me toward the brownies after him.

Chapter 20

I had intended to use Saturday as a day of sleuthing, but Rob was bummed not to have heard back from his boss about the email he'd sent. I pointed out that it was Saturday, but it didn't make Rob feel better to think he'd have to wait till Monday at the earliest for any word.

I suggested that we do something fun, to take our minds off everything. I had turned in my editing, early for once, and was feeling free and ready for a day of total enjoyment.

"Bowling?" Rob said, kicking at the futon legs. "Denny's?"

He didn't sound enthused about either.

"Crazy Taxi," I said, waiting for a reaction.

"Heck, yeah." That was the one I'd been hoping for.

We drove out to the arcade and spent far too many quarters driving clients into the San Francisco Bay, until a line of irritated prepubescent boys suggested that we had had taken more than our share of turns.

We wandered around the arcade, trying out various ticket-earning opportunities. Rob scored big at Skee-Ball, so when our quarters ran dry, we cashed out our earnings for two huge handfuls of Frootie Tootsie Rolls and a half-dozen Pixy Stix.

We downed them all in the car on our way to a celebratory dinner at Steak 'n Shake. I warned Rob not to drive like we were in Crazy Taxi, because the laws of physics once more applied.

I was deep into a Frisco Melt and a chocolate chip cookie dough shake when Hal and his girlfriend slid into our booth on either side. I scooted over to make way for his girlfriend's hips, enveloped in a tie-dye maxi-skirt.

"Fancy seeing you here," Hal said. His girlfriend smiled more reservedly, hugging her bag, made of some sort of Mayan fabric, to her bosom.

"Hal," I said. I turned to his girlfriend and stopped short.

"I don't know that you've met Laura," he said. "Rob and Christine."

"Hi." Laura reached out her fingertips for me to shake.

"Well, we just thought we'd say hey." They both began to stand again.

"Feel free to join us," Rob said quickly. It was unlike Rob to suggest spontaneous fellowship, so I wondered if he'd be playing bad cop again. But he was smiling and waving a skinny fry welcomingly.

Hal and Laura resumed their positions and placed their orders when the waiter saw them there and came around.

"Please, though, keep eating," Laura said to us. Unnecessarily, since Rob's and my mouths were both full.

"How long have you been going to New Vision?" Rob asked Laura once he'd swallowed.

Oh, I got it. Rob was good cop this time. I decided there could be two good cops, then, because today was my day for relaxing. I licked some steakburger grease off my fingers and picked up a fry to dip in the cheese sauce.

"For about two years," she said. She gestured to her

boyfriend. "Hal's been going since, what, June?"

"May," he said, smiling at her. "Laura brought me in."

That squared with Hal's presence in the summer photos of One-on-One.

"What do you do, Laura?" I asked her, trying to be conversational.

"I'm a hairdresser."

I tried not to think ill of her long, dull gray ponytail. "Oh, how nice."

"And where do you guys live?"

"I live in Draper." Laura emphasized the first word. "Hal lives in Royal Heights."

"Oh, nice." I couldn't think of a better adjective.

"I live with my parents."

I couldn't muster up even a "nice" for that. "Oh?"

"They're elderly," Hal explained. "Laura helps take care of them. But I'm hoping someday she might let me marry her and move in with all three of them."

Laura blushed and bent her head but looked pleased.

The waiter arrived with their orders at that point, and I had to watch them dig in. Despite having just polished off a burger, fries, and a shake, my taste buds wanted to do it all over again.

I busied my mouth with conversation. "Has either one of you been married before?"

Laura said "no" quickly. Hal shook his head and smiled. "No, no, though I had a few chances back in the day."

Laura looked at me with earnest, Golden-Retriever eyes. "Hal had kind of a rough life before he met me."

Hal snorted some of his soda, then laughed out loud when he'd finished choking. "That's your spin on it, honey."

"Well, you had several live-in girlfriends."

Hal shrugged and took another sip of his drink. "I enjoyed each one," he said finally.

Laura frowned and stabbed a bite of salad. I wondered if she was dieting in expectation of a summer wedding.

"I have two kids, though," Hal said, reaching around to the butt of his faded jeans. "Wanna see?"

"Sure," Rob and I both said. Hal drew out a couple school pictures from his well-worn leather wallet. The wallet itself was embossed with the kind of stamps that kids use at summer camp, and I wondered if it had been a gift from one of his younguns.

I accepted the two wallet-sized photos of unexceptional kids, a boy looking to be in middle school and a girl a little older, and passed them along to Rob after I'd had a look. I recognized them from Hal's picture in the InSight Newcomers Corner.

"Oh, nice," I cooed. I really needed to come up with another term. I noticed neither had inherited Hal's ponytail.

Hal told us about his kids' personalities and escapades over the rest of their meal. He later explained that they both lived with their mom, Hal's ex-girlfriend, in Kentucky.

"Kentucky," I said. "I wonder how Tammy's memorial service went."

"Yeah," Hal said. "That's a downer."

"She seemed to be really active in One-on-One," I said. "She was in a lot of pictures on the website."

"That's because Jim was taking the pictures," Hal laughed, looking at Laura, who laughed along with him.

"Was there something there?" Rob asked.

"Not yet," Laura said.

"Not officially," Jim said. "Not for want of Jim's trying, though."

"Hey, random question," I said. "You and Blaine were moving boxes during the search for the cough drops. Any reason?"

Hal looked at me and paused. "No, no reason. Why?"

"I was just trying to piece together everyone's movements that night. I wondered if you saw anything odd behind the boxes, or if that's why you were rearranging them."

"Nooo," Hal said slowly, shaking his head. "No. I was just thinking maybe the kids had hidden the purse back there or something."

"How did you know the kids took the purse?" Rob said in surprise.

Hal shook his head again but responded without tension. "I didn't know. But I have kids of my own, and I know how they work." He winked.

Hal scraped up the last of his chili-topped spaghetti. "It might have been Blaine's idea," he suggested. "I forget now. Maybe I was just following his lead."

I smiled politely, remembering that Blaine had said the opposite. It was hard to tell when people were lying and when they were just remembering wrong.

Laura pushed her half-finished salad away. We all stood and took our leave.

As Rob and I were driving home, I felt relaxed and sated.

"It's hard to believe there's a murderer loose in the church," I said. "It all seems so unreal."

"Maybe it's all just a big practical joke," Rob said dreamily, "and Tammy will come back in tomorrow."

"Oh, church is tomorrow," I said. "I forgot."

"It's easy to lose track of time when you have no job."

"Isn't it, though?" I said, patting him on the leg.

The Sunday morning sun crept in through the cracks in our living-room blinds and bothered me awake. I couldn't fall back asleep, even though I was uncharacteristically ahead of our alarm clock.

There hadn't been a murderous attack for an entire

week, I thought as I washed my hair in the shower. And rehearsal on Thursday had gone well. All the mayhem still seemed like a bad dream.

I was making my face more presentable when I heard Rob snoozing the clock radio. I decided to be generous and tiptoed in to switch it entirely to "off." Thirty-five minutes later, and with plenty of time still to spare for him to perform his abbreviated ablutions, I woke him with bagel and peanut butter in hand. We ate sitting comfortably on the futon, enjoying the peace of a Sunday morning. Even our neighbors' bass was remarkably silent. Maybe their stereo was taking a sabbath.

The junior high seemed quieter than usual when we arrived, no music coming over the sound system yet and the volunteers chatting in low tones.

One group folded bulletins industriously, barely stopping to converse, but at another table Jared Scheele, the co-editor of the InSight newsletter, sat alone, tapping a bulletin impatiently against the surface.

He looked up at me eagerly when I came into his line of vision. "Oh," he said, his face clearly reflecting disappointment. I wasn't sure whether to feel offended.

"What's wrong?" I checked my watch, and I had time to kill for once before rehearsal began.

Barb stopped by on her way to the stage. "Christine!" she sang. "Am I late?"

"No, I'm early," I assured her.

Her face creased in confusion, and she checked her wristwatch, looking between it and me. Apparently convinced there hadn't been a rift in time and space, she continued on her way to join the other early-bird praise team members up front.

Jared was still looking up at me. His brown hair looked like he had raked his fingers through it one too many times. "Valerie Dejong's not here yet." I knew Jared did a little of the reporting for InSight and a lot of the layout, but Valerie handled the nuts and bolts of finishing up. She was in charge of printing out and copying each edition. "She's supposed to have the papers here to fold and get ready to hand out before the service. She's never late." He worried with the bedraggled ties of his hoodie.

"I'm sure she'll show up soon," I said. It gave me pause, though. Valerie had been nothing but poisonous to a lot of the church members. Rob and I really should have given her some more consideration in terms of whether she had a motive to be the killer. What if she was late because she was setting some new trap?

I would have to remind Rob that we needed to have a talk with Valerie this week, assuming no one was arrested before then. I had avoided talking with her at the Bible study on Friday, mostly because she seemed like the kind of person I'd prefer to avoid. But that was no way for a P.I. to think.

I headed off toward the front of the auditorium and found that being on time for practice was even duller than being late. I made small talk with Kirsten and Hal while the sound team worked on hooking up all the cords. Various team members filed in, the singers warming up their voices by chatting with each other and the guitarists plugging into their amps and strumming experimental chords. Barb was slowing down the sound techs by asking questions and suggesting alternate arrangements of the cords.

Listening with half an ear to the conversation with Kirsten and Hal, I searched past the brightened stage lights that the lighting volunteers had just inconveniently decided to test and tried to make out the figures at the back of the auditorium, where the bulletin stuffers had been working. I saw Jared as an antsy, silhouetted outline still sitting and fidgeting at the same table, his hair getting spikier as he continually pulled his fingers through it. Two figures were approaching him from the doorway, though I couldn't tell if either was the errant Valerie, or perhaps a late-arriving praise team member. Suddenly, the lighting crew cut the floodlights on the stage, and I could make out faces instead of just body outlines.

One of the figures speaking to Jared was indeed a woman, but it was not Valerie or anyone on our team. It was Detective Madari. And by her side was another police officer, in uniform.

This couldn't be good.

Chapter 21

"Where are you going? We're almost ready to start!" Barb called after me, but it barely registered as I rushed down the steps wheeled in front of the stage each week for easier exits.

As I raced across the length of the auditorium, set-up volunteers were draping black fabric over the windows. The room grew dimmer with each hurried step, so that I had trouble making out facial expressions and not a prayer of lip reading until I was close enough to the threesome that the horrible acoustics were overcome.

"What's wrong?" I panted.

Detective Madari turned and looked at me with her inscrutable gray eyes. She was wearing an immaculate dress suit again, effectively making her the most dressed-up person at church, with Walter up on stage in his collared shirt and actual tie a close second. Once a principal, always a principal, I guessed, particularly when your church service is held in a school.

"Christine Randal," Detective Madari said. "How does this concern you?"

I nodded and smiled.

"How does this concern you?" she reiterated, face impassive.

My smile faded.

Ignoring the good detective for the moment, I studied Jared's face. Not good.

"What's wrong?" I asked again.

Detective Madari forbore to interrupt as Jared spat out, "Valerie is dead!"

"Dead!" I exclaimed. "What—how?"

"Some sort of accident with the copier." Jared shook his head. I mused if he nobly wished he had taken her place, or if he was glad Valerie always took care of the mundane tasks.

An accident, he'd said. I looked again at Detective Madari, who was looking steadily back at me. Who sends out homicide detectives to notify co-volunteers of an accident?

Suddenly, the music started up. I couldn't believe it, but there were the opening bars to "King of All Kings," and lo and behold, the singers all started in on the tag as ordered. I almost applauded my good little team but caught myself in time, sliding my eyes over to the detective. As I suspected, she was watching me keenly.

"This is horrible," I said to Jared, trying not to get distracted by the music blaring through the speakers throughout the assembly room.

Fortunately for my wandering attention span, a bulletin volunteer had finished stuffing and came over to see why the police were conversing with the newsletter staff. I left Jared in comforting hands, nodded at Detective Madari and her sidekick, and started back toward the stage.

I couldn't wait to find out more about Valerie's death, but from Jared and without the fuzz present. I also couldn't wait till Rob came in and we could discuss this staggering new development.

But, when I say I couldn't wait, obviously I was overstating. I had to wait, because our worship team had to finish up our practice. Barb was gesturing to me wildly to come up on stage in between raising her hands in worship. It was an effective sight. I hurried up the stairs to go through the motions of directing my team. I only hoped Jim and Walter didn't forget all the syncopation I'd drilled into them at the last few rehearsals, because I was in no shape to concentrate on what was going on.

After we'd departed the stage, I was reasonably satisfied that we could muddle through the morning's worship. I spotted Rob making his way in through the back doors. He was far away and his face was turned down, but he always leaned back a little as he walked, and I would have recognized his particular gait anywhere. I called his name and hurried to meet up with him at the bulletin table.

"Valerie's dead," I told him with no preamble, accepting the bulletin he handed to me from the stack.

"Valerie the newsletter editor?"

"The same."

"In what way?"

I blinked. "In the dead-as-a-doornail way."

"No," Rob said, "I meant, how did she die?"

"Foul play. I think."

"You think?"

I craned my neck to look past Rob and around the auditorium. Finally, I spotted the group I was looking for. "There's Jared," I said. "I need to go pump him for information."

Rob, appropriately subdued by my sleuthing leadership, trotted along after me.

Jared was in a group of half a dozen people, some of whom were crying. Two had their hands laid on Jared's shoulders as he sat on a folding chair turned the wrong way in their midst. It looked like the group had just finished a prayer. Jared looked shell-shocked.

"Jared," I said in as undertaker-like a voice as I could manage. I was going for smoothly sympathetic and trying not to cross the line into unctuous. "What terrible news about Valerie. What happened?"

Jared repeated the news robotically, as if he had retold the story several times now, although it didn't seem like he had quite taken it in yet. "Valerie was in the church office sometime last night making the final copies for the newsletter." The church rented office space on Route 30 in Murphy, on the way to the middle school. "Melissa Hernandez found her this morning when she went in to collect the craft supplies for PB&J."

"She was just...lying there?" I said. I was rolling and unrolling my bulletin as I anxiously awaited his response, and I made myself stop so I wouldn't distract him.

"It was worse than that, apparently," Jared said, his face white.

"She was very badly burned," said Gordon Whitehorse, one of the church members who had kept a hand on Jared's shoulder, either as a prayer technique or a comforting one, I didn't know. "And sort of in a strange position."

Jared swallowed, and Gordon hurried past the gory details. I would have to get them from Blaine later, I thought. Assuming he wasn't the killer.

"She had been somehow...electrocuted"—Gordon whispered this word to make it less offensive—"by the Xerox machine."

"Faulty wiring?" I asked.

"Deliberately faulty wiring," Gordon said.

"Another booby trap," I breathed.

Gordon and Jared nodded in unison, and several of the rest of the group simultaneously shook their heads in disbelief at the horror.

"I'm so sorry for your loss," I murmured in my undertaker tones. "Valerie will be greatly missed." I raised my voice to represent a vision of impending justice. "I hope the police quickly find who did this terrible thing." Everyone in the circle nodded vigorously, and I started to move away, Rob following.

Then I had an idea and turned back to face Jared and his circle. "Um." I wasn't sure how to broach this. "Any chance I could get a copy of the latest issue?"

Jared looked puzzled and perhaps slightly offended.

"I'm looking for clues," I said.

"I could mail you one," he said, "assuming they didn't all get burned up."

"Ah," I said, nodding and feeling more than a little awkward. All I could say was "Thank you," and then I did scram.

I needed to talk about this whole thing but badly, and I couldn't do it amidst the mourners.

"Valerie Dejong," I said once we were a safe distance away. "Was she a target or a hapless victim?"

"We said we needed a third attack, but I don't know if this clinches anything," Rob said, also immediately in the analytical spirit. "It's just like the cough drop and the stage accident. Was it intended for a specific person, or was it random malevolence?"

"Valerie certainly ticked off her fair share of people," I said.

"It would be hard to think of a church member without a motive for shutting her up," Rob agreed. "What do you hope to find in the latest issue of InSight?"

"Maybe she'll have left some indication of who's been most recently annoyed."

"An editorial titled 'Why I Will Be Murdered,'" Rob said.

I whacked him with my bulletin.

There was nothing for it but to continue on with the morning's worship service. I could see that Pastor Chris was visibly shaken, but I knew he would make sure the show went on as planned.

I made my way backstage to use the girls' room in the back hallway.

I heard someone enter the bathroom while I was ensconced in my stall and suddenly felt all over spooked. I even flushed the toilet with some trepidation, in case it had been booby trapped to spray acid on my face or something equally insidious and random.

Valerie had angered so many people that if her death had been the original one, I would have assumed it was intentional. But even this latest copier incident might not have been targeting her specifically. I had more than once spent time in the church office late on a Saturday night while I was reproducing last-minute sheet music for my team. I shuddered. But, just as Tammy had announced her desire for a cough drop before being handed a poisoned one, and just as Gavin's drama skit was planned well in advance of the weakening of the stage, it was possible that the killer knew Valerie would be the next to use the copier. It was also possible that the intended target had been someone who would come in to the office on Sunday morning, such as Melissa Hernandez, and that Valerie's late-night arrival was unexpected.

In any case, who would be next, whether targeted or accidental? And would anyone—police or otherwise—stop the next death in time?

I was washing my hands when I nearly jumped a mile at the crashing open of a stall door behind me. Penelope emerged, the toilet flushing behind her. She didn't have Gopher with her for once, though she still had an empty length of fabric tied around her. I found myself wildly hoping she hadn't just flushed him down the toilet.

She met my eyes in the mirror. "Terrible thing about

Valerie, isn't it?"

I nodded.

"How could someone do something like that?"

I found my voice. "But you must be relieved to have her stop her gossip about you."

She stopped in mid-lather and glared up at me in the mirror. "You can't seriously imagine I would kill her to get her to stop talking."

"Well," I said, "someone did."

"You don't know that," she said, turning her gaze back to the sink, wringing her hands under the water to get all the soap off.

I was still cleaning my hands, too, now sterile enough to operate with sans gloves. I shut off the water.

"Aren't these deaths random?" she insisted, holding her wet hands aloft in the air as if waiting for me to glove her.

"Maybe," I said. "What do you think?" I skirted widely around Penelope to get to the paper towels, and nearer the door.

She followed my arc, continuing to face me no matter where I went. "I think you think too much," she said.

"Would Walter kill to protect his secret?" I kept my voice low and even.

Her pale face blanched enough that the freckles stood out in relief. I at least felt I'd regained some of the power in this scenario.

"Walter is the father of Gopher, isn't he?" I persisted.

Penelope unfroze, lowering her wet hands to wipe them compulsively against her long skirt. I now regretted blocking the paper towels, but I didn't want to break the moment by offering her one.

"No one knows about that," she whispered, still wiping up and down compulsively. "Valerie was the only one here who guessed."

I hadn't been sure Walter could even get up to such

hijinks with his heart condition, but I was pleased my guess had landed. "And now Valerie's not bothering either of you. And you have your new job, and everything's all right for now."

Penelope's coral lips twisted. "Nothing's all right. I won't be at that job or New Vision for long, not once Gopher's old enough to ask who his father is." She shuddered a deep breath. "You're wrong about one thing: Walter would never kill for me. He won't even get a divorce for me or acknowledge his kid. So you can drop that line of thought."

I wasn't sure how to respond to that, and I needed to think over Penelope's reasoning once I had a clear space to do so. I tossed my paper towel and lurched into the bright hallway, where Dylan and Avery leaned against the backstage door and watched coolly as I made my way toward them, followed closely by Penelope. They finished up in hushed tones whatever conversation they had been having. Avery stopped slouching to move away as Dylan opened the door and held it for all three ladies to enter.

Entering the darkened backstage from the sunlit hallway, my eyes hadn't yet adjusted to the dimness before I bumped into a figure.

"Mrs. Randal...Ms. Randal."

"Detective Madari," I said. "We have to stop bumping into each other like this."

I wouldn't be able to see a smile in the dim light, but I imagined its absence. "I would like to request an interview," continued the detective.

"Absolutely," I said, my stomach doing a flip. Here's what I had angled for all week, and now that she was finally talking with me, but on her terms, I felt almost sick. I hated to be in trouble, and being questioned by the police in a murder investigation was the worst I'd ever had it with authority. "Can it wait until after the service? We're about to go on."

Detective Madari gave one curt nod. "Please set up a time for this afternoon." She handed me a card. I looked and saw the familiar number of the police station, along with the address. I gulped.

I tucked the card in the pocket of my Sunday slacks and gave Detective Madari another smile. I confirmed this time that it was not returned. She swiveled on one shiny heel and headed out through the wings to the side door.

Chapter 22

Pastor Chris didn't mention Valerie's death at all beyond a vague plea for God to be with New Vision and its members during these trying times. Maybe he thought it was too soon to explain what had happened. Maybe he worried about causing a panic over a serial killer at loose in the congregation.

After the service, as everyone milled about in the back near the displays, I looked around for Detective Madari, but she was nowhere in sight.

I handed Rob the card and told him of her directive to call. "Let's go," I said. "I want to get this over with."

I called the number with my cell phone as Rob drove toward the station. I never could get hold of Detective Madari, but this time at least one of her stony-faced assistants answered instead of the voicemail and scheduled me in for an hour in the future.

I related the timing to Rob, and he swung into a drive-thru Pizza Hut so we could fortify ourselves with breadsticks while we waited. We parked in the lot after receiving our garlicky purchase. I thought I was too nervous to eat but found myself munching away, dipping the sticks into the marinara sauce and reaching around for a tissue from the box in the back seat to stanch the grease off my hands, since the cashier had neglected to give us napkins. I handed one to Rob, too, for good measure. I would hate for our thirteen-year-old car to get trashed, I thought, as a little red sauce slopped onto the gray upholstery. I blotted it up as best as I could and continued chewing.

Reluctantly, we eventually made our way to the police station and found parking in the visitor lot.

"Does she want to see me too?" Rob asked when we were in the lobby, eyeing a couple perps coming in in handcuffs and one man arguing loudly with a clerk about what proof he needed of adequate insurance to dismiss a ticket against him.

I had no idea, and told Rob so. "But come anyway," I said. "I want moral support."

"I could always pretend to be your lawyer," Rob said.

We checked in at the front desk after the loud man had been mollified and left to obtain proper documentation, and I felt a little like an errant schoolgirl heading, again, for the principal's office.

Fortunately, the police station was much more office-like and bland than gritty and tough. Our interview was conducted at Detective Madari's desk in a tidily cubicled room, not in an isolated chamber in the back. I had never been in a police station in my life, but I kept feeling I had, as if I were now living a movie I'd seen before.

Detective Madari looked neither pleased nor displeased that Rob had shown up beside me. She gestured for us both to sit down. Her dark hair's remarkable shifting hues were even more evident under the fluorescent lighting, but she had it screwed back into an obedient knot as usual.

"Do we need a lawyer?" I asked her.

"I don't know," she returned evenly. "Do you?"

"No," I said quietly.

"Good." She tapped some papers together on her desk. Her unpolished nails were evenly trimmed and buffed to a shine. "Let's get down to business. I have a few questions to ask you about last night. But, first, let me fill in your particulars."

She directed all her questions to me, so I took it that Rob was beneath her radar right now. I wondered what made me more suspicious than he was but put that away to mull over another time. Detective Madari had pulled up a form on the desktop computer in front of her and now began to ask my life details, which I gave automatically but with some trepidation that even my date of birth might be used against me in a court of law.

When she got to former residence, I gave her the address of our first married apartment in Illinois, near Blanchard College, where we'd met.

"When did you come to Indiana?" she asked. "And what brought you here?"

"We moved last year. Rob transferred jobs." I waved toward him where he sat, button-lipped.

"But not you?" She looked up, fingers poised over the keyboard.

"No." She waited. "I work from home."

The keys started tapping again. I wondered what she thought of my home-business status. I tried to distract myself by glancing around her cubicle, but it gave no clues as to her personal life. There were no family photographs, no decorations, just neat gray fabric and a disconcertingly bare desk.

She asked a few more seemingly innocuous questions about Rob and me, and I answered each one factually, trying not to embellish or sound nervous.

She stopped typing and pushed her wheeled chair back.

"Now," she said, looking me in the eye. "Where were you last night?"

I wished I had something more interesting to tell. "We went to the Hollywood Arcade and then to Steak 'n Shake."

"You and your husband?" Detective Madari interrupted, ignoring Rob's nods. She wheeled forward and began to type again.

"Yes, that's right," I said.

"At what time?" she asked.

I tried to piece together the timing of each element. I asked Rob for confirmation, and he whispered a response, as if helping me cheat.

"Can anyone vouch for you?"

Rob started nodding again, and I picked up on it.

"Hal Dormer and Laura, his girlfriend, met up with us at Steak 'n Shake," I said.

"A planned meeting?" Detective Madari said, keys once more paused.

"Uh, no, just random."

She asked for the address of the restaurant and typed it in.

"And at the arcade?"

"Excuse me?"

"Can anyone vouch for your presence there?"

I stared at her. "Well, some other kids were there. No one we knew." I had a thought and stood up slightly to dig around in my pocket. I worried suddenly that she might think I was reaching for a piece, but she waited with her plainly manicured hands loose on top of the desk, apparently unconcerned at my potential for violence. Why was I a suspect, then, I wondered?

I pulled out my little credit-card holder that, along with my pockets, functioned as my purse, since I was too lazy to carry a real one and not forget it somewhere. I set it on the desk, then dug deeper. Lip gloss emerged next, and then a partially used tissue. Stuck to that, though, was what I was looking for.

I handed her a wrapper for a Frootie Tootsie Roll, watermelon flavor. "We won quite a lot at Skee-Ball," I bragged.

She dutifully accepted the little waxy scrap and laid it on the desk.

"I know it's not much," I said, "but you could check that that's the kind of prize they give out there."

She didn't respond. Maybe I sounded too defensive and should just let her figure out that sort of thing on her own. I didn't want to come off like one of the crooks in a Columbo episode, giving the detective ten good reasons why it couldn't have possibly been me.

"What did you do after you ate?" she asked.

"Went home. Watched some TV and did some stuff online. Went to bed."

"What did you do online?" She zeroed in on that aspect.

"Just...stuff." I waved my hand and shrugged. "Just goofing off."

Her keys tapped some more. I wished I could angle my head to see what she was typing, but it would have been too obvious. Was she going to subpoena my computer for evidence that I'd played Text Twirl and looked up the latest celebrity pregnancy gossip before watching some detective shows on Hulu with Rob?

She asked some other questions about my movements for the day before and Sunday morning as well, and then she asked some rather pointed questions about my knowledge of electrical equipment. I told her I knew how to operate an on switch. Then again, wouldn't anyone who'd rigged a copy machine to electrocute someone pretend to know nothing about electronics?

Finally, she clicked a key with finality and stood to scoot around us and over behind the cubicle wall. We could hear some vague movements on the outside, but Rob and I stayed put since we hadn't been released. Detective Madari reemerged with a thin stack of printouts, which she laid on top of the papers on her desk and once more tapped them all into alignment before looking up at me.

"Thank you," she said, tan hands folding on her desk. "You're free to go. We'll contact you if we have further questions."

"Wait," Rob said, the first time he'd used his voice at a normal level since arriving. "We didn't tell you about the latest threat."

"What's that?" Detective Madari asked, unimpressed.

"Someone got me suspended from my job."

Detective Madari wordlessly pulled a blank notepad out of a drawer and a pen from a sparse holder on her desk and began to take notes as Rob outlined the situation.

"Thank you," she said when he finished, laying her pen down at a precise line along the top of her stack of paper.

She seemed to be dismissing us again, but I remembered there had been something else I had wanted to tell her. "Barb Vanderwal told me she'd seen Valerie at the school the night before the floorboard incident," I said. I wasn't sure of the significance of that anymore. "Did she tell you that?"

"I have spoken with Mrs. Vanderwal, yes."

"Oh, okay." Detective Madari was staring at papers on her desk, apparently of the impression that we had already left. "So...should we do anything about these threats?"

She looked up again and folded her hands in front of her on the desk. "If you'll just leave all the worrying to the professionals, everything will be all right. Thank you."

I saw Rob's jaw twitch. "Losing my job isn't everything being all right," he said, half-standing.

"We will investigate that," Detective Madari said unflappably. "Thank you for alerting us to it."

With that, she physically left her desk again. When we stood, we saw her slipping through a far doorway, so we had no choice but to depart. Rob halted to ogle several skankily dressed ladies in the lobby.

"Do you think those were real hookers?" he said as we exited into the bracing January air.

"Probably," I said.

"I had forgotten that Barb saw Valerie at the school. What does that mean?"

"I don't know," I said. "Maybe she was with someone else."

"A co-conspirator?" Rob asked. "That would explain how so many attacks could be accomplished in just a week and a half, not to mention all the threats."

"Or she saw the person doing it," I said.

"Or…," Rob said meaningfully. "Or we're just assuming that this is all one killer. Maybe Valerie did the first two, and someone killed her as retribution."

"Did you get the feeling Detective Madari knew more than she was letting on?"

Rob's breath showed in a puff. "Too bad we didn't get any information out of her."

I pressed my lips together. "Should we have?"

"Well, Miss Marple would have."

He was right. As detectives, we were a little disappointing.

Chapter 23

That night, a booming crash and a rumble woke us up. I sat up on the futon in the darkened living room and looked over at Rob, who was struggling upright as well. The noise seemed to have come from the parking lot on the other side of our window.

I was afraid to go outside, but I inched over to the window and peered out the blinds. I jumped a little at what I saw: an unlit headlight, inches from brushing the glass. I opened the blinds a little wider, and there was no denying it: Our little green car was on the small stretch of lawn in front of our apartment. Behind it, a souped-up white station wagon, of all things, was disengaging itself from our rear bumper, bouncing back down the curb, and then tapping both cars next to where ours was before squealing away.

Rob and I looked at each other. "This is the third time our car's been hit in the parking lot this year," he said.

I went to get the phone to call our friendly officers of the Mansardville Police and rethought our decision to renew our lease in this complex.

We spent a couple of the wee hours of Monday morning filling out the accident report and describing the vehicle we'd seen drive off. We hadn't gotten a plate, and I knew from experience the perpetrator would never be caught, but we would need our insurance to kick in this time so we went through the motions.

We hadn't reported the previous and much milder hit-and-run, or the ding we'd gotten before that that must have been a swing with a baseball bat, because we hadn't wanted our premiums to rise. But the impact of the station wagon into our rear bumper had crumpled one of the wheel wells on the passenger's side, rendering it undrivable. We watched the tow truck haul our poor little Corolla away and went back inside.

Rob and I were too wired to go back to sleep, so we munched on some melon cubes while worrying aloud that this attack could be related to the murders. The Mansardville police officer hadn't seemed to think so, given the propensity for reckless driving in this area.

We finally got some extra shut-eye for a scant hour or so before our neighbor's bass woke us back up for the day. I let Rob loose on my computer while I caught up on some of my television watching. I liked to watch any show about other people's unruly kids, to gloat.

Finally Rob traded with me, and I groaned as I saw three more editing jobs waiting in my inbox.

"It's not fair," I whined. "I should get to be off work, too."

Rob yelled back to ask where I'd stashed the remote.

I went out to help him search. It was right in front of him, which made me wonder what kind of observation skills he'd been working on.

"If I accept all the jobs, I'll have barely any time to sleuth," I whined.

"Well, obviously, I have nothing but time on my hands," he said.

"No one from work wrote back yet?" I asked.

His expression gave me all the answer I needed.

Just then, a phone rang. I dithered about picking it up, since not having the last threat recorded had proved to be unfortunate.

But Rob recognized the ring and raced back toward the office.

"Hello, hello," he panted into his cell. "I'm here."

I listened to his side of the conversation but couldn't tell much beyond the fact that he was agreeing to something.

"What was it?" I said.

"Mr. Wheeler wants me to come in tomorrow to discuss the suspension," Rob said. He looked wide-eyed, like a bunny facing down a rifle.

"That's good, right?" I ventured, crossing my fingers behind my back.

"I don't know what it is."

"Maybe Detective Madari called them."

"Already?" Rob shook his head.

"Well," I said heartily, "if you're back to work and I'm working, who's going to catch the killer?"

Rob didn't respond. His look of concern deepened. "How am I going to get to work?"

He unceremoniously turned my laptop to face toward him instead of me and stood at my desk to start typing into the web browser.

"Hey," I said, ineffectually as it turned out. I craned my neck to see what he was looking up. Bus schedules.

"Unnnh." Rob let out an inarticulate moan. He clicked another page. "Unnh," he said again, this time louder.

"What?"

"The best I can do to get there takes an hour and a half and makes me get there an hour early. The next one would get me there ten minutes late."

"Well, that's no good."

Rob sighed.

"We'll just ask around for someone to drive you," I said reasonably.

Rob sighed again and stalked off. The phone call really had not left him in a good mood.

I pulled up my email account and started typing addresses into the To: field of a message, starting with the groups I'd created for praise team and the worship planning committee (or the Sunday Makers, as at least one person called us) and adding in a few extras I could think of. I explained the situation with our car and sat back to wait for a reply. When none came within five seconds, I decided to do some editing in the meantime.

Rob wandered back into the office. "I don't want to ask someone to drive me," he said morosely.

"Too late!" I was going for chipper.

He sighed again and walked back out.

I had gotten ten minutes of editing under my belt, punctuated by checking my stubbornly unrefreshing inbox, when Rob made another round to the office.

"If I do go back to work," he said, with his first ray of confidence, "we'll just have to confine our detecting to the weekends."

"Let's just hope the killer isn't caught by then," I said, and then wrinkled my brow when I realized what I'd said.

At least I got Rob to laugh for the first time that day. "That would be a shame."

I clicked over to my email again and saw a new message. Someone had come through.

"Barb's going to drive you to work tomorrow on her way to taking me to the worship planning committee meeting."

Instead of thanking me, he gave me a dour look and said ominously, "One or the other of us might end up murdered before we reach my work."

"Beggars can't be choosers," I replied sweetly.

He muttered something unflattering as he wandered

back off to watch TV.

Later that afternoon, my phone's ringing was a welcome respite from my editing. Even though we had no reason to go anywhere, I was feeling confined from being carless. I yawned and stretched in my office chair and checked the caller ID.

When I saw a local number, I took a gamble and picked up. It turned out to be Jared Scheele from InSight.

"The police have confiscated all the copies of the current issue of InSight," he said.

"Oh, that's too bad," I said.

"Yeah," he said.

"Is it online, by any chance?"

"No," Jared said. "Valerie had a thing about making sure it was printed. She thought if we didn't put it into people's hands, they wouldn't read it."

I remained silent, thinking over the number of InSights that had gone from my hands straight into the recycling bin.

"But, you know, I could email you a PDF of the layout instead," Jared continued. "Would that work?"

Would it ever!

I gave him my email address and waited for it to come through. Rob was reading a thriller out in the living room, so I called him back to the office to look through it with me.

I printed out two copies and handed him one.

"What are we looking for?" he said. "It's usually too boring for me to want to read it all."

"I have no idea," I said. "Just look."

"That's the problem with real-life mysteries," Rob said. "You have no idea what's going to be important. If this were a novel, whatever story I flipped to would give me some clue that clinches the thing."

"Or we'd see a help wanted ad from the killer."

Rob started laughing. "'Assistants needed to set booby

traps. Previous electrical wiring experience a plus.'"

"Just read your paper," I said.

It was boring as all heck, of course. I waded through an interview recounting a recent conference one of our members had attended, a photo story of a silly hat party for the moms group, congratulations to the Volunteers of the Year (I was not included), and the minutes from the latest Watchkeepers meeting.

A paragraph teeming with repressed curiosity mentioned Tammy's death in a neutral fashion, giving the address for sympathy notes to be sent to. I had a feeling someone—perhaps Pastor Chris, or even Detective Madari—had vetoed any further details. I couldn't imagine Valerie censoring herself on such a juicy topic.

There was a Newcomers Corner that boasted photos recent attendees must have sent in to Valerie, presumably as a result of constant hounding. Hal was posing with two tweens, and Jim was next to a young woman close to our age, or perhaps a couple years younger. It's funny—I'd never thought of them as parents, but clearly they were.

There was a longer profile on Marjorie DeHaan. She had met Gavin "presumably after his divorce," as Valerie had written it, at an event at the girls' dance school, where she was a teacher of little kids' ballet and jazz. Even the camera couldn't catch her full on; her photo had her thin blond strands obscuring half her head, which was tilted slightly away from the viewer as it was. There was a photo of Gavin, Avery, Wren, and his first wife that I thought was a rather tasteless accompaniment, but I supposed that was Valerie's specialty.

I scrutinized the rest of the articles and even checked out the masthead. "Valerie Dejong, Editor. Jared Scheele, Editor. Gordon Whitehorse, Reporter. Walter Kapas, Contributor." Misspelling of his name aside, what did being a contributor amount to? Was it just the Watchkeepers minutes?

It went on. "Jim Vegter, Photographer. Anne Kuiper, Advertising."

Advertising? I flipped through the newsletter again. There was a one-inch-square box on the back page touting Alex Ruiz Auto Dealers. That must have been a hard sell. I wondered if Alexander and Mora were financing the paper, and how that could mean anything if they were.

"Jim's the photographer," Rob pointed out to me.

"Yeah, I noticed that. I guess that means he would have camera equipment, then."

"And it explains why there were so many pictures of Tammy and so few of him on One-on-One outings."

"See anything else?" I asked.

"Nope, just that the youth group will be holding a car wash next week."

"Thrilling."

There was a knock on the apartment door. Rob and I looked at each other.

"Beats reading the InSight," Rob said.

I shrugged and followed him, both of us walking silently, into the front room. Rob crept to the peephole. I was uncomfortably aware that someone could shoot him through the little glass hole if they knew his eye was pressed against it.

Rob turned back to me and shrugged. "Someone's forehead," he mouthed.

"Christine!" came a shouted call from outside the door, and I jumped, shrieking a little involuntarily. "It's Hal. Are you there? Sorry if I startled you. I was just in the neighborhood."

"Hal," I called back, my voice quavering. "It's good to see you again."

But of course we weren't seeing him at all. Rob and I held a hurried, silent conference. Finally Rob made up our minds and unlatched the chain and deadbolt.

"Oh, hey, Rob," Hal said. "I thought you'd have been

at work still."

"Hi, Hal," Rob said evenly. "What are you doing here?"

"I wanted to talk with Christine, and you, too, if you'd like. Is that okay?"

"Let's go to the clubhouse," I announced.

"What?" Rob turned back to stare at me.

"Let's go out to the clubhouse," I said enthusiastically. "Sorry, Hal, it's just the apartment's a mess." And you might be a murderer.

"Sure," he said amiably. "Where is it? Can we walk?"

"Yup. Just a sec and we'll get our coats."

I locked the apartment behind us, and then the three of us made our way down the hall toward the entrance farthest from the parking lot, the one that led into the center of the apartment complex, where there were tennis courts perpetually without nets, and swimming pools that swarmed with children in the summer, and where, several buildings over, there was a clubhouse that anyone in the complex could use. I remembered from delivering the rent that there was a lounge area that didn't require reservations and that seemed to be always deserted. I was counting on having a public but quiet space for this conversation.

I looked at Hal's black leather coat. Was his the form I'd seen crouching in the parking lot? Was that person even the one following me?

I paused to make sure my phone was to hand in my coat pocket, and I pulled it out for a moment to check that it was on and charged. Then I hurried to catch up with the other two, my breath puffing in the cold air and my feet scuffing on ice-rimmed dead leaves underfoot.

When we gained the overly warm interior of the clubhouse, I nodded to the receptionist, then led the guys along to the lounge on the left. There was a television set playing an advertising loop for the complex, but it was set to nearly inaudible. I had a vision of the staff having grown tired of listening to it daily, forcing down the volume, and then telling their supervisor they had "lost" the remote.

Rob and I perched on a floral loveseat so overstuffed it almost spit us back out, and Hal chose to perch on the less cushioned arm of a nearby chair. I felt a little at a disadvantage now that he loomed over us, and his back was to the window, which made it hard to see more than his silhouette. But I glanced over to my left and saw the reassuring presence of a receptionist and another apartment complex worker, as well as a couple electricians fixing some wiring. They had shiny black jackets on with a handyman company's logo, and I noted with surprise that it was Jim's company.

Hal noticed it, too. "He gets all the business," he said with a crooked smile.

Was that a motive for revenge? I wondered. The company Hal worked for was staffed solely with electricians, while Jim's company offered general maintenance and repair. It must sting even more to have Jim's company take over Hal's specialty.

"Well, we're bigger in Illinois, and he's taken more of Indiana." It was as if Hal had read my thoughts. I nodded.

"I wanted to talk with you again," Hal said. "I was thinking of telling you more yesterday, but...it didn't seem like the right time."

I caught my breath, wondering if we were about to hear a confession.

"I'd rather not bring it to the police at this point, because I don't know if it's the kind of thing that warrants that." Hal shook his head, his gray ponytail swaying slightly.

"What is it?" I said, both disappointed and relieved that it was probably not going to be a confession.

"Valerie came to see me that night Tammy...you know...before practice began."

"Valerie?" I was surprised.

Hal nodded. "She must have followed my truck. She confronted me in the parking lot, and started insinuating all this nonsense. She had a little green diary—one of those calendar dealios—"

"A day planner?" I suggested.

"Right," Hal said. "She had it out and it was like she was reading from it. She told me stuff from my past—oh, like that I'd had two kids with my ex-girlfriend, a big secret"—he guffawed—"or that with our third pregnancy she'd had an abortion, stuff like that. And I realized—this b...chick is trying to blackmail me!" He raised his eyebrows and spread his hands.

I nodded sympathetically.

"Who did she think she was messing with?" Hal went on, warming to his subject and becoming more agitated. I noticed Rob dart his eyes toward the witnesses to make sure we were still publicly visible. "I mean, the nerve of her. I thought Christians were supposed to be all accepting and sh...crap. Sorry," he muttered.

I shook my head. "No problem. I know very few Christians who blackmail, if it makes you feel any better."

"Oh, I know, I know," Hal said, subsiding back onto the arm of the chair from whence he had risen in his furor. "It just made me so mad. I smacked that lousy green book out of her hands and told her to go f...boil her head." He chortled a little. "My grandmother used to say that."

Rob and I gave a nervous titter. "So what did she say to that?" Rob asked.

"She left." Hal looked pleased with his accomplishment. "She took off running like a sissy. I guess I was the first one to stand up to her."

"She was bothering a lot of people," I confirmed.

"So there were others," Hal said, nodding his head.

Was I not supposed to let that slip? I glanced sideways at Rob. It was too late now, regardless.

"I thought as much from the notes in her book," Hal

264

said.

I was dumbfounded, although not for long. "You still have it?"

"Kinda."

"What does that mean?"

"Well, the night that poor Tammy..." He trailed off, a frown on his face.

"Yeah," I said.

"It was that night, like I said. We were all looking for those cough drops, and I went ahead and tucked the book behind some boxes in the rehearsal room."

I blinked. "Is it still there?" I asked, hardly believing it.

"Yeah," Hal said, "along with another one."

"Another one?" Rob echoed.

"Well, she came back to me last Thursday. All ticked off that I'd stolen her first one, demanding it back, saying she'd let everyone know that I was a thief. Well, what could I do?"

There was a pregnant pause. "I don't know. What?" I said finally.

"I knocked that one out of her hands, too," Hal said, spreading his hands wide as if to say, what else.

"And then what?" Rob said, as riveted as I was by the recitation.

"I dumped it in the same place. I'm pretty sure I saw the first one there still."

"Do you think they're still there?"

Hal shrugged. "I imagine so. I haven't looked since Thursday."

"Why not tell the police?" Rob said simultaneously.

"And let the killer know I know about the blackmail?" Hal eyed us in disbelief. "I know as well as you that the killer's someone on the praise team. I wasn't going to pop the book out in front of everybody, and I haven't even wanted to go some other time. I haven't been sure that someone hasn't been following me around lately. You ever get that feeling?"

Rob and I said, "Yes," in heartfelt unison.

"Someone was upset enough about whatever was in that notebook to kill Valerie," Hal said.

"How do you figure?" Rob said.

Hal looked confused.

"Valerie was the third attack," Rob continued. "Why kill Tammy and try to kill Gavin and Blaine first?"

"I don't know," Hal said. "But the Tammy death seemed random. And the stage thing was just weird, haphazard. The Valerie death seemed intentional. The miswiring—that's not easy to do. You'd have to have some good electrical skills to pull that off. Like me." Hal laughed a little. "I don't know. I don't care. I know someone out there must have hated Valerie's guts—that's all I know."

"But why?" I said. "You didn't care about what she was trying to scare you with. Why do you think someone else did?"

Hal laughed. "Are you kidding me? You church people are so uptight. I made the choices in my life that were right for me, and I don't regret a single one. I mean, I'm not proud of everything, but all told, it's made me who I am, you know?" He pointed to his chest so we'd know about whom he was talking. We nodded obediently. "But all I hear from you church people is moaning and groaning about how terrible you are and how much you hate yourselves and on and on. It drives me nuts."

"Then why are you even going to church?" I asked in a small voice.

"I thought maybe I could help you," he said magnanimously.

I heard Rob choke beside me but couldn't trust myself to look to see whether it was laughter or shock that he was suppressing.

"All right, it's because of Laura." That made sense.

"She's so good for me, and she's so good, too. She doesn't think much of my life before I met her, but she's just trying to live the way she thinks is right, and I respect that." He paused. "And I love to play the drums. It's been a while since I got to play the drums." He pantomimed a short drum solo, finishing up with a vocalized cymbal crash.

I couldn't help but smile. "You've got it figured out," I said. "But why do you think Valerie was blackmailing people? Did she ask you for money specifically?"

"Well, no, I just figured. Why else would she throw stuff in people's face?"

"To make them feel bad?" I suggested, feeling a little sheepish myself. "We haven't heard from anybody that Valerie demanded money. I was just wondering if she had from you."

"Are you kidding me?" Hal exploded. "You Christians are uptight enough that someone just knowing a bad secret about you would be enough to send you into a tailspin?"

"Well, she threatened to tell other people," I said timidly.

"Still!" Hal roared.

I caught movement as the receptionist and a renter dropping off a check looked over our way.

"Do you mind if we try to get the notebooks?" I asked.

"And hand them over to the police," Rob added.

"Better you than me." Hal stood up, looking relieved. "Hope she didn't have anything on you two."

"Nope," I said. Rob shook his head.

"I figured as much," Hal said. "Somehow I knew I could trust you."

He held out his hand, and we stood to shake it in turn.

"Thanks for meeting with me," he said formally. "See you Thursday, yeah?"

"Yeah," I said, giving him a small smile.

He turned and took off.

Rob and I sat gingerly back on the overfilled loveseat, adjusting our weight until we were stable.

"So you think he was telling the truth?" Rob asked me.

"I imagine so," I said. "I guess we can check easily enough by going to look for the day planners."

"You don't think that's a trap, do you?" Rob said.

"Why would it be?" I said, eager to get my hands on those little books that Valerie so compulsively scribbled in. For once, a verifiable clue.

"Well, every other death so far has been a trap," Rob said reasonably, if a little edgily.

That shut me up. "I guess we could call the police and have them go find them," I said slowly.

"There's a thought."

I pulled the cell out of my coat pocket and caught a pursed-lip look from the receptionist. Whatever.

I stood and pulled Rob to his feet after me. "I'll call outside," I said.

Once more, the person who answered said I would be patched through to Detective Madari or one of her minions, and once more I was cut off in mid-Muzak.

"Arrrghhh!" I said, in primal-scream mode.

"Problems with the cops again?" Rob said sympathetically as he pulled his jacket off and dropped it by the door. My time on hold had given us sufficient cover to return to our apartment.

"Why do I even bother going to them?" I slammed the deadbolt home behind us. If the police didn't want those diaries, I sure did. This was the worst day ever to be sans automobile.

Chapter 24

Both of us woke on Tuesday morning before the sun, but it turned out my early rising was pointless. Debbie rang through to cancel the worship planning meeting for the week due to an issue with her septic system. I didn't want to ask for too many details. I confirmed with Barb that she could still play chauffeur, and she was fine with it. I knew Rob was consumed by thoughts of the suspension hearing when he didn't pester me about sending him off alone with a potential murderess.

Rob dressed carefully in his snazziest work shirt and even unearthed a tie. I pointed to an ink stain on the pants he'd chosen, and he cursed and went to change. In an unwise fit of philosophizing, I asked him what the big deal would be if he lost this job, that it wasn't necessarily his dream job anyway. Rob stared at me stonily and said it was the principle of the thing. I shut my trap after that and just tried to stay out of his way, except to hand him a peanut-buttered English muffin wrapped in a paper towel to eat on the way in case his appetite returned.

Barb appeared at the door, cheery despite the early morning errand we had asked her to run. When I kissed

Rob goodbye, he was as nervous as a teenager on a first date. I wished him luck.

Then he was gone, and I had nothing to do. I was too squirrelly to go back to sleep. I didn't have the worship planning committee to kill some of my day. I checked my email, but I had no clients banging down my door. I could work on some online ads or update my website, but...

Those dang diaries were so tempting. If I left them till Thursday, someone snooping around at practice might discover them. I could almost smell the leather, or maybe it was fake leather, but whatever it was was in my nostrils but good. They might have the clues that would help us solve the case. Valerie might have seen the killer and written about it. And if I let the police have them, I might never get a peek.

I stared at the phone, then away, fighting temptation.

Finally, I wrenched up the handset. I repeated my routine with the receptionist, asking first for Detective Madari and then for her assistant.

And, once more, after a full nine minutes this time of easy-listening saxophones, the familiar silence.

I slammed my finger on the disconnect button, jamming my nail. "Ouch!" I yelped. Now I was really mad.

I put my phone back in its charging dock none too gently and got up to get dressed and ready to go. I ripped off my PJs and left them where they fell, retrieving my jeans and sweater from yesterday that I had conveniently slung on a doorknob.

I ran a brush through my dark hair, ignoring the wild errant locks, and dabbed on some foundation. Now I looked pale. A little blush. Now my eyes looked undone. A little brown eyeliner to bring out the blue?

A full face of makeup later, I was ready to go. I grabbed a chocolate chip granola bar and a can of diet cola and swooped up my jacket on my way out the door.

I had gotten used to this bus thing. On my way to Fazoli's to meet with Jim, I had noticed that the same number bus took me past our praise team rehearsal building. I wasn't sure exactly where the stop was, but I figured I could fake it.

I ended up jumping the gun and pulling the cord well before I needed to. After trudging for a block and a half on the uneven verge, my shoes getting wet in the damp grass, I discovered a stop directly in front of the parking lot to the building. Well, what do you know? I thought, and wondered at how you never notice things you don't need at the time.

I walked through the parking lot, which was usually nearly empty when we came for praise team but which was now half-full. I knew there was a midwife business that took up the ground floor, and I wasn't sure what was on the other ones.

I took the elevator up to the top floor, which was deserted except for me. This floor had one empty suite down the other end of the hallway, the restrooms, the water fountain, the stairwell door, and then our large, rectangular practice space. The hall lights were on the dim security levels, and there was no noise, even from the other floors.

My key card opened both the front door downstairs and our office door. I assumed that each office's cards were keyed to open only their own spaces, but I'd never tried it out.

I walked into the room, daylit by the sun through the large windows. I saw the stack of boxes pressed against the wall, just as Hal and Blaine had left them after the search. I approached the stack I remembered Hal being nearest and tipped the stack toward me, out from the wall. I could see something. I rested my stomach on the top box and leaned over, reaching my arm down between the boxes and the wall. I could feel one of the thin leather-covered books, caught on the edge of a box a couple down from the top. My fingers brushed it, and I leaned a little farther, feeling the cardboard of the top box dent in a little from the pressure. Oops. But, there, I had it. And right next to it, I sensed the other. I turned onto my stomach so I could use both hands. Slowly, slowly, I slid them out of their hiding hole.

And that was when I realized I wasn't alone.

How had I missed the click of the key card opening the door? Unless he sneaked out of the stairwell and caught the door just before it closed behind me. I was so intent on getting to the day planners that I never thought to keep an eye out behind me. After all those detective movies I'd seen, how could I have been so foolish?

"Hello, Christine," he said.

"Hello, Jim."

Chapter 25

I held the diaries in a loose grip in front of me. Jim walked up and wrenched them out of my hand.

I wasn't as surprised as I thought I should be. I guess my subconscious had figured out who it was before my conscious mind had. The clues whipped through my mind: Jim's shiny black jacket, his vehement endorsement of hymns, his uncharacteristic sorrow at Tammy's death. Too late now.

Somehow I expected to see a gun in Jim's other hand, but there was instead a thin wire cord dangling from it. My mind balked at seeing it as a weapon, even though my stomach's roiling showed that it knew what it was intended for.

Jim flipped through the kelly green day planner, coming to a stop where the entries did, then backtracking.

"Here I am," he said proudly, pressing his index finger to the page he'd found. He mouthed along as he deciphered what Valerie had written. "It's just initials and a few notes, but I'd guess that people could piece it together if they wanted to."

"Piece what together?" I said nervously. I tried to edge

toward the door without alerting Jim to my motions. I wanted to do whatever I could to distract him.

"Valerie had seen me with a bag of Barb's cough drops. She certainly was too nosy for her own good. 'They learn to be idle, wandering about from house to house; and not only idle, but tattlers also and busybodies, speaking things which they ought not.'"

Uh-oh, I thought. When the psychotic murderer started quoting Scripture, you knew you were in trouble. I took another shuffling step toward the door, pivoting inch by painful inch while Jim continued to examine the diary, occasionally looking up to make eye contact. Fortunately, he seemed to be in a mental world of his own, and he pivoted along with me without seeming to notice he was turning.

"Once the first sacrifice had taken place, Valerie started following me, hoping to confront me. And then she saw even more."

"Is that what you call Tammy's death?" I said. "A sacrifice?"

"I never meant for it to be Tammy," Jim said, and I noticed with horrified shock that tears had started rolling down his face. "I was such good friends with her. I thought maybe... But the Lord chose her, and who am I to question his will?"

My stomach felt like it had just eaten itself. "It was God's will that you killed her?"

Jim stared at me, and I stopped moving, as if caught in a deadly game of Red Light–Green Light. "I did not kill her," he declared. "I am an instrument. God is the destroyer."

"Right," I said, my lungs constricting so that it came out as a breath of hollow sound. "Why?" I managed.

"Why does God destroy?" Jim laughed, but it wasn't a happy laugh. He flung his hand expansively around the office, and the thin cord whipped around with it. My eyes clung to the cord, paralyzed that the motion would remind him to use it, but Jim continued with his rant. "Look around at the painted whore," he yelled. "See the antichrist luring God's chosen away from the flock!"

I hoped someone from a lower floor would hear the yelling and be annoyed enough to call in a noise complaint, but from the absolute stillness of the building on this floor, I didn't have much hope of an unexpected rescue.

"Am I the painted whore?" I asked weakly. I could feel the makeup on my face like a thick mask of shame.

Jim shook his head in derision. "This church," he spat. "This abomination."

"Who's the flock, then?" I said, trying to stay meekly curious.

"The true churches, the authentic churches of God," Jim explained, as if to a child. "Like the church God called me to leave temporarily so that I could carry out his work here, in the realm of Babylon."

"Is this all about the praise choruses?" I said in a small voice.

"No!" Jim thundered.

I jumped.

"It is about that and more!"

I took in a shallow breath once more.

"It is about the falsifying of the Bible. It is about the weak, insipid sermons that do not teach the Word but merely scrape its surface. It is about the dramas that lead God's people to expect heathen entertainment in the place of true liturgy and holy meditation." Sweat beaded on his bald head.

I nodded, trying to appease him so that I could take another step or two toward the door.

Jim noticed this time. "Stay where you are," he ordered, holding out the hand with the cord. I imagined running for it, and I could almost feel the cord being whipped around my throat from behind, digging in... I stayed still and played for more time.

"Why didn't Valerie go to the police when she knew it was you who had set the traps?"

"Valerie was influenced by an evil spirit," Jim said, "the spirit of gossipers and busybodies."

I wanted to laugh at the thought of where such a spirit must rank in the full army of evil, but it would have been a hysterical laugh.

"She was forever trying to find the shameful in people and hold it against them." Jim shook his head at the sins of his former sister in Christ. "She reminded me of my wife, who was also led astray. I found Valerie's yellow book when I went to check that she had perished"—I dimly found it interesting that he used a euphemistic expression for having killed her, but I couldn't dwell on it—"but the books containing the details about me weren't there. Thank you for leading me to them."

I had to keep myself from politely responding with "you're welcome." "Did you know you were going to kill Valerie then?" I said instead.

"Valerie was an evildoer. She chose herself, unlike the other sacrifices." Jim stared at me. "Like you."

Oh, that didn't sound good. "Me?" I squeaked. "What did I do?"

"You have not heeded God's warnings to stay away, to allow his work to progress. He is not pleased with you."

My heart flew up to my throat and made a little squawking sound. "I got you the diaries," I hedged.

"I like you, Christine." Jim looked at me sadly. "You remind me of my own daughter. But I cannot deny the work of my Lord. Do not ask me to."

He tucked the diaries into the pocket of his shiny black jacket. Both hands free now, he wrapped the cord around each hand in turn while I stood there like a dummy.

I searched my mind for survival tips from my self-defense class at Blanchard. But all I was calling up was a frantic humming, as if the engine of my brain were about to explode.

"Shouldn't you kill me another way?" I blurted out in desperation. "Something that looks like an accident?"

"I tried." Jim shook his head sadly, and I had another inappropriate urge to say I was sorry it hadn't worked out. "With your car."

"You hit our car?" I said. I knew that was fishy.

"No," Jim said, a disgusted look passing over his face. "That would be so crude."

Ah, I thought, a murderer of distinction.

"I tampered with the electrical system. It would have stopped responding to you once you went over a certain speed."

My breath caught in a little choke. "You would have killed Rob," I said, my voice strained.

Jim shrugged. "Whichever. I knew it would stop you, either way."

My nostrils flared as rage pulsed through me, forcing out some of the fear.

"When you wrote us all of the hit-and-run," Jim continued, "I knew I must prepare myself to be more...direct."

Jim lunged at me, and I was at least thankful that I was facing him. The cord wasn't going to go the right way around unless he could get my back up against his chest.

He wrenched at my shoulders, throwing me off balance as he tried to turn me. As if my muscles remembered what my brain did not, at a break in his momentum, I spun back to face him and my knee thrust up into his groin. When he bent over slightly in surprised pain, my forehead came forward to crack against his.

"Ouch!" I gave an involuntary shaking of my head, seeing spots of light in my vision. I ran toward the door, but now he was behind me.

Fearing the wire noose, I turned again. He had lost one end of the wire, so that it flapped down toward his injured groin. But with the other hand, he grabbed hold of my hair at the roots. I heard ripping and wondered if later I would feel the pain. One of my eyes started blinking in an annoying way, and when something dripped onto the ground in front of me, I realized it was because blood was running into it.

I stopped trying to run from his clenched grip and instead reached up with both hands and took hold of his. I bent forward and then around, twisting his arm as I refused to let go. I could feel the pain in my scalp now, searing and making me cry out as I intensified my own pain. But the twisting of my body forced him to release his hold to relieve the strain on his arm.

I had let go of him to fumble behind my back with the door, and now he used both hands to grab hold of the front of my jacket. I only wished I were wearing something as slippery as his black company jacket. I didn't see the wire cord now, which was a minor relief, but I knew it was nearby.

"Come...back...in," Jim panted.

I didn't have the breath to respond one way or the other.

He had hold of my left arm as I fiddled furiously with my right one to open the door, my own body against me. I let him pull me forward a little so I could get it open, but now I couldn't get loose to leave through it. One half of me was in the doorway, holding it open, and the other half was being wrenched back into the practice room by Jim's iron grip. He used his other hand to grab once more at my hair, and I cried out again in agony at the tenderness of my assaulted scalp. I hoped someone down the stairwell might hear me, but it was a dim hope.

Against all inclination to protect my tender scalp, I leaned my full weight away from Jim, until his arm holding my captured one was pulled and locked out straight in the opposite direction. We were in a bizarre tug-of-war, with the rope being my hair and body.

I flung the door off me and in the split second before it slammed back against my body, I whirled with my free right fist and slammed down—crack!—on the flat of his forearm. I felt something give beneath the impact and hoped it was bone.

He howled in shock and let me go.

I had a minuscule moment of opportunity, and I took it. I lurched against the heavy half-open door and plunged into the corridor, hesitating a split second in the corridor before making my choice of the stairwell. I remembered dimly some edict against being caught in a stairwell, since they were soundproof, but at this point speed was my friend, and that leisurely office elevator would never beat someone running down the stairs at full tilt.

Speaking of which, I heard the door open again above me and steps thundering down behind, along with the grunts and moans of an injured beast in pursuit.

I burst out of the stairwell on the first floor, my lungs heaving for mercy. I saw the door for the midwifery clinic ahead to the left but, whether through unstoppable momentum or an instant of moral clarity that kept me from endangering mothers and babies, I launched myself out the front door instead and raced across the parking lot, worried that any moment might bring a cold steel wire around my neck. Or maybe he had a gun with him, too, and I would feel the impact of a bullet in my back.

I wove in and out of the cars and rounded the corner into a convenience store parking lot. Fair enough, I thought. They must get their share of criminals in here, so they'll be used to it.

I ran through the door, and the bell jingled indifferently above me.

The sudden quiet of the shop struck me. My breath

whistled in and out of my lungs in a rattling wheeze. The cashier looked at me with bored eyes over the head of a customer picking out cigarettes. My chest aching, sticky wetness trickling down the sides of my face, I continued speed walking to duck behind the row farthest from the door. I peeped around it, but I didn't see Jim immediately on my tail.

I dug in my pocket and pulled out my cell phone to punch in 911.

I looked toward the door again. Someone was entering, but it was just a customer wanting to pay for gas.

I caught the cashier giving me the stink eye. "Call the cops," I hissed over to him. His eyes widened, and he seemed to have pressed some sort of button under the counter, because suddenly lights flashed and bars descended over the bulletproof glass that surrounded him.

I wished I could be on the other side of that glass. Instead, I sank down by the Twinkies and gave my location to the efficient operator who answered my call.

Chapter 26

The police cars pulling into the lot, sirens blaring and lights flashing, had reassured me. Seeing Detective Madari emerge from an unmarked car and walk calmly up to me, where I huddled in a blanket perched on the back of an ambulance, was even better. That surprised me, but it must have been how assured she seemed, and how not one piece of lint marred the smooth navy wool of today's trench coat, and how the belt was pulled snugly and, were it not Detective Madari, I would say jauntily, into a knot instead of utilizing the provided buckle.

I giggled that I was considering Detective Madari's fashion quirks, and she looked at me with furrowed brows, apparently concerned at my state of mind.

"Where is he?" she asked.

I pulled off the oxygen mask and handed it back to the EMT. He held it at the ready, should I collapse again into hyperventilation or a severe case of the giddies.

I started giggling again, and Detective Madari's frown lines deepened. I was surprised her face had enough skin to form such an intentional frown.

"I don't know," I said, trying to will my face into

solemnity. "He was right behind me."

I couldn't help it—I started laughing again. It was all just so dang funny.

Detective Madari turned and started barking out orders to her minions. "Fan out," she said, and then she directed each squad car to a different section of town. The sirens, which had been temporarily stifled while the cars sat in the parking lot, started wailing again as one after another peeled out of the convenience-store lot.

Customers stared after the departing police cars, and at me in my blanket. Some of them carried cartons of orange juice or were scratching lottery tickets in between peeks. I found it hilarious that even a scene like this wasn't keeping the customers away. I started giggling again.

Detective Madari bent over to my level, and I began to worry her pristine coat might drag in the mud of the parking lot.

She actually snapped her fingers in my face to bring my gaze up from the ground to her eyes. My annoyance quelled my giddiness.

"What?" I said.

"Where did you last see him?" she asked.

"Jim Vegter?" I said.

"Naturally."

Had I told the 911 operator the name of the person pursuing me, or did Detective Madari know on her own? I tucked this conundrum away to examine later. Maybe all my detecting had been pointless in the extreme.

For now, I told her what had just transpired up on the top floor of the office building. A uniformed officer stood behind her, taking notes and occasionally relaying information into a shoulder radio to the squad cars, I supposed anything he thought would be helpful in tracing Jim's whereabouts.

"Should I call Mr. Song?" Detective Madari finally asked.

I blinked, wondering why she would contact my father-in-law. Then it sank in.

"Oh, Rob," I said. I hadn't even gotten my mind power up to full enough speed to have called him yet, although several times I had wished he was there. Clearly I still had some mental recovery to do.

"I can do it," I said, pulling my cell out of my coat pocket and waving it at the detective.

"All right," she said. "Stay safe." She turned on one navy pump and started to walk away.

Before she could disappear into her unmarked car, I yelled after her, "Will you let me know when he's captured?"

She gave a little salute, which I took to mean yes.

I called Rob's cell, my giggles giving way to sobbing as I tried to speak. Finally, the EMT took pity on me and took over the phone to tell Rob to meet me at Graybeal General Hospital.

And then off I went for evaluation, with all the novelty of riding in a real ambulance and none of the scariness of thinking I was actually going to die. For now.

I was wheeled into Graybeal on the gurney, though I tried to insist that I was well enough to walk. The EMTs ignored my protests. And then everyone ignored me altogether.

Apparently I was indeed better off than most, because my gurney was rolled against a wall while more urgent cases were triaged. The EMTs had already bandaged my head and stopped the bleeding, so I wasn't in any immediate need of medical care. I watched with more interest than concern as the wrist Jim had trapped turned different colors and grew increasingly swollen. The ER was exceptionally crowded today, I heard one of the ambulance folk remark to a fellow EMT before they headed back out on their route. A passing nurse explained that negotiations had once again broken down and the threatened nurses' strike had just started, cutting into the workforce.

I wondered if she was a scab, and for some reason the juxtaposition of that term within these injury-laden confines almost sent me into a new fit of giggles. I kept it together by looking at all the injuries I could determine. Several people, children especially, looked indeterminately feverish or lethargic, but for other people blood stains and makeshift bandages marked their wounds.

I had the best view in the house, because I was in a hallway next to the nurses' station, where I could look into the emergency room head on. I considered getting off the gurney and taking a seat like a normal person, but I realized that my seat was padded and the waiting room seats were not. I stayed put, perched on the edge. I kept busy playing my observation game, noting everyone's position and apparent malady, then closing my eyes and trying to place them all again.

It was frustrating—for me, if not for the patients being helped—that people kept disappearing from my grid, or they got up to use the restroom or grab something from the vending machines, and new people entered. I concentrated on performing my mental list as quickly as possible so that the fewest alterations would have happened.

After one particularly pleasing round, I opened my eyes to check and stared straight into the eyes of a bald-headed man, one arm hanging at an odd angle from the elbow down. He saw me, and time stopped.

Until I launched myself off the gurney and ran the few yards into the waiting room. I leaped over a chair, startling the mother and toddler sitting beside it and kicking their diaper bag out of my way in mid-air. My momentum sent me catapulting into Jim Vegter, and we were lying on the floor within seconds.

I could feel his chest struggling to rise underneath my

weight, and heard the whimpers as I put pressure on the arm I had pleasingly broken.

Security came over to drag me off him, and I yelled and pointed, "Arrest that man! He's a murderer!"

Jim lurched unsteadily to his feet, trying not to use his arm for assistance, turned, and tried to run. I screamed again and struggled to free myself. The guard took a better hold of my injured arm, and I screamed louder.

The two security guards clearly didn't know what to do. Finally, the one holding me must have gestured to the other to capture the other suspect, because he belatedly set off toward him, but Jim was almost to freedom.

He had reached the automatic doors, and I yelled to anyone who would pay attention. "Catch him! Stop him!"

I willed the patients to stick out a foot and trip him, but maybe there were too many sprained ankles in the house. I twisted against the security guard's grip, yelping when he struck the same nerve again and again with his tightening clasp, but apparently I seemed too much like the crazed violent lady in this scenario.

Jim ran headlong out the door—and smack into an empty wheelchair, mysteriously pushed into his path. He tumbled head over heels over the seat and landed, splat, on his back on the concrete. The other guard had reached him by now and flipped him over to pin him to the ground while he radioed for backup.

Good enough, I thought, relaxing in the guard's manacle grip on my battered left arm and whimpering a little in relief and continued pain.

Stepping past the prostrate form of Jim and in through the automated doors was Rob, my Rob.

I grinned and waved with my free hand, and then he was there, and the security guard let him hug me, apparently reassured that I'd stay put for now.

"Was that you?" I whispered.

"Hey, what are crime-fighting partners for?" Rob said.

Indeed.

Chapter 27

The next day was Wednesday. Rob's meeting with his boss and a committee of other higher-ups had gone well, he thought, but they wouldn't give him a definitive word until they'd conferred with each other further. Rob was given the impression that they had found no evidence of misconduct, and Detective Madari or one of her minions had come through on the phone call to alert them to a potential motive for someone to frame Rob.

In light of everything else, Rob was willing to wait peacefully until he found out one way or the other. We both spent the day continually gazing meaningfully into each other's eyes and reaching out for spontaneous hugs, happy to be alive and together.

It was just as well that we spent it at home, then, with the phone unplugged and my laptop turned off. We played Yahtzee and watched DVDs and ate medicinal sherbet.

I had finally received medical attention, which culminated in several stitches in my scalp and a reassurance that the missing patch of hair would grow back. My left wrist was sprained and splinted, and I was given two gel ice packs and some ibuprofen to take home with me to help with the swelling. They suggested not visiting further trauma upon it for a while, a tip I would be glad to follow, as long as security guards and murderers left me alone. Various other scrapes and bruises were examined and found superficial, though they offered to bandage them all if that would make me feel better. I declined, even though I thought it would. Pain in my chest prompted an X-ray that determined I had also cracked a rib sometime during my exertions, but they weren't doing much about it except to advise me to take it easy and continue to breathe.

That I could do.

The night before, Barb had left a message that a memorial service for Valerie was being held today, but I didn't feel up to going. I figured I had already done what I could to send her off in peace, whether she deserved it or not.

The next day was Thursday. Rob and I wallowed happily until the afternoon, when his boss called to announce that he had been reinstated and asked if he would mind doing some makeup work from home and coming in early the next morning.

I laughed at the conflicting emotions on Rob's face.

That evening, I considered giving praise team practice a miss, but as the leader, I'd still have to call everyone to cancel. Going seemed less of a hassle.

Our insurance company had come through with a rental car while ours was in the shop. Rob told me he'd drive, since my wrist wasn't up for activity, and that he'd pick me up, too. We were both feeling a little tender about being separated.

I committed to getting to the rehearsal on time. Seven p.m., I told myself over and over as I got ready, experimenting with winding a scarf to cover my missing patches of hair and putting on a full face of makeup to distract from the scarf. Seven p.m. At precisely seven p.m., we were in the rental car, on the way. Shoot. I guess I should have had an earlier time in mind.

The parking lot was nearly empty when Rob let me out. I looked around behind my teammates' cars as I passed, but there were no monsters lurking there tonight. Rob waited till I had swiped my card and entered the building before driving off.

The lobby to the building was dark, and I remembered racing out past the midwives' door, Jim on my tail. I took the elevator this time, partly to avoid the stairwell and partly to favor my still-aching body.

I stepped off the elevator into the dim corridor and approached the lighted door. I could hear voices within, so at least everybody hadn't decided to boycott tonight's rehearsal out of embarrassment that their leader fancied herself a vigilante.

I gingerly pushed open the door, bracing myself for the bright fluorescent lights and hot stares.

"She's here!" someone shouted.

"Christine," cried Barb, swooping in for a hug. I cringed from the pain in my cracked rib but hugged her back anyway.

Kirsten, grinning, struck up a few phrases of "For she's a jolly good fellow" on the only slightly out-of-tune piano.

I stood, Barb's arm around me from one side and Walter's from the other, feeling my face flush brightest red and the goofiest expression freeze across my face.

"How did you do it?" Barb wanted to know after the cheering had died down.

"How did you know it was Jim?" Zachary asked.

"Well," I said modestly, "just piecing together a few things here and there. Blaine helped immeasurably"—I gestured toward him—"by being our police liaison." I thought that sounded better than criminal hacker. Blaine ducked his head and blushed but looked pleased at the accolade.

"Why didn't you go to the police when you knew who it was?" Kirsten asked, sensibly.

"Well, um...I didn't exactly know that far beforehand."

"We heard you fought him here," Dylan mercifully interrupted. "There's even still blood stains on the carpet." He pointed them out eagerly. I was surprised that he was interested in someone besides himself but tried not to show it.

Avery picked up the thread. "How did you get away?"

"Self-defense," I said solemnly. "I recommend you all take a class, especially the women."

"I already take taekwondo," Avery said, tossing her blue-streaked head.

Then she could probably take me, I thought. I ignored the blood-stained area of the short-nap institutional carpeting. I didn't want to remember how uncomfortably close I came to not being here tonight.

"Thank God for his protection," Barb said fervently, and I echoed a heartfelt "Amen," along with several others.

"Let's pray," Walter said spontaneously.

We all bowed our heads, huddling together in a circle. I felt part of the group for the first time.

After Walter thanked God for justice and prayed for the grieving families of the two dead women, continued healing for Gavin DeHaan, and even blessings in whatever way God saw fit on Jim and his loved ones, I thought we could get down to practicing finally. But the group had other plans.

"We heard you found Valerie's diaries," Kirsten said, carefully examining her short nails. "Did you look inside them?"

"No," I said, in awe that mother-of-five Kirsten might

have a dark secret in her past. "Jim caught up with me just as I found them, and the police confiscated them when they arrested him."

"Do you think they'll be read at the trial?" Barb asked, affecting a disinterested air that went ill with her general conviviality.

"I couldn't say," I said, surprised again. "I can't really imagine why they would need to be, except for how they implicate Jim in Valerie's death."

I thought I sensed a collective exhale.

"So he killed her on purpose?" Walter asked. "The attacks all seemed so random."

"The others were," I said. "They were traps Jim set for God's will to be wrought."

All twelve pairs of eyes were staring at me.

"I mean, that's what he said. But Valerie's death was intentional on his part, to stop her from interfering with God's plan. And...well...mine, too. He tried to mess with our car's electrical system first, and when that was foiled, he went the more direct route."

"So those are the ones he used his electrician skills on," Blaine said. I had to admire his deductive abilities. He'd make a good partner, now that I knew he wasn't a psychopathic murderer-stalker.

I stopped myself, realizing I was thinking as if this sort of thing might happen again. This was the only time I would ever involve myself in crime solving. I had learned my lesson. Besides, I had a renewed commitment to keep busy with my paying work and with proving to the church that I could be worth compensating as praise team leader. I'd leave P.I. dreams to someone else. Honest.

"He had to be sure he killed Valerie," Walter said, shaking his head. "She was certainly...a loose cannon." He and Penelope looked away in opposite directions, studiously avoiding eye contact.

"It did seem like the other deaths were more amateurish," Dylan said.

"And in the case of Avery's dad," Zachary said, nodding toward her, "hit-or-miss."

Catching Avery's expression, Walter hurriedly finished for him, "Fortunately, miss for him."

"He wanted God to be able to choose his sacrifices," I said, my lips twisting even at repeating Jim's claims.

"Why did he hate the church so much?" Walter asked.

"He didn't hate just any church," I said. "He hated this church, New Vision, in particular, and all churches like it."

"But why?" Barb wailed, genuinely perplexed.

"He came from Nederland Christian Reformed," Kirsten said from her place on the piano bench. She was the only one among us ready to get down to business if the time called for it. "Just like several of us did. Only he still really liked the old style of things. He was always talking with me about which hymns I knew and if we could work any into the instrumental interludes."

"His wife left Nederland Christian Reformed for Saddleback in California, and took their daughter with her," I added.

"That's enough to give anyone a complex," Blaine said.

I nodded. "It wasn't just the personal connection, though. He talked to me a lot about hymns versus praise choruses, as Kirsten said, and not having dramas and such, but I think his main beef was that seeker churches were shallow and interested in entertainment only." Barb gasped. "That they were stealing away real Christians from honest churches instead of actually accomplishing what they'd set out to do, which was attract nonbelievers."

"That's ridiculous," Barb said, breathless with indignation. "We do too attract nonbelievers. Look at Hal!" She pointed boldly toward the drummer. Hal winked at me once Barb wasn't looking.

I could agree with Barb on one thing. "He definitely was mentally ill." I shuddered, remembering my final conversation with the man, in this very room. "He left threatening messages on my machine, telling me to back off, but he didn't try to kill me until he thought I'd gone too far. It was all part of what he thought God was telling him to do. Until God told him to kill me, he couldn't."

"Weird," Dylan breathed.

Dylan was listening to something I said. That was a miracle right there.

"Why didn't the police catch him sooner?" Avery wanted to know. I figured she was probably still thinking of her dad, the second would-be victim.

"I don't think it helped that almost everyone I spoke to had something to hide, so getting people to be honest and open was challenging." I wondered if I had been diplomatic enough in how I worded that.

The team members looked around at one another, eyes wide, and Hal smirked at me. Apparently not.

"Let's get practicing," I said briskly. "We still have a service on Sunday to prepare for."

There was some good-natured groaning from the younger contingent. Walter rubbed his hands together and eagerly took his seat. Kirsten spread out today's pages across the piano's stand, while Hal tested the tuning on his drums. Potter began tootling on his horn to get his spit flowing, and Blaine and Dylan plugged in their guitars and adjusted knobs on the amps. Penelope shifted her baby to one arm and picked up her music with her free hand, deftly avoiding having Gopher snatch it out of her grip. Zachary picked out a tambourine and gave an experimental jingling. Oh, dear heavens, I thought, his mother's going to give me the dressing down of my life—a tambourine had to rank well below congas in prestige value. Avery flamboyantly scrawled notes to herself on her music, and the elderly German twins started doing warm-up vocalizations of their own accord.

"Mee, may, mah, moh, moo," they sang in unison, one

soprano and one tenor.

Suddenly, Heidi's voice broke off in mid-moo in a fit of coughing. Her sister whacked her on her rounded back with one veiny hand.

Barb rummaged through the handbag that she now kept safely tucked under her seat. "Hang on, honey!" she called, her voice muffled as she ducked down to search. "I have a cough drop right here."

About the Author

Amanda Caldwell lives in Seattle with a husband who loves junk food and mysteries as much as she does, three delightful kids, two fluffy cats, a snuffly hedgehog, and a chubby frog.